DEEP NIGHT

ALSO BY THE AUTHOR

The Fat Man's Daughter

CAROLINE PETIT

DEEP NIGHT

SOHO

Published by
Soho Press, Inc.
853 Broadway
New York, NY 10003

Library of Congress Cataloging-in-Publication Data

Petit, Caroline.
Deep night / Caroline Petit.
p. cm.
ISBN 978-1-56947-530-0
1. Young women—Fiction.
2. Hong Kong (China)—History—20th century—Fiction.
3. China—History—1937–1945—Fiction.
4. Macau (China)—Fiction. I. Title.
PR9619.4.P47D44 2008
823'.92—dc22
2008019892

10 9 8 7 6 5 4 3 2 1

FOR
ALYSSA
AND
REBECCA

"I am not an adventurer by choice but by fate."

—*Vincent Van Gogh*

October 8, 1941

WHITE CLOUD MOUNTAIN, NEAR CANTON, CHINA

Tokai Ito seriously doubted he'd see anything in the grey fog. The rain had cleared, but the mist still swirled. His Italian leather shoes were soaked and his socks clammy around his ankles. By his side was the Japanese captain boring him with army slogans straight out of the training manual. For the second time, the captain insisted on dragging him around the plywood installations representing the British defences in Hong Kong, Kowloon and the New Territories.

The captain crowed: "We were able to do this because of the loyalty of Japanese businessmen in Hong Kong."

Tokai nodded. In Tokyo, his father religiously harangued their managers to be vigilant and report anything, anything at all that might help the great war machine of Japan. Striving managers then scurried around foreign cities, notebooks in hand, collecting information. One of Tokai's duties was to read their reports. Most were totally useless or repeated things that were already public knowledge. A few were valuable. These he discussed with his father and took credit for, proving himself to be a worthy son of a steel magnate and ammunitions manufacturer. As a reward, his father insisted he witness first-hand the nation's fighting spirit and that was why he was now standing on this peak, one of the most beautiful spots in all of China, waiting for the training exercise to begin.

The captain cocked his head and his eyes moved to the mountain's edge. "Can you hear them? They've begun the climb. Let's go see."

Distantly, Tokai heard the soft grunts of men straining to climb up rope ladders. The sun peeped through and began to burn off the mist and haze. Tokai worried about grass stains on his English worsted trousers as they tromped through the long grass to peer over the ledge. Far below were hordes of uniformed men wearing dark glasses to simulate a night attack on Hong Kong.

The men climbed slowly, hand over hand, their heavy packs weighing them down. Their grunts grew louder as they struggled upwards. Finally, Tokai saw the faces of the men—boys really, country lads—sweating and straining. One soldier froze when he looked down, his companions clogging up behind. The captain bellowed to get a move on, he wasn't sightseeing. For a second, Ito thought the soldier would let go of the rope and fall, but the men behind shouted patriotic words of encouragement. Slowly, the frozen man began to move.

The first soldier to reach the top flopped onto his belly, red-faced, gasping for breath. Others joined him. The captain yelled for them to attack. Hundreds of men in khaki zigzagged around the make-believe British fortifications, firing their rifles and shouting bloodthirsty cries as they jumped across an intricate network of gullies. The captain watched with satisfaction.

White Cloud Mountain was a magical place: clouds forming and re-forming into dreamy mystical landscapes. Now it was ruined by ear-splitting gunfire, the poisoned stench of cordite and blood curdling battle cries, robbing Tokai of the ability to absorb its true beauty. Still, he was going to make a killing.

1

From her bed Leah watched Jonathan dress in his Hong Kong volunteer uniform. She never tired of looking. His skin had the texture of finely worked ceramic clay, smooth and compelling. His year of toiling up and down the hills of Hong Kong had defined his calves and hardened his belly. The fine blond hairs on his legs and arms were bleached to a silvery softness. He tanned easily and, naked, she could see the boundary between his pale solicitor's skin and his browned soldier's hide. When he returned from training, sweaty and bruised, he gave off such an intoxicating musky scent that she was suffused with desire.

Jonathan buttoned his shirt and cleared his throat. As casually as he could, he said, "I want to put your name down for the next evacuee ship to Australia. Things are not getting any better here."

"I'm not going anywhere. This is my home," she insisted.

"You're not Chinese. I want you safe," he said.

"Safe. No one is safe any more. They'll kill us all." She threw a pillow, as if to underscore her point (or to soften her refusal), and hit him in the head.

He caught the pillow and crushed it to him. "Then marry me for God's sake."

"We've been through this before."

"I'm asking again."

She ran a long-fingered hand through her sleep-tousled hair and he could feel his heart stop for an instant. How could she do this to him, cause him to lose his heart all over again? He had made love to her over the last three years at least one thousand times. Not that he counted, but he reasoned that by rights she should be his, only she remained just beyond his grasp. At the beginning of their romance, for that his how he chose to characterise it (it was not an affair), he was overwhelmed that he had been chosen to be her lover from amongst all the eligible and ineligible men who yearned and lusted after her. Sitting in his offices of Everston, Hallawick & Deebs, thinking about her, he was filled with wonder and pride. He was breaking her unwritten rule now, trying to stake his permanent claim.

"We have plenty of time," she said, deflecting his proposal again, unwilling to have a scene, to cloud her day with anxiety. She had made a space in her life for him and he filled it with his beauty, kindness, and willingness to take her as he found her. She had no intention of changing the rules. She was happy as she was. He made her happy. "You'll be late and be put on report," she teased.

"It doesn't matter."

"I'm closing the shop today. My customers won't mind. Huang fu says the packing materials have arrived. Goddamn the Japanese. Who wants to buy in this climate of fear?"

"You're sending your precious antiques away to the Freer Gallery to America."

"Here, they might be looted or destroyed."

He sat beside her on the bed and put his arms around her, drawing her close. "So could you," he said.

She wiggled free. "So could we all, Jonathan. I'd hate Australia. I don't want to watch a herd of kangaroos hopping around." She gave him a dismissive kiss on the cheek.

"It's a mob."

Perplexed, she asked, "What?"

"A group of kangaroos is a mob, not a herd."

"Thank you, Mr. Hawatyne, for clarifying that issue."

Her smile lured him into saying more earnestly than he had intended, "The offer remains open. I want to make an honest woman of you."

Bristling, Leah pushed him away. "You shouldn't listen to Hong Kong tattle tales," she said coldly.

"I didn't—it's a figure of speech. A joke."

"It's not funny."

"No. It was a stupid remark. I love you." He tried to capture one of her hands, but she tossed the sheet aside and stood.

"Theo was a good man. A good father. He raised me by himself. I have nothing to be ashamed of."

"It's jealousy," he agreed. "Hong Kong's a backwater. People concoct things to make themselves feel better. I wish I had known him."

"It's the anniversary of his death in a few days. I'll visit his grave then."

"I'll go with you."

"No," she said. "I'd rather go by myself." She turned away and opened her closet to survey her clothes.

Jonathan looked longing at her back. He could tell from her rigid stance and her tightly crossed arms that their conversation was finished. Why had he mentioned Theo? He knew better. She never talked about Theo, only gave oblique hints about growing up in this extraordinary house designed by China-loving Theo and his obsession with oriental art while the most precious beautiful object, his daughter, was flowering beneath his gaze. Watching her stand, Jonathan was filled with yearning: the graceful curve of her back, the taut breasts, the delicious roundness of her bottom. He wished she'd swing round and say I love you, but he knew she wouldn't. He told himself words were not important. He had crossed so many barriers in the last three years. It was only a matter of time before he breached this one. He wished he didn't mind so much. She was only unguarded and abandoned in their lovemaking. For most men that would be enough, but he hungered for more. He so wanted to protect her. It was why he had joined up the minute the Colonial Government asked, tangible proof of his love. He sighed deeply and left without kissing her goodbye, shutting the door quietly. He'd have to hurry to make parade on time.

Leah stared blankly at her dresses, glad he had gone. She liked their current arrangement. Jonathan kept his flat in Mid-Levels though he spent every night in her bed. It was evidence of her independence, that she could come and go as she pleased. Only, she pined for him when he was away and when he came home early and she discovered him lounging in the living room in his sharkskin suit, long legs out, sipping on a G&T that Huang fu had obligingly made, she was often overwhelmed by such an intense feeling of joy that she could only nod in his general direction before fleeing to their shared bedroom to take a few breaths to compose herself. Legalising the relationship, becoming Mrs Hawatyne, might sour her love. He would feel honour bound to oversee her antiquities business and this she did not want. Jonathan could be so irritatingly pedantic. She pictured him, hovering around her study, offering to sort out her ledgers and accounts, obligingly reading her correspondence. He'd want to see bills of sale or chains of title—a legitimate provenance—for various treasures dug up even now, in the midst of the Sino Japanese war, by archaeologists and sold by people unconcerned about proper procedures. He would never understand her complicated business arrangements. Her business was her own, her last tangible link to Theo and everything she had learned from his beguiling, scheming hands.

Her old school acquaintance, Hope Cuthbert, recently married to Charles Lewis, had smugly told her as they drank cocktails in Hope's gaudy, expensive apartment: There are no secrets between husbands and wives. Leah had feigned agreement, even as she tingled with revulsion and choked and spluttered over her drink, finally managing to say coolly, "How nice for you," avoiding Hope's eyes. Jonathan was acting for Charles over the scandal of the huge cost overruns and shoddy workmanship of the city's air raid tunnels—many had collapsed.

Charles lined his pockets with kickbacks. Leah doubted very much if Charles told Hope where all his money came from. Everyone had little secrets. Or, at least she thought they did. Theo did. He had schooled her to keep her own counsel. It was a lesson she had learned well as an only child, although she believed it was his secrets that had gotten him killed four years earlier. She no longer looked for answers about his death, but she still missed him terribly and had never felt completely safe since. Having Jonathan near calmed her fears. She'd never leave Hong Kong. Let the Japanese come.

Hurrying now, she dressed in an old skirt and worn silk blouse, then grabbed a faded blue smock to prevent the cotton fibres clinging. She hadn't finished packing, the boat was sailing tomorrow, and then there were infuriating customs and insurance forms to fill in.

◎

SURROUNDED by enormous tea chests, Leah knelt on the hard wood floor of her Hollywood Road antiques store with her skirt hiked up, wrapping the kaolin figurine of *Hsüan-ti*, who was invited into heaven to battle the demon kings laying waste to the universe. The Saturday noise from the street hawkers screeching out the wonders of their own trashy curios penetrated into the rear of the shop. Was there any more room in the chest? She picked up two yards of cotton wadding and tucked it on top. No, another layer was required.

Finally satisfied, she leaned back to rub her aching spine, dreaming that her treasures were already displayed in a gallery in glass cases with discreet white cards attached, acknowledging her loan, her taste and perhaps, attracting new clients to expand her business. Business was bad. She blamed the Japanese. Everyone talked of war; or rather, no one talked of war, only evaded each other's eyes and changed the subject.

Damn, why hadn't she ordered steel waterproof lockers to protect them better? It was stupid to penny-pinch, but also too late to change. She wiped her hands on her smock and felt a needle of throbbing pain in her thumb. She blew away the cotton dust to see a long splinter poking out of the skin. She pulled the splinter out with her teeth as the shop bell tinkled.

A man's voice called out, "Miss Kolbe?"

"In here," she managed.

A Japanese man walked in and bowed. "We had an appointment? The sign says closed for inventory."

Leah dusted her hands against her smock again, leaving

behind a small trail of blood. They shook hands. He took off his Panama hat. A Japanese woodcut, she decided: the straight black eyebrows, the long face and sharp chin. He wore a hand-tailored linen suit so unlike the boxy, cheap ones favoured by Japanese businessmen who hung around Hong Kong, hungry for any opportunity. Who was he? She bestowed a welcoming smile, as if she knew exactly who he was, but had become so engrossed in her packing she had forgotten the time. "I'm so glad you have come," she said. "I"—she gestured toward the disarray.

"I am pleased you received Monsieur Martin's letter introducing me and setting up this appointment. I was worried that you might not have received it."

Martin's letter from three months ago came flooding back and thankfully a name, Ito. Martin had written: 'Mr Ito is a collector. He is a very charming fellow, very un-Japanese and very knowledgeable about all Chinoiserie. I'm certain you will like him, besides he has money.' Then he had suggested a date, 21 November 1941, today, and she had forgotten in her rush to ready her boxes for the ship's sailing. She must make up for this lapse.

"It's a pleasure to meet you, Mr Ito. I have been looking forward to it."

She continued explaining about the packing cases and the Freer Gallery. He seemed impressed that her collection was going to be seen by Americans. Good. She might be able to charge more.

"Oh," he said sadly. "I'm only interested in the best," and looked longingly at the tea chests, but was too polite to ask to see their contents.

His pronunciation was flawless, English and not American. Leah relented, figuring that if she let him look at one chest, he might be induced to consider one or two special things she kept at the Peak and couldn't bear to part with. At least she'd understand his taste and could be on the lookout for something unusual, now that she had an affluent buyer.

Ito asked permission to remove his jacket and began unwrapping objects like an expert. As he admired each piece, he explained his situation, although she hadn't asked. He was in steel, shipping it to new factories in China. "There has been widespread . . ."

Leah waited, keeping her face animated and interested, and realised he was searching for an inoffensive word.

Finally, he said, "Pilfering on the Hong Kong docks. It's important war materiel."

She masked her displeasure. Japanese ships docked in Hong Kong on their way to China loaded with armaments. He might have a connoisseur's appreciation of Chinese objects d'art, but he saw no contradiction in the fact that his country was slaughtering Chinese. She must remain pleasant and not alienate a wealthy customer. What had Theo said? There is no politics in business, only the exchange of money. "Must be distressing," she said, neutrally.

Ito bobbed his head at her understanding and delicacy. "I'll be travelling frequently in China and then home to Tokyo. I'm going to use Hong Kong as a base. I want a few good pieces in my pied-à-terre here. They'll keep me company. One can't be lonely surrounded by beauty." He gazed into her eyes.

Leah was surprised. She hadn't expected flattery from a Japanese.

Ito wasn't interested in the painted porcelain, although he carefully rewrapped the *mei-p'ing* vases decorated with sprigs of plum blossoms. Or the figurine of *Hsüan-ti*. Leah smiled broadly at his lack of interest in the warrior god. Then again, maybe his allegiance to the Emperor Hirohito precluded it. One could only worship so many gods of war. What was wrong with her? Here was a ready buyer and already she was passing judgment on him. It was a ridiculous way to do business. War infected everything.

Ito held up a pot, declaring, "Late *K'ang-his* reign."

"No. It's earlier. A true example of the Golden Age."

They argued. She was amazed at his encyclopaedic knowledge, a brilliant amateur.

"It's the metallurgist in me," he explained. "The invention of monochrome porcelains intrigues me. So subtle, each so different. So evocative, the glaze names—peach blossom, tea dust, *clair de lune*. It must be difficult to part with them."

Shrugging, she said, "They will be safe at the Freer. I mean . . ." Her words trailed off.

"The times we live in," he said as his eyes settled on an exquisite celadon vase.

Leah saw the lust to own it flicker across his face.

"I must have it," he declared. "Name your price."

Leah apologised and explained it was the star of her collection. The Freer had asked for it especially. "I'm sure I could, given time, locate a similar one."

His greed overcame him. "But I want this one. I'll pay in Swiss francs."

There was something obscene in his wanting it so much. In his hands, its graceful neck and slender body, glazed apple green looked both tempting and sullied. Already, she liked it less.

"It's the lines that appeal so much. Simple, but speaking of centuries of craftsmanship. Others might not see what I see in it. I would appreciate it more than curators with their dry desires or with the idle curiosity of museum goers. It belongs with me."

Under pressure from Ito's desire and his ready cash, Leah's resolve melted. The vase might never reach the States. Jonathan had patiently explained that her insurance would be worthless if the ship were bombed and sunk. It would be an act of *force majeure*, an act of war. Insurance companies didn't pay out for acts of war. She wasn't surprised. A figure jumped into her head. It was astronomical. She lowered the price by ten per cent. She didn't want him to think she was a complete bandit. Though why she should care what he thought, she couldn't say. Though he was very un-Japanese.

"Eighteen hundred Swiss francs. Cash. I don't know how I'll explain this to the museum."

He winced, but didn't haggle. Hurriedly, before he could change his mind, Leah wrapped the vase. She watched him pull out his billfold and count out the money. It made a thick pile on top of the tea chest.

When he finished, he said breezily, "Don't bank the money."

"Why? Is it counterfeit?"

He laughed, his brown eyes dancing with good humour. Then he was serious and cold, all business. "Of course not. But these days, cash in a good currency is always useful. The Hong Kong dollar fluctuates so."

He meant that the Hong Kong dollar went into steep dives when rumours of war heated up. What did the charming Mr Ito know?

"It's just good financial sense," he said lamely, as he saw her withdraw to hold the packaged vase as a barrier between them. "I look forward to doing more business with you on my return. I won't be away for long."

He made it sound like a promise. Leah was surprised that she was glad. She handed him the vase.

His face glowed with acquisitive pleasure. "Thank you. The world would be a better place if there were more trust."

Leah was taken aback. It was such an odd thing to say. "I feel I've betrayed the Freer."

"No," he declared. "You have simply found a safer place for an object of beauty." He dazzled her with a smile. "I'm sure the Gallery will understand."

He had a female understanding of the effect of his handsome face when he showed his delight. She had never seen a man wield this kind of power before. It had its desired result but she met his gaze.

Ito bowed goodbye as Leah extended her hand. Awkwardly, he shook it. His hand was dry and his grip strong. Then he bowed again, as if wanting to make a point about customs and goodbyes. He placed his Panama hat firmly on his head.

Leah watched him walk down Hollywood Road with the vase tucked snugly under one cradling arm, his other hand in his trouser pocket. He had a rolling gait, slim-hipped, jaunty. A boulevard stroll. She doubted he had been raised in Japan. She was relieved to see he didn't bother to look into the windows of the other antique and curio shops that crowded the street. He had what he'd come for.

At the customs office the next morning, Jonathan and Leah rechecked the paperwork for the Freer Gallery.

"You have to sign here," said Jonathan, "and attest to a witness, that's me, that the list of objects is accurate."

Leah scanned the paper. Her hand hovered over the listed apple green celadon vase. No, she wouldn't cross it off. Things got stolen in transit all the time. Probably, the director would write to apologise and offer payment. And, of course, she would have to accept the cheque with reluctance. It was the honourable thing to do. She imagined Theo's broad smile on his large face. He would have been so pleased that his training was being put to such good use. Everyone cheats; cheat first had been his precept.

"It's all in order," she declared, teasingly holding up her right hand as if she were in court.

2

THE FOREIGN AUXILIARY of the Chinese Red Cross was housed in a squat nondescript building on the outskirts of Chinatown, not far from Narrows Road. To Leah, the headquarters looked furtive, as if the Europeans inside were ashamed of their support for the Chinese army dying to save China. Socially prominent colonists volunteered for the International Red Cross near Central, staffed by paid workers. On principle, the International Red Cross refused to give desperately needed medical supplies and aid to the Chinese army, proclaiming its aim was to help only Chinese civilians. Leah sighed as she entered the Auxiliary. She was becoming a boor about the Sino Japanese War.

At parties, or dancing at the fashionable Gripps Room atop the Hong Kong Hotel, she complained bitterly about the colonial community's lack of support for the Chinese. Men, who she knew would willingly sleep with her, crossed to the other side of the room to avoid her harangue. And Hope declared in her high-pitched, fluting voice she used to score points: "Leah, stop nagging. No one is interested."

Unrepentant, Leah retorted, "Hope, it's the Chinese army that is keeping Hong Kong safe."

Hope sniffed and turned to Charles for support. "Isn't she a scream? Everyone knows the Chinese make terrible soldiers."

Then Jonathan, for the sake of peace and because his firm was representing Charles, diplomatically ordered more drinks and asked Leah for a dance.

On the dance floor he whispered, "Darling, they're impossible. Don't argue with her and that fool Charles. They're not worth it." He pulled her against him, his arm tight around her back, their legs deliciously intertwined. "The Government should be giving money directly to the Chinese army. The Japs are at our back door. Hope is an idiot. You're doing a wonderful job."

But Leah knew her motives weren't pure. After her first refusal to evacuate to Australia, she had to find a war-related reason to stay. Joining the Auxiliary was the solution. Sometimes, she resented having to spend two days a week in its run-down rooms, sitting in battered uncomfortable chairs, sweating as the squeaky fans failed miserably to push the air around. Then there were the boxes, boxes of prized medical supplies that made the place seem more like a chaotic post office than a workplace, and her antique business was suffering from her absence. But it was the maverick women—women, who scorned the usual female pursuits of bridge and gin and cared about what might happen—that made the place bearable. She liked many of them and admired tall, angular Delia for her ruthlessness. Delia would stop at nothing to aid the Chinese army. When Delia discovered she could speak and write Cantonese, she was pressed into composing endless begging letters to wealthy Chinese.

If they failed, Delia invited the would-be donor to dinner. The Chinese businessman accepted because Delia's husband, Carrington, was high up in the Colonial government. It was an honour to be invited. It was also gruelling. Delia was merciless, stopping at nothing to obtain a donation. Cornered, the man would agree to donate hundreds of Hong Kong dollars to the cause as Carrington nodded, implicity promising future government favours, and Leah flirted and praised. Later, after the cheque had been cashed, Leah wrote to thank the benefactor for his generosity and discreetly tucked in her business card: Miss Leah Kolbe, Proprietor, Asian Objects D'Arts for the Discerning. The benefactor would either go himself or send an assistant to her shop and acquire a treasure he didn't necessarily want. It was how business was done in the Colony. The donor understood this; Leah capitalised on it; and Delia let it pass because the coffers of the Auxiliary were increasing exponentially.

Today, Delia's hawk face was wreathed in smiles as she greeted Leah and propelled her toward the back room. "See, the sulfa medicines have arrived. They need to be labelled in Chinese. And our generous Mr. Wo is coming this afternoon to have his picture taken with them for the *South China Post*. I want you to emphasise to Mr. Wo how many lives will be saved."

"Delia, not me, please. I don't think Mr. Wo has forgiven me for ruining his suit."

The Wo dinner party had been awful. Wo was so wealthy that he didn't bother with normal courtesies and growled commands that everyone obeyed. He worked day and night, his money talked. He kept a string of concubines who were always fighting amongst themselves. During dinner, under the table, Wo had stroked her knee. Torn between her desire to wheedle as much money as she could from the old tyrant and the urge to slap his wandering hands, she'd knocked over a glass of wine. It stained Wo's elegant suit. Wily Mr. Wo realised it wasn't quite an accident. Nonetheless, to save face, he pledged five thousand Hong Kong dollars. Leah wrote to thank him for his generous donation, apologised effusively for spilling the wine, and included her business card. Wo sent his son to Leah's shop. The younger Mr. Wo bought a trinket, an elm tree pen stand containing inferior brushes. The son knew this token purchase was beneath his father and kept his head down. Leah was not looking forward to seeing the senior Mr. Wo again.

Delia laughed. "He deserved it. He's a scheming old dog. But I do want your face in the picture. A pretty face always helps."

Leah ignored the dig. At school, her teachers hid her beauty in the back row of the tall plain girls or cast doubt on her looks. Some focused on her high cheekbones and grey eyes, demanding to know if she were British. She lied and said yes. Why should she have to explain about her long dead White Russian mother or American Theo? Others, smug in their blue-stocking ugliness, sneered: Pretty is as pretty does.

Now, she said, "I'll be wide-eyed and beautiful."

"Wonderful," Delia declared as a note of regret crept in. "Use your power. I was always the plain girl, the prefect. I would have given it all up to be the pretty one."

"I don't believe you," said Leah. "You like power."

"Do I? Who knows?" She gave Leah a sharp-eyed stare.

Delia had ugly hands, large, with big knuckles, and ungainly, bunioned toes, peeping out from her sandals. Leah pictured Delia in her petticoat staring into a closet full of unbecoming print dresses that bagged over her bony chest and did nothing for her sallow skin and asked too quickly, "Do I have time for the labelling of supplies?"

"Gathering public support is important," Delia admonished. "An English reporter is coming. He's going to interview you about our Chinese war effort. Hands across the border, that sort of thing."

"Shall I put the bite on him?"

Delia grinned, her large teeth visible. "Appeal to the snobs," she said savagely and handed Leah a pen with a thick nib. "The India ink is in the cupboard."

☙

THE late-afternoon heat made Leah drowsy. She had to concentrate to remember how to write 'sterile' in Chinese characters. She was blowing on the ink to prevent it smearing, when Benjamin Eldersen walked in, glowing with delight. He scooped her up and held her to his chest. She relaxed in his arms and kissed his cheek, muzzy with the familiar smell of stale cigarettes. She pulled away and examined him. It must be three years since she had seen him. His fingernails were now permanently stained nicotine yellow and his hair was thinner, hanging lank around his ears. He needed a good haircut. The lines on his face were deeper. There were purple pouches under his eyes and his slouch was more pronounced. Apart from that, he was about the same: rumpled suit, badly ironed shirt, cheap tie, hatless.

"You arranged this, didn't you? You're the wire services reporter."

"Wanted it to be a surprise. Take you unawares."

"You could have written."

For a moment, his face dropped and he looked guilty. "Wasn't sure of the assignment . . ." He shrugged as if he could dismiss the half-written desperate letters he had begun in too many Asian cities. "Lately, I've been covering the 7th Army on the plains of Shaokwan. Bad postal service," he joked.

"You should have written. I see your by-lines and think of

you. It's no way to treat an old friend."

Delia strode in with Mr. Wo and a very young, overawed photographer, who barely had the nerve to raise his camera as he backed into a distant corner. Without prompting, Mr. Wo draped his arm over Leah's shoulders, gave a hard smile, and ordered the photographer to proceed. In the flash of the bulb, Mr. Wo's hand sneaked toward Leah's breast, then the pressure was gone and Delia rearranged them in another pose.

Finally, the photographer ran out of bulbs and Delia ran out of suggestions. Delia said in a rush, "The board of the Red Cross is expecting us. The car is ready."

Mr. Wo held out his arm to escort Leah to the car.

Delia shook her head, "Sadly, Miss Kolbe won't be joining us. She has kindly agreed to be interviewed for our British fundraising campaign."

Wo snarled his displeasure to Leah in Cantonese and said in English, "Another time?"

Leah smiled as if this might be possible.

Delia laid her hand on Mr. Wo's arm and Wo was forced to escort her out.

"You shouldn't do that," cautioned Eldersen, "you'll end up as his fourth favourite concubine."

"Don't you mean his first?"

"Without a doubt," he said, his eyes full of admiration.

"Don't look at me like that." She could feel herself blushing.

"At least the old reprobate has taste."

"That's not a compliment."

"Sorry. How's Jonathan?"

"You're well informed."

"Hong Kong is a small place."

"Small-minded. Shouldn't we get on with the interview?"

She sat down and patted the chair next to her.

"Let's forget the interview."

"The Auxiliary needs the money."

"Conscientious. Gotten new clients for your shop?"

"The Chinese deserve our support and you have become even more cynical."

"Guilty," he said and fumbled around in his jacket for matches and a cigarette. He inhaled deeply and spoke in a funny radio broadcast voice: "The pretty"—he stopped, reconsidered—"make that the ravishingly beautiful Miss Leah Kolbe is a staunch supporter of the Chinese army war effort. She well understands that China's fight is our fight and to fight well, troops must be equipped . . . That what you want?"

Leah clapped. "But truly, Ben, you don't need to include the beauty part . . . it makes me sound like an empty-headed debutante. I believe in China."

"You once told me beauty was very important."

"I was talking about art."

"You've grown into your beauty."

"Have I?"

"Don't fish. I want you to meet some good friends of my mine. They're at a party."

Why spend the evening here? She had almost finished labelling the boxes. Jonathan was working late and she didn't fancy dinner alone on the Peak. She liked Eldersen. He was the perfect companion: clever, witty and full of accurate news about the war. So what if he looked like an old shoe, old shoes were very comfortable. "I'd love to."

ELDERSEN led the way, searching for room 315 down the

thick-carpeted hall of the Peninsula Hotel. Through a half-opened door, they heard female laughter and a jumble of male voices. A woman could be heard above the din, "Hong Kong is the safest place to be. The Japs don't want war with England." A man hooted in reply, "They don't want to fight Europeans. Wouldn't stand a chance." There was a peal of drunken laughter.

"The natives are restless," said Eldersen, putting a firm hand around Leah's waist to steer her through the room. He attempted to cut a path to the double bed where a couple lounged. The man looked vaguely familiar, but Leah couldn't place him. Midway, a uniformed waiter with a loaded drinks trolley and demanding drinkers blocked their way. Bottles clanked ominously as the insistent crowd called for whisky with soda, straight whisky, gin and bitters, sloe gin.

"There is a queue," declared an irritated major in full army dress pushed beyond his endurance by people stepping on his toes and thrusting out their hands insisting on being served before him.

A young woman in a bright green dress elbowed past to grab a bottle of gin. She poured half a glass then added a splash of tonic. "Help yourself," she said, slurring her words.

The waiter blanched and stood still as eager hands snatched full bottles and began pouring drinks for friends. The military man handed the distraught waiter ten Hong Kong dollars and said, "I'll sign for it. Leave the trolley." The waiter bowed deeply and left as the crowd cheered.

Eldersen parted people with a polite "Pardon me" and thrust Leah towards the couple on the bed. Leah stared at the man.

Eldersen whispered, "They've just come back from the Chinese front."

The man's arm was around the shoulders of a good-looking blonde woman in a silk blouse and grey trousers. He had a full head of dark hair, thick moustache and a large mouth. His hand toyed with the buttons of the woman's blouse. The woman flicked his hand away. He flashed alarmingly white teeth in a disarming seducer's smile as he said, "Ben, so glad to see a friendly face. Welcome to the dog and pony show."

"Leah Kolbe, please meet Ernest Hemingway and Martha Gellhorn," said Eldersen proudly.

"Enjoy the honeymoon?" he then asked Martha.

Martha made a face. "Camping out on Chinese battlefields makes marriage a breeze."

"Isn't she wonderful?" beamed Hemingway.

He sat up and patted the bed. Eldersen and Leah sat. Hemingway reached for a large bottle. "A present from the front," he said. "Very handy on the battlefield. Cures everything." He shook the bottle to show that the two curled dun-colour snakes inside were dead. "Don't worry," said Hemingway, "It wasn't the rice wine that killed them."

"It tastes foul," said Martha.

"You have to drink from the bottle but don't tilt it too much. You'll swallow a snake," said Hemingway and eyed Leah, daring her to drink.

He had a flat, loud voice. Everyone in the room was watching him perform. Leah sniffed the wine. It had a dead smell. She tilted the bottle—the snakes remained coiled at the bottom—and took a good slug, her eyes on Hemingway's, answering his taunt. Martha was bemused. Leah forced herself to swallow the bitter wine and handed it back. "The snake drank the best part."

Hemingway guffawed. "Glad to see someone has life around here. You want to try, Ben?"

"Pass."

"Quite right, Ben. Don't let him bully you," said Martha.

"The troops swear by it," Hemingway persisted.

"Rice would help more," said Eldersen.

"Yeah," said Martha. "They were starving. It's hard to fight on an empty stomach."

"They hate the Japanese," said Leah. "With good reason."

"Leah was in Manchuria. We met there in late '37, early '38," Eldersen confided.

Hemingway's big face reflected lively interest. "How was it?" he asked, his writer's instinct aroused.

Leah said nothing. The room was stuffy. If she turned her head even slightly, she would meet the staring faces of strangers who had arranged themselves along the edge of the bed, not daring to sit next to the chosen few. Despite the noisy babble that ebbed and flowed, the spectators could hear every word. "Cold," she replied. "It wasn't a good place for a holiday."

At first, she thought Eldersen was going to contradict her, but he seemed wary of the crowd of hangers-on and changed the subject, asking, "What did you make of Chang-kai-shek?"

"Hard to say if the man is telling the truth. Still the good thing about the Sino Jap War is that it keeps the Japs tied up while the United States builds up its arms," Hemingway pronounced like a god, then sank back onto a pillow to watch the partygoers' reactions.

Many of the spectators nodded in agreement. Angry, Leah said, "It's not a prelude for anything for the Chinese. They're the ones dying, being raped, having their land confiscated. Did you even speak to any ordinary Chinese? Of course not. You don't, as they say, speak the lingo." She looked to Martha for support.

"You tell him, honey. Mrs Chiang-kai-shek is a piece of work."

"You going to write that?" asked Eldersen.

Martha sighed. "I don't know. It wouldn't help the Chinese

cause, would it?"

"You Brits ought to supply the Chinese better. They're tough fighters. Or at least dogged if futile," said Hemingway.

Leah understood it was a kind of game. He was teasing her, making fun of her. She blurted out hotly, "No one here cares. It's all about England and how to maintain Hong Kong's neutrality."

Martha smiled in friendly agreement. "Ben, this is a young woman who cares passionately. Don't let her get away. Sign her up to write an article." Martha dropped her voice, "Something is going on here. There are too many Japanese in Hong Kong. God knows what they're up to. They have spies everywhere. You can't bend over backwards for thugs."

Leah nodded. There were hundreds of Japanese in Hong Kong, including Mr Ito. Mr Ito would like this party, but he'd probably be asked to leave. Two days ago, she'd received a picture postcard from him. It was a photograph of a wide boulevard containing a dozen baronial houses in the German concession of Hankow. There were no people on the street, just the empty wide street and the enormous houses. He wrote:

Dear Miss Kolbe,

I will be returning soon.

Yours faithfully,
Mr. T. Ito

It was a strange card to receive. Troubled by his need to communicate with her, she had torn it up and thrown it away.

Hemingway gave a slow clap. "Isn't she good?"

Martha made a face. Leah thought she looked put out by

Hemingway's patronising words, but what did she know about marriage. Did they have secrets from each other? Hemingway appeared pleased to have a beautiful young wife. But what did Martha get out of it? An important writer, Leah supposed. Life was a bargain.

"You want to become a stringer for Hong Kong, Leah?" asked Eldersen, not quite joking.

"What?" said Leah, caught off guard talking to people she had only read about. "No, I have a job."

"Good," said Martha. "There are too many writers in the world, anyway."

Hemingway flashed his large teeth. "Martha is very ambitious."

"So are you, darling," said Martha and kissed him lightly on the cheek.

A giggling girl in a polka-dotted dress pushed through the worshipping crowd and grinned with adoration at the Hemingways. "I'm such an admirer," she gushed. "I've read all your books." She thrust a book at Hemingway. "Please sign my copy."

Hemingway frowned politely. "I haven't got a pen."

A flood of people began searching their pockets, opening handbags and slyly sneaking out their own books.

Eldersen nudged Leah, "We're in the way."

They moved to stand by the closed bathroom door. There was the sound of a toilet flushing. A man in a suit came out shaking his hands. "No towels. Best damn hotel in Hong Kong and no towels. Or they've been stolen." He stared at the excited crowd. "They ought to charge, like the zoo to look at the monkeys." Then he strode away and helped himself to a generous whisky.

"He doesn't mind drinking the monkey's whisky," noted Eldersen.

"You're full of surprises," said Leah. "What other famous

people do you know?"

Ben scanned the room. Wedged next to him was a fat man with a large bald head haranguing a female in an electric blue dress about self-promoting American authors, stabbing the air to underscore his point. The man spilled his drink down the front of Eldersen's jacket. "Awfully sorry," the fat man apologised and daubed at the whisky stains with his pocket-handkerchief.

"It needs cold water," said Leah and led Eldersen into the bathroom, taking the fat man's handkerchief with her. As she turned on the tap, Eldersen kicked the door shut. He watched Leah's long fingers pat the widening stain.

"Forget it, Leah," he said. "It doesn't matter if I smell like a brewery. Part of the reporter image." He took hold of her wrist. "Stay. I have to ask you something. In private. It's important."

There was a sharp knock on the door.

"In use," called Ben.

"But that poor man—" said Leah.

"We know a Mr Ito visited you."

"Who's we?" she demanded. "He bought a vase. He's a customer. I don't know him."

The doorknob rattled. "Come on, old man. I can't make it across this crowded room," a voice called.

"He's left Hong Kong," she added.

"He'll be back."

Leah nodded slowly, her attention focused on Eldersen's face, stern and insistent. "What do you want?" she asked. His nicotine-stained fingers tightened around her wrist. Her wrist looked small in his grasp. She didn't struggle.

"You want me to spy?" she said, amazed, feeling unsure and very young.

"Ito is important. He knows a great deal about Japan's arms

shipments, steel. The things that make war possible."

Gently, she unwound his fingers from around her wrist. "Can I think about it?"

"There isn't time. I need to brief you."

"It's late. I'm tired."

"It's war. You said so yourself. Or are you another armchair patriot," he mocked, and reached for the door.

"I meant what I said."

"Actions speak louder than words."

There were loud kicks at the door. "Steady on," said Eldersen.

"Come to the house tomorrow. It's the best I can do. I just want one night to think about it. That's not too much to ask."

"You're going to say yes."

"Do you know me so well?" she teased and dropped a small swift kiss on his tobacco scented mouth.

Before he could respond, she whipped open the door and a desperate man, his hands already fighting with the buttons of his fly, rushed past them, declaring: "You could have picked a more romantic place."

"Prig," said Leah. Eldersen hooted.

The Hemingways had left. The noise level was unbearable. Someone had switched on a radio. A few couples were dancing in a tiny space, bumping into people, while a few leftover men stumbled around humming and swaying and the rest were getting seriously drunk. A man appeared in the doorway and asked for quiet. Leah recognised the hotel manager, Mr. McIntyre. Those at the front shouted for silence; a dancer snapped off the radio in mid tune.

"I'm sorry, to interrupt. There is a practice black out tonight. We can offer transport for those who require it. Alternatively, you may wish to be our guest for the night, only some may have to share rooms."

There were scattered drunken catcalls, followed by indignant cries. The partygoers trickled out as McIntyre thanked each guest and apologised repeatedly, saying, "It's the war."

Out on the street, Leah invited Eldersen home. "You can stay the night. Jonathan can lend you pyjamas. We can talk in the morning."

Her invitation disarmed him. It was so matter-of-fact, no lying about why Jonathan was at her house, in her bed. It made him feel old. How ridiculous he would look padding about in Jonathan's pyjamas. They were bound to be too tight. He was nearly forty and, despite his inadequate diet on the plains of Shaokwan, had a definite paunch. In the morning, he'd look worse because he wouldn't have slept. He'd stay awake listening for the sounds of Leah and Jonathan having sex. Pathetic, but he knew he would lean against the wall eager to hear, or even more degrading, might attempt to loiter barefoot outside their closed bedroom door. Disgusting. In the morning, there would be the added indignity of Jonathan treating him like a disreputable uncle one has to humour, or at least lock the liquor cabinet against. "No, I'd best go back to my hotel. I'll get you a taxi and see you in the morning," he managed in a voice he hoped sounded normal and not collapsing under the weight of his futile desire.

Leah let Eldersen talk on as they waited in the queue for a taxi, lost in a wave of conflicting emotions. She was under no illusions about what it meant to be a spy. She would be trading in secrets. Who knew where that might lead? Jonathan would never understand. She would have to build tight, new walls around her love.

They moved to the head of the taxi queue and Eldersen

opened the door. Leah blew him a kiss through the window.

He caught it in his hand and watched the cab meld into the light traffic. He touched his cheek and started to walk towards his modest hotel in Shah Tin. At least the usual whores wouldn't be hanging about. He might have been tempted tonight.

3

SHEEPISHLY, JONATHAN RAISED his head from the legal brief he was pretending to be absorbed in as Leah entered the bedroom. He felt guilty, caught out waiting up for her. "I was worried. The blackout. Thought you might not be able to get home."

"I've had fun," she volunteered, "I went to a party. I met the Hemingways. Amazing. I liked them. Ben Eldersen is in town. He invited me." He was looking at her so hard. Had he guessed something was amiss? What was he looking for? Signs of drunkenness or the kisses of other men?

Jonathan laid the papers aside. "You could have called. I might have been able to come."

"Could you, darling? But I had no idea the Hemingways were going to be there. Ben surprised me. It was a lovely surprise."

She decided to let him play out his petulance. Part of the problem was Eldersen. He didn't like him or didn't trust him; or, perhaps it was an English schoolboy kind of snobbery. It was difficult to know. Whenever he saw Eldersen's by-line, he made fun of it: It's *your* friend again, getting mixed up in something he knows nothing about. Leah would defend Ben and then the conversation would screech to a halt.

"Had a good time?"

"Mmm." She let her clothes fall in a heap on the floor, and got into bed. Nestling into the crook of his arm, she told him about the snake wine, how people had ringed the bed in awe. "It was like an audience with the Pope."

"I wouldn't be surprised if Hemingway bought the wine off a street stall at the night market. It must be hard to think of new gimmicks to impress the locals."

"He wasn't interested in me. He's got a new wife."

"Fool," muttered Jonathan as they began to make love in earnest.

Leah woke in the inky darkness and listened to Jonathan's regular breathing. She ran a finger along his back and licked it. He tasted salty, slightly fruity. She resisted the urge to poke him in the ribs, wake him, and reveal what Eldersen had asked. What good would it do? He would be adamantly opposed and livid with anger at Eldersen. He couldn't advise her. It was her life. Theo taught her to think for herself. If Theo wanted something, he went after it. Life is dangerous, he'd said. In the end we all die. As soon as Ben asked, she knew she'd do it. No one was safe anymore. The fan purred; Jonathan tugged at the sheet. Jonathan must never know. She tucked herself in against his warm back. Mr. Ito was the enemy. She'd get him.

LEAH waited for Eldersen in the garden. It was her favourite place, lush green shrubs, and bright flowers framed by the moon gates. Tranquil and peaceful. All Theo's doing. He had planned it meticulously, fussing over the views, where the pond should go. How he would loathe the deep trench that now ran through the lawn, a precaution against the rumours of war, somewhere to cower when the bombs fell. A ladder rested against its entrance. It made the garden seem makeshift, as if a fleet of workers were waiting at the gates with their wheelbarrows, rakes and shovels to demolish it and start over.

Eldersen's eyes went straight to the gash when he arrived.

"I hate it too. We were forced to do it. The servants might not make it to the shelters in time . . . I had to make provision."

"Sign of the times," said Eldersen, trying to read her face, how she stood, to see if she would agree.

She held up a blue notebook. "I'm ready."

Eldersen blinked at the swiftness of her decision. "You mustn't write anything down. That's a rule."

Leah took a seat at the bamboo table with its striped umbrella and gave Eldersen the notebook. He sat with it on his knees, riffling the blank pages with his thumb, feeling as though the end of the world had come. "You don't have to do this."

"You've changed your tune."

"No, I just don't want to think I bullied or tricked you into it."

"You haven't."

"What about Jonathan?"

"What about him?"

"Nothing. It was a stupid question." He bit his lip and turned away to pull out a pad of yellow lined paper from his battered briefcase.

The top piece of paper was covered in doodles and a scattering of words. Leah couldn't read them upside down. She remembered the first time she'd met Eldersen in the dining car of the train going to that terrible place now called Manchukuo by the triumphant Japanese. He had a notebook then, a tiny red thing, full of scribbles, held together by rubber bands and stuffed full of God knew what. He referred to it jokingly as his little black book, pretending it held the secrets of all the women he had abandoned in exotic places. They both knew that was a lie. He was a lonely man, never quite at ease. He had a pensive look now, his thick eyebrows forming a caterpillar line across his forehead. On his chin was a shaving nick. As he spoke he rubbed the cut continuously, but it didn't bleed.

"It's settled," she said.

Gravely, he nodded, pushing down a lump of regret.

With a tray of tea and sandwiches, Huang fu trotted across the grass neatly side stepping the ladder.

Not missing a beat, as though it was exactly what they had been discussing, Eldersen said, "You're right. A fine day. Hong Kong is best in early winter. Cool and sunny."

Huang fu, his face smooth and polite, set the tray down. In Cantonese, Leah thanked and dismissed him.

Eldersen waited for Huang fu to cross the lawn and shut the French doors noiselessly. He resumed their previous conversation asking, "When is Jonathan coming?"

"He won't be home for hours. He's training with the Volunteers."

"Well, then," he said in an authoritative voice. He peered down at his doodles. "Let me tell you about Mr. Tokai Ito."

Leah appreciated Eldersen's clinical detachment. It was like examining Ito in a Petri dish: inert, pinned down, giving up his secrets. Unusual for his time, Tokai's parents had made a love match; they were part of the small, but growing upper middle class. Japan was shedding its feudal past. They married while his mother was still at university. His father, Hiroyuki, was an engineer, a man of increasing substance owing to the country's rapid industrialisation. Then tragedy struck: Ito's mother died giving birth to him. Hiroyuki retreated from the world. His emotional reaction shamed his father.

"How do you know all this?" asked Leah.

"It's in his dossier."

"Do I have a dossier?"

"Yes," he said. "That's the kind of world we have now."

"Yes, of course," Leah acknowledged, all the while knowing that facts don't mean much. No one knew she traipsed around curio shops and stalls searching for a Japanese woodcut of a handsome prince with a sharp chin and rich clothes. She couldn't find what she wanted; now, she decided, she wouldn't look any more.

Eldersen discussed Japan's desperation at the turn of the century to obtain the know-how of the West. Hiroyuki was an ideal candidate to live abroad and bring the new technology back. For his father, it solved the embarrassing problem of his son's overreaction to his wife's death. His grandson, Tokai, would remain in Tokyo to be educated like a proper son of Japan.

"This is where it gets interesting," said Eldersen. "Hiroyuki insisted on taking his son with him. Tokai has visited Japan many times, but he has never lived there. He's a foreigner in his own country. He speaks German, French and English as well as Japanese. You can see why we picked him."

"You don't think he's loyal."

Eldersen drew more doodles and eyed Leah nervously. "He's loyal to his father. It's a national trait, subservience to the father."

Leah watched Eldersen backpedal. What was he really saying? That 'they,' whoever 'they' were, had chosen her because she was like Tokai? She didn't fit in either. Icily, she said, "I am my own person. I am not like Tokai Ito at all."

Agitated and upset, unable to continue with the briefing, Eldersen got up and inspected the trench as his thoughts collided. He was such a fraud. He couldn't remain detached. Even as he discussed Tokai calmly, without emotion, he pictured Tokai and Leah together. His mind was a cesspool; just like the ditch it offered only limited protection. Oh hell, he was a pimp. The higher ups had put it about, well actually had looked uncomfortable over their teacups, as they let it be known that they expected Leah to seduce information from Ito: where the Jap plants were in China, when large shipments were going to be made, what kind of ships were passing right under their noses in the port of Hong Kong loaded with armaments. In a minute, reality would hit Leah too. He wished he were a thousand miles away, holed up in a rat trap of an Asian newspaper office, banging out stories, not responsible for someone he cared so deeply about. Love in wartime was shit.

Leah watched Eldersen scrutinize the trench. He walked up to it and tapped his foot against the side, as if trying to determine if it would cave in. It wouldn't because Huang fu had overseen the project. Leah suspected Jonathan provided Huang fu with generous squeeze money to ensure that the trench was dug and braced properly. Several times she caught Huang fu and Jonathan, deep in conversation, pacing around the garden. They both looked guilty when she asked them what they were plotting. Eldersen had the same look, caught in the act. In a flash of mortifying insight, Leah realised Eldersen's spying was whoring. He wanted her to become Ito's mistress. Ito's loyalty to his father was absolute. Eldersen was asking her to wheedle information from Ito in bed, or later, as he slept, to go through his private papers. They might be written in Japanese but she would be able to understand more or less what they meant and figure out the rest. Livid, she said, "Do you get excited at the thought of my bedding the cosmopolitan Mr. Ito?"

Eldersen lost his balance and fell onto the roof of the trench. He rose awkwardly to his feet and brushed off the dirt. He came to stand uneasily by her side, catching hold of both her hands, and gazed into her eyes, knowing he mustn't fake this. He spoke from the heart. "There are no rules about . . ." He searched for an appropriate word. None came to mind that he felt like saying aloud and he muttered like a coward, "This sort of thing. We rely on your own judgment."

"I screw him and you learn his secrets."

He dropped her hand. "You don't believe that."

"No," she said. "I believe you are my friend and wouldn't hurt me."

Her words made him feel worse. "Forget it. You aren't cut out for this."

"You know I am."

"We need you," he said by way of an apology. He dug around in his battered briefcase and brought out a tiny camera. "To photograph Ito's papers."

She took the camera and squeezed his hands. "I won't tell you how I got the information. If I have to fuck him, I will."

He fumbled as he lit a cigarette and inhaled too deeply. The smoke caught in his lungs. Coughing and gagging, he drank the now cold tea to soothe his wounded throat. "Let's leave it at that," he said, flame-red with embarrassment.

She didn't care she had made him look small. She had a right to set the ground rules. Look what he was asking her to do. "What do I do with the film?" she asked.

"Right, to business," he said, not looking up. "Nathan Thwaites is your contact. He's a clerk in charge of new accounts at the Hong Kong and Shanghai Bank. Open a trading account in the name of New Lotus Enterprises. The funds are there for anything you might need." He sighed, "For bribes or asking anyone you can trust to find out things. You give Thwaites the film, verbal reports, anything at all of interest. I respect your judgment." Then he launched into technical details on how to read bills of lading to understand what actually might be found in the ship's hold. Even as he talked on, he was consumed with a creeping despair, his explanations growing shorter and more precise until he couldn't speak any more.

The sun hung low in the late afternoon sky; the garden was getting chilly. Leah rubbed her hands against her cold arms. Half-eaten sandwiches and cakes littered the table. She was surprised at how ordinary a spy briefing was. She didn't know what she had expected. Ben looked ragged; she felt exhilarated, agitated and overwhelmed.

Finally, he said, "I have to leave tomorrow. Another assignment. Any questions?" and rolled cake crumbs across his plate, waiting for her to answer. Her face was obscured by the long shadows. He lit a cigarette to prevent himself from reaching across the table to touch her petal-soft skin. Christ, why couldn't he stop these thoughts?

Leah leaned closer so he could see her clearly. He was keeping something back. If they wanted her this badly, then they were more afraid than Eldersen was letting on. She must know. "When will the Japanese invade?"

He paled and stared intently at the trench. "Our best intelligence is that nothing will happen before early June 1942, over six months away. More troops will be stationed here and defences improved by then."

"Really?"

He ground his cigarette into his plate. "Go to Macau. Portugal is neutral and so by extension is its colony, Macau. Don't try for Free China. God knows what will be happening in China.

It won't be safe. Whatever you do, don't fool yourself you can remain in Hong Kong, it's—" He stopped.

Jonathan strolled across the garden in his uniform: khaki shorts, open collared shirt, his hat jammed onto his head at a jaunty angle. Leah sprang up and went running to his side, entwining an arm around his waist.

Eldersen stared at the handsome couple. Jonathan looked like a bloody recruiting poster, even to the sweat stains that ringed his armpits, as if the ad man wanted to prove the model was a man of action. Jonathan kissed Leah on the cheek. Eldersen wanted desperately to leave.

Jonathan plonked a bottle of whisky on the table. "What have you two been plotting all afternoon?"

"Ben has been telling me about his travels. He's off to Burma tomorrow."

"Must be off. Have to check the telegraph office to see if there have been any last minute changes."

"Stay for a drink at least."

"Sorry, another time. Have to check the wire services too."

"Ben," said Leah, "we're going to hold you to your promise to visit more."

Eldersen trotted out his wise uncle smile and said, "Next time. I'll drop you a postcard before I come. Don't bother to see me out." He walked quickly away, not wanting to turn around and see them together. It would be a memory he couldn't remove.

"I didn't mean to scare him off," said Jonathan as Eldersen reached the garden gate and left with a backward wave.

"See you soon," called Leah.

"Cheers." The gate banged closed.

"No," declared Leah, "he was getting ready to go. He had packing to do."

Jonathan shook his head. "He doesn't pack. He sleeps in his suit. Probably has only two pairs of underpants. He always looks the same."

Leah laughed, but felt a stab of guilt at ridiculing Eldersen behind his back. The man really did carry the weight of the world on his shoulders. "Actually, I think he's aged and he's lonely."

"He could quit anytime he wants. Settle down, marry. No, he likes the life he leads."

"Things are never that simple. You don't know what drives him."

Each time Jonathan saw Eldersen, he wanted to explode. Instead, he was unfaltering polite and chummy. If he were honest, he disliked Eldersen because he had been in Manchuria with Leah and shared a part of Leah's past he wasn't privy to. Leah never talked about Manchuria. He changed the subject, determined not to probe further about why the reporter had been hanging around all afternoon. "Things are looking up. Everyone says the Japanese will come by land. They've reinforced our defences on the Heights. The Canadian troops are going to man it. The Japs hate the sea, prone to seasickness and they can't swim. So, it's good the Canadians are here."

"What nonsense, Jonathan. They live on an island."

"Leah, marry me."

Leah's face paled under her tan and her grey eyes grew large with terror.

"Don't look like that. It makes perfect sense. I can't go on in this . . ." He looked around the garden with its ugly gash and the imposing house. There was nothing of his here, except the woman he loved. "I think if you don't, I will leave. If I do it now, I know that I can. Otherwise we'll be in this infernal no man's land I can't stand."

His eyes raked her face. He looked so lost; her heart lurched. She couldn't imagine life without him. He made her feel safe, filled up her heart, her house and chased away old ghosts. With the coming of war, no one was truly safe. And she recalled Theo's bleak words: In the end, we are all dead. She moved into Jonathan's arms, showering him with kisses. "It's nearly Christmas. Let's have a Christmas wedding."

A shock of joy spread across his face, the look of a drowning man unexpectedly rescued. Hand in hand, they went indoors to celebrate their love and their decision.

In her bones, Leah knew it was the only decision she could have made.

4

LEAH WALKED DOWN Queens Road in the full glare of the sun. She had arranged to meet Jonathan at the jewellers to pick out rings after she went to the bank to settle some accounts. Jonathan hadn't suspected a thing. It was a normal day; he was going to his office first.

She stood in front of the imposing new headquarters of the Hong Kong and Shanghai Bank, known affectionately by all as Honkers and Shakers. The building radiated money and power, and towered over the island. She walked through the heavy brass doors and asked the man sitting at an enormous mahogany desk to direct her to Nathan Thwaites.

Thwaites was a thin man with glasses, probably not yet thirty. His brown hair was plastered to his head with water and his eyebrows were raised in a perpetual look of surprise. He led her to one of the inner sanctums of the bank, containing a portrait of King George VI and a baroque table with uncomfortable Chinese ladder-back chairs. She declined his offer of tea.

"Your line of credit has arrived for New Lotus Enterprises," he said genially.

They did not discuss its purpose as he handed over signature cards and forms to be filled in and waited patiently. When she finished, he asked if she knew when Mr. Ito might be returning to Hong Kong. She told him about the meaningless postcard.

"Our friend wants to maintain contact," he concluded. "An encouraging sign."

On alert for sexual allusions concerning her future relations with Mr. Ito, Leah stiffened. Thwaites kept talking without innuendo. He was exceedingly courteous as he asked if she had any other information to report.

"Do you know about the newly opened wholesale tea business on Queen's Street? It's a supply front for the Chinese Communist 4th Battalion fighting the Japanese."

"It has just come to our attention. Your sources are good," he said and counted out $500 in Hong Kong notes. "The bank is always at your service."

At the jeweller's, Jonathan was enthusiastic. "Show me your best," he requested, squeezing Leah's hand with excitement as they sat on plump chairs painted gold. The bald, white-gloved jeweller unrolled a black velvet mat on top of the glass case. He arranged a row of diamond rings to demonstrate their clarity and cut.

"The choice must be right," the jeweller said, looking at Leah for encouragement, extolling the virtues of the diamonds: the clarity, the cut, the colour and the carats.

Leah was unmoved by their brilliance. Her soft-skinned, long-fingered hands were Theo's genetic gift. Like his, hers were crowned with perfect nails, buffed pearl pink; just visible underneath the clear varnish were flawless half moons. You have connoisseur's hands, Theo gloated. Gimcracks and gewgaws must not spoil them. He would be happy she was marrying for love; he would have been repelled to see a diamond on her finger. "It's a short engagement. We just want wedding rings."

"I want to do this," Jonathan pleaded.

"I want to be married, not engaged."

It was an arrow to his heart. Conquered, he agreed.

The jeweller sucked in his cheeks, swallowing hard to avoid showing his disappointment and swept the diamonds back into the glass case.

They chose two wide bands of gold and asked that they be engraved: Jonathan & Leah, 23 December 1941, their wedding date. High on a tidal wave of happiness, Jonathan said, "Engrave the word 'Love.'" Then he kissed Leah and even the jeweller minded a little less about losing a big sale. The engraved rings would be ready on Tuesday.

Out on the pavement, Jonathan linked arms with Leah. They grinned at one another, feeling slightly drunk and totally happy. Jonathan's friend, Tony Pentley, was hosting a dinner in their honour in the Gripps Room, but it was too early to go there. The ring-buying had taken so little time. They had planned to change at Jonathan's Mid-Level's flat, but if they went there now, Jonathan's giggling, under-worked houseboy would be in the way.

"Let's go to a film first," she proposed. "I can't face Pan Ling. He'll simply ooze all over us."

Jonathan laughed and agreed. He didn't mind. If the film were slow, he would daydream about the evening: Tony's party would be fun with magnums of champagne; Leah would be heart-rendering beautiful and everyone would be pea green with envy. To cap off the night, they would sink into bed on the Peak in a mutual embrace of lust and desire. Life was perfect.

They went to the newly-opened cinema on Nathan Street. The seats still give off a new leather smell and the carpet underfoot was a deep, unspoiled red. The film was *Bringing Up Baby*.

Everyone said it was screamingly funny: Cary Grant ran around like a lunatic, trying not to fall in love with an ebullient Katherine Hepburn, as a lion (a present from Katherine's brother in Africa) ran amok. Cary Grant ended up in jail until Katherine sorted things out. In the dark, Jonathan pulled Leah close and stroked her neck and fair hair.

Already Leah regretted her decision not to go to Jonathan's flat. To hell with Pan Ling. She'd tell Jonathan that they should leave. It would be a delicious end to the afternoon. She whispered, "Let's go—"

Instead of the sudden rush of music heralding the film's beginning, the screen went blank, then flickered. The audience groaned. The screen flickered again, then lit up with an announcement.

---

8 December 1941

ALL MEMBERS OF THE MILITARY AND VOLUNTEER UNITS ARE TO REPORT *IMMEDIATELY* TO DUTY

As the house lights came on, there was a collective gasp of disbelief. Leah and Jonathan looked at each other, uncomprehending and slightly mad with suppressed desire and grief.

"Perhaps it's a false alarm," said Jonathan.

There was a great deal of pushing and shoving as people attempted to say goodbye and others struggled to get to the aisle. Leah hugged Jonathan. An old man hissed his annoyance as they blocked his way.

Gently, Jonathan unwound Leah's arms. "I'll get leave for a few hours. Nothing is going to happen yet. The rings don't matter."

Tears welled in Leah's eyes. "Do it."

Jonathan kissed her again, then stared, memorising every inch of her face. When he joined the tide of men moving towards the door, he didn't turn around.

Around her stood deserted, dazed women reeling in the brightness of the house lights. She recognised the look. She had seen it in newsreels. It meant her world was falling apart.

At home, Leah directed the servants to tape the windows to prevent them breaking. She and Huang fu wrapped the porcelain in sheets, placing the pieces underneath the furniture, and then scattered cushions to stop them rolling. Exhausting the supply of cushions, they resorted to overturning chairs to make tents for the brasses and stone carvings. She surveyed the mess and felt foolish and chilled. If a bomb hit—the house made an easy target, squatting large and vulnerable atop the winding drive—everything would be blown to smithereens. As to her shop, well, it was locked and bolted and there was no way she could protect it. Even if she could find a truck and men to haul her antiques up here, they wouldn't be any safer. Besides, she reassured herself, she had sent her best pieces away.

"No more," said Leah. "It won't help."

"Tea?" asked Huang fu.

Leah nodded and sank down on the hard base of the cushionless sofa. Out the window, she saw the ancient gardener and his wife creeping around the garden supervising the two younger gardeners, making sure it remained exactly as Theo designed it.

It must be a false alarm. Everything was quiet. Jonathan was probably busy obtaining permission to get a car and lining up a magistrate to marry them. Maybe their engagement party could be cobbled together as a wedding party when the men straggled back from the call up.

She was raving. It must be shock.

Six of the servants finished taping the windows and appeared in the doorway of the living room, shifting from anxious foot to anxious foot, awaiting her orders. The radio was on, playing forgettable music as Leah listened, eager for any scrap of news. Huang fu came in with a tray of tea and scowled at the idle servants huddled in a nervous clump. The ancient gardener and his wife entered, holding onto one another like clinging vines.

An authoritative male voice broke into the radio program. "The Japanese have bombed Pearl Harbour in a sneak attack. There have been confirmed sightings of Japanese planes heading towards Hong Kong. We are now at war with the Japanese." Afterwards, *God Save the King* filled the room. Huang fu translated the announcer's words into Cantonese for those who hadn't understood.

The gardener and his wife cried. Leah looked at their tear-streaked faces and decided there was still time for the servants to go to the shelters in town. They were too vulnerable here. Victorious Japanese might harm Chinese who were loyal to Europeans. "You should all go to your families now," she said. "You must use the shelters in Central. It is safer."

The servants nodded; the gardener's wife stopped crying. Wordlessly, Huang fu handed Leah a list of all the foodstuffs. He had calculated how much food was on hand and how much each servant would be entitled to if he wanted to leave. Leah agreed, surprised that Huang fu had been secretly stockpiling supplies and humbled that she hadn't thought of it herself. Huang fu oversaw the dispensing of the rice and canned food.

Leah raced upstairs. She opened a Chinese box, pushed on the concealed knob to release the secret compartment and retrieved a wad of Ito's Swiss franc notes. Downstairs, she pressed a hundred Swiss francs into each outstretched hand, explaining it was real money and the moneychangers would give them many Hong Kong dollars. They should wait to change it as long as possible. The war could go on for a long time.

The gardener's wife clung to Leah in gratitude. "You should go, Auntie. It is dangerous to remain here," said Leah.

The old man held out his arm for his wife and the couple shuffled out and padded down the hall. Finally, only Huang fu and the cook, Tung, were left.

"I'm staying," declared Huang fu. "It is my job to look after the house. The shelter is good."

"I am grateful for your company," said Leah and turned to Tung. "Aren't you going?"

Tung thought of the cramped, crowded shelters in Central, full of terrified old men, women and children, crying, talking and shitting. Here was plentiful food and a kitchen he could still cook in. "I'm staying."

"If anything happens . . ." began Leah. She stopped, staring at the jumbled living room, "Well, you take what you want."

Huang fu gasped and eyed Tung. "Nothing will happen. We are safe."

The waiting was terrible. She couldn't stop worrying about Jonathan. She entreated the heavens that he be spared and delivered safely back. When the air raid siren blared, she greeted it with relief.

❧

DURING the early night, the fighting was loud and fierce— bombs detonating, spot fires burning, the roar of big guns. They had candles and a kerosene lamp, but Huang fu cautioned that the light might trickle out between the beams of the trench. They sat huddled on a large tarp with a blanket each to keep off the chill. Tung sat on his haunches and screamed, "You wait dwarf monkeys, you'll be dead soon." Leah jumped up too, cursing in rage and anger that they were forced to squat in the damp earth and pray they wouldn't be killed. She would never forgive the Japanese. Huang fu watched, nodding his approval, too dignified to join in.

The fighting stopped some time during the night. They slept fitfully. Leah awoke to quiet, except for Tung's snores, and a desperate need to pee. She stepped over the two dozing men and, positioning the ladder, climbed out.

The misty air smelled foul: cordite, gasoline and a burnt stink. The stars were invisible because of the haze and she couldn't locate the fire. It could be a downed plane. The noise of the battle would have drowned out the crash. She shivered. Was Jonathan all right? Perhaps he was camped on a ridge in the Heights or sound asleep, exhausted from fighting. Or, was he awake like her and nervously watching the false dawn? Maybe he was right: the Japanese didn't fight well at night and were hopeless swimmers. But as she moved stealthily towards the house, she listened for soft-shod Japanese footfalls and imagined them creeping up on Jonathan and his men, bayoneting them as they slept. She raced across the garden to the house and was sick in the toilet.

Holding her head under the tap, she tried to wash away the taste of sick and fear. She stripped off her clammy, earthy clothes to burrow naked under the covers in the too large bed and prayed she would have a dreamless sleep.

THE war had no rhythm. The days melded together. Thursday had no more meaning than Sunday. They spent long hours in the trench trying not to think.

During a lull, Huang fu and Leah risked a journey into Central to find fresh food. They leaned against a shuttered store in the empty street market waiting for the stallholders to arrive. An old woman peeked through the shutters and beckoned them into her son's empty repair shop. She served them tea, clucking and moaning about the war. A few peddlers drifted into the street, lugging baskets of tired bok choi, chillies and bean sprouts. Huang fu attempted to bargain hard, but the word had gotten out, and a rush of people poured in, making haggling impossible. The vendor gave Huang fu only a pound of vegetables and demanded ten times what they were worth.

"Pay him," said Leah. They would eat less. There were no fish; the fishermen were spooked by rumours of mines and human-flesh-eating fish.

Huang fu insisted he escort Leah to the jeweller. Bad people might be on the streets. The jeweller's shop was steel shuttered and padlocked with three locks. Huang fu pounded on the heavy door demanding the man open up. He called, "Miss Kolbe has come to pick up her wedding rings." There was no answer. Leah was certain the jeweller and his family were hiding inside, hunkered down, afraid.

"It's no use," said Leah, as other people leaned out of their windows and shouted at them to go away.

"When Mr Jonathan comes home, he will get the rings."

Leah smiled at Huang fu's fiction and agreed.

Silently, they trudged back to the Peak, their ears alert for the sound of planes or gunfire.

Living on the Peak was like living in a distant country. No

one knew what was happening. In between the bombing and the guns, Leah telephoned everyone she knew to get news. Delia refused all calls. She was flat out at the hospital, working twenty-hour days. When Leah called Hope, Hope argued that Charles and Jonathan would be fine; only the Canadian troops were in danger because they were raw recruits and didn't know the terrain.

Upset, Leah said, "Which is why we should have enlisted the Chinese."

There was a significant pause at the other end of the line. Then Hope said, "Leah, don't be ridiculous. They couldn't meet the height requirements."

"Well, they should have lowered them. The Chinese are good fighters. They hate the Japanese, especially those who escaped from China."

"Don't be a romantic. The Chinese make terrible soldiers," said Hope in a told-you-so tone. "They run away. What the Colonial Government should do is declare Hong Kong a Free City. Like Paris. We should be neutral. Let the Japs come and go and stop the fighting. It's not our country. And I don't want to be a widow."

Hope was a defeatist. All she cared about was her own skin and getting her easy life back, thought Leah as she toyed with the cord. She heard Hope's voice crackle over the wires, "Leah, Leah are you still there?" Leah pressed the disconnect button. The telephone rang again five minutes later. Leah let it ring.

Huang fu was convinced that any day, Chinese Nationalist troops would pour into Hong Kong to save their brothers and its strategic harbour. A free Hong Kong was indispensable to the Nationalists to get guns and food.

After the electricity stopped working and Hong Kong's water supply had been bombed, Leah and Huang fu stopped speculating about when Chinese troops would arrive.

Tung set up pots and pans outside to collect rain. Leah rationed herself to a cup of water daily for a sponge bath. Her hair was greasy and lank. A small cooking fire was kept going with bits of furniture she never liked. She wandered away from the sound of Huang fu chopping up a stool. For once, she was glad Theo was dead. He'd hate to see his treasured house being picked apart. It was like nibbling at his carcass. Anxiety rumbled around in her head all the time, leaving her exhausted and without any interest in food. Eating was a cruel joke. They existed on congee, a rice porridge that dwindled to mostly rainwater. She wore a pair of discarded black Chinese pyjamas; every few days she drew the drawstring waist tighter. Still, the house was standing, unlike the Beechworth's further up the road. Their roof had been destroyed and, if she looked into the sun, she could see its blackened timbers. Where the Beechworths were, she had no idea. Perhaps they had taken shelter in town.

The war raged on. Some days it was closer and they huddled underground as large clumps of dirt fell on the shelter, but the rafters held. Other days, the fighting was further away, and the drifting black smoke made them choke. Ritually, Leah crossed off the days on the Tiger Balm Company calendar in black ink. On the 22nd of December, Huang fu suggested they take the calendar down and put the new 1942 one in its place. Leah refused. She didn't want to rush into a new year. War was unpredictable. A miracle could happen. On the 23rd, Huang fu stared unhappily at the blue printed number circled in red to signify Leah's wedding. He foraged among the ruins of the Peak and discovered an escaped chicken. They roasted it over the outdoor fire and ate it greedily with their fingers.

Afterwards, Leah wandered into the kitchen and lit a candle to examine the almond-eyed girl who represented Tiger Balm's December. She sat, half-turned, on a high-backed chair, her head tilted to one side, the beginning of a possible smile on her lips. The girl was certainly waiting for something or someone. Neatly, Leah tore the picture in half and touched it to the candle flame. It caught fire. She flung the burning picture down and stamped on it.

ON the 25th of December 1941, the Hong Kong Government surrendered to the Japanese.

5

December 8, 1941

My darling Leah,

I'm mad for worry about your safety. Did you get home all right? If things get bad, you must go to the shelters at Central. Have you got enough food? Let some of the servants go home. They'd want to be home. So much hanging about. War is waiting. I'm hunkered down in a corner, writing.

The call-up was disorganised. Tony and I milled around the garrison as the chaps trickled in. Good we came early. Hated leaving you. Had our pick of the equipment—what we had trained with. Others like Stan and Wes issued only with mortars. Charles took his time. Probably stuffing away his banknotes. When Stan complained about his equipment, old Charles banged on about Dunkirk and having to make do. He became aggressive in that nasty way of his, puffed up and superior. Everyone wanted to take a punch at him. Before it got out of hand, Tony began to tell one of his rude jokes. No. I'm not going to repeat it. Won't get through the censors. Even Charles managed a smirk. Everyone on edge.

Please stay in the shelter. I know it's safe. Keep the bath-
tub full of water. The mains could be bombed.

I'll post this when I can.

Love, Jonathan

*

Day 3 Dec. 10 1941

My darling dearest Leah,

Have a minute to jot. Am on Gin Drinkers Line, near
neck of bay in Kowloon. Transport a nightmare. The big
guns had to be carried by mules. Who planned this? Am
fine. A little Jap strafing. We fired back. But okay. Our sap-
pers have blown all the bridges and entry points to Honkers.
You will be safe. They can't get to you. The Japs decimated
Kai Tak airfield and our six planes. Anyway, what bloody
good is it to have six ancient planes?

*

Sorry, interrupted. More shelling and random bombs.
Later, after dark, major came. Said every day we hold out,
we are beating the Japs. Bollocks. Sky is hazy like the mist
we get on the Peak. Stinks, though. I put my arms around
you and in our eyrie, you are safe.

*

Day 7, 14 Dec '41

Royal Scots magnificent. No idea of progress, squatting here and doing a bit of this. Cloud cover good. Ate in
peace. Weary. Stray thoughts—my tin soldiers on mother's
Axminster carpet. Soldiers in full battle dress of the Crimean
War (another lost cause) and miniature cannon. Marching them here, waging war, going boom. Like the damn

nursery rhyme about that bastard the Duke of York. Was he a good general? Can't remember. Better than sitting still. Big hit then. Must be our oil dumps. Sky black with smoke.

*

Sorry paper smudgy. Waiting for ferry, not sure where we are going. News: Japs are not afraid of the dark or the water. Remember your silvery laughter. I kiss you. Even Charles no longer believes Chiang Kai-shek's army is going to rescue us. Heard rumour. Japs coming from the New Territories through the rough country. You must get away. Maybe you could stow away on a ship, a boat, a junk, a sampan? How could I have left you!

*

Another day

(In pencil) Repulse Bay. A rout. Crawled here, unhurt, abandoned house. Inside a cupboard. Haven't moved a muscle—Japs down below. Heard 'em rampaging. Thugs. Bastards. Terrible shrieks from Chinese women and a man outside.

Gunfire. Grunts of satisfaction, laughing on the lawn. Unnerving quiet. Chanced it, ate my M&V ration—cold meat & vegetable stew. Feel better. Are you safe? Must be safe.

*

Sundown

Must have slept. Peeped outside. Japs marching in little bands or in noisy belching vehicles. Saw a lorry piled high with furniture. From Repulse Bay Hotel? One heaved a piano on the road. Big joke. Thirsty. Need water. Should have stayed on the Peak with a machine gun. Am raving.

*

Maybe 22 Dec '41

Hiding in toilet block near football ground. Water foul, but water. Saw bodies 10 Chinese women & a young boy—10,12? Hanging from wire mesh around field. Shot. Bayoneted. Shouldn't tell. Writing. Keep brain ticking. Darling. Jap businessmen betrayed us. Built concrete floors in their port warehouses. Japs used them for gun emplacements. Didn't stand a chance. Leah, my lovely Leah.

*

Must be a whole day without shooting. This terrible quiet. Am going mad.

*

Japs sniffing around again. Lying in a drain. Heard our chaps' voices. Head up.

*

SAVED: Moving at an inch a minute manoeuvring around craters, saw one of the army staff cars carrying a large white sheet. An officer shouted: We've surrendered. Didn't know whether to laugh or cry.

*

Crept out of the culvert to the potholed, rubbished road. Gave me a canteen of water and told where the collection point was. No salutes; no name. No one cares.

*

Near Collection Point:

A man who looks like Huang fu's brother waits. Gave him my watch to deliver this. Japs won't get it. Have seen one Jap with six watches on his arm. Keep these scribbles for our children. Get out of Hong Kong. Leave. Darling, I can survive if I know you are safe. Have this terrible longing to see you. Man impatient. Have to go. All my love always, J

෨

THE man took Jonathan's scrawled notes, stuffed them into his pocket and strapped on Jonathan's gleaming watch. Every few steps, he lifted his arm to his ear to listen to the ticking. He smiled.

Farther along the road, a Japanese soldier steered a motorbike with a sidecar cautiously around the craters in the road. The other soldier sitting in the sidecar caught sight of a coolie wearing a watch. He aimed his pistol and shot. The motorcycle driver stopped and grinned at his friend's deadly marksmanship. Jumping out of the sidecar, the shooter liberated the watch.

"Search his pockets," ordered the driver.

His friend found only useless bits of scribbled paper in the dead man's pocket. In disgust, he threw them away. The sheets fluttered in the breeze and disappeared down a steep hill.

6

LEAH STARED AT the strings of lacy cobwebs hanging from the ceiling of her once immaculate bedroom, listening to the insistent rain falling. Maybe it was a good time to be dead. It was a dead time, pearl dawn. Even Huang fu must still be asleep. She didn't remember dreaming. What would the Japanese do with the defeated soldiers? One thing was for certain, they wouldn't be released and she could not rescue Jonathan. The rain eased. To escape her thoughts, she pulled on a robe and walked out into the wet garden.

The sky was ghost grey, as if signalling that her world had changed. An escaped canary, a blur of yellow, perched in the peach tree, singing. She half expected it to fall down dead at her feet or talk in English because nothing was as it should be.

The roof of the trench was now a sea of mud; someone else's roof tiles littered Theo's flowerbeds. A length of copper tubing embedded in the soft earth poked up like a periscope to survey the changed landscape. The outdoor furniture lay abandoned and soaked cushions littered the grass. Soon they would go mouldy. In that overturned chair, warmed by the sun, she had sat on Jonathan's lap and been happy. Was he alive? It was rumoured that several units had gotten away, slipping over the border to join forces with the Chinese. Jonathan could have done it. He was resourceful and his men were loyal. How she hungered for news. There was only a brief surrender announcement on the short wave radio, a last minute gift from Eldersen sent by a Chinese boy. All night she twisted and fiddled with the knobs and the antennae as it whistled and crackled until, exhausted and distressed, she had collapsed into bed.

The French doors opened and Huang fu stood in the doorway dressed in casual clothes, cheap cotton pants and a clean short-sleeved shirt.

"Are you going?" asked Leah.

Huang fu shook his head. "Breakfast, Tung has made breakfast."

Leah smiled with relief. It was such a generous thing for Huang fu to remain without being asked. "Mustn't keep him waiting, then," she said, as if expecting the pre-war breakfast of stewed tea with milk, toast and perhaps eggs.

Tung, Huang fu and Leah sat at the kitchen table eating the rainwater congee slowly, sucking each spoonful dry. Huang fu shifted in his seat and shovelled in the last mouthful.

"You can't stay here," he declared.

"No," replied Leah, trying not to think about the future. Then it came to her—what the Nazis did when they took over a defeated town. It was possible. She spoke eagerly, willing it so. "The Japs will order me to report to the police and register. That's the way it was done in Europe."

"That will not be the Japanese way," argued Huang fu.

Leah forced a spoonful of congee down her throat. "They don't want chaos."

"You are fooling yourself."

"When I was in Manchukuo, I could move around freely," she asserted, disturbed by Huang fu's certainty.

"You were not the defeated enemy," said Huang, crushing her with searing truth. "Tung and I will go to Central and see what is happening. You must stay here. It's not safe for women."

Huang fu's voice had new authority. In the past, he accepted everything she said and kept his opinions to himself. Welcome to the new order.

Tung, his eyes on his congee, mumbled, "I'm going to my cousin's. He owns a restaurant. He needs a cook."

Huang fu protested.

Leah interrupted. "Tung has every right to go where he wants. He will be safer there."

"It's not right. Tung has been paid to the end of the year."

"No, Huang fu. Let him go."

To show he was grateful, Tung offered to clean up the kitchen before he left.

All three stared at the kitchen. It was a disgrace. The pantry door was open, its shelves bare, and a mountain of discarded tins littered the floor. All the glass jars were lidless and empty and the pots black from cooking on the makeshift brazier Tung had fashioned from the bricks of the garden path. "Let the Japanese do it," said Leah.

Huang fu banged the table. "No!"

"Yes," said Leah, "you already told me I won't be safe. If I'm nothing, then they'll commandeer the house. They'll think it's their right to own the best houses in Hong Kong."

"They make the rules now," he agreed, his face brimming with resentment. "Huang fu will find a hiding place for you. The Japs will never find you."

How vulnerable she must look, sitting here in her bathrobe, unwashed, slurping down rice gruel, unable to protect herself, while a servant, a man who had served her with dignity and resourcefulness she had taken for granted, was willing to put his life at risk and help her. She sat up straighter and met his eyes.

"Macau. I'll go to Macau," she declared, as if it were as easy as buying a ticket and sailing away.

"They'll bomb Macau too," countered Huang fu. "Hong Kong is better. I know many people in Hong Kong. Triads in Macau."

"There are triad here too. It is not triads I'm worried about," said Leah through gritted teeth.

"You stay," ordered Huang fu.

"I can't, Huang fu."

Stricken, he said, "I can't go to Macau. I must stay here with my family. I will help you get to Macau."

Leah bowed her head out of respect for Huang fu's generosity and courage. What secret reserves the man had. Why hadn't she noticed? "The Japanese might be willing for you to remain here and work."

"No," cried Tung. "Huang fu not work for squat ugly monkeys. My uncle in Shanghai, he work for a cook for a Japanese army man. The army man didn't like Chinese food. He chop off that man's head. My uncle run away. He's still not able to eat dumplings. He cry all the time."

Leah gasped; Huang fu's face was ashen. Tung crossed his arms and dared Leah to contradict him. The rain began again, pounding on the roof and beating against the windows.

"Did this really happen?" demanded Leah.

"My uncle is an old man. He cry a lot."

"Yes," acknowledged Leah. "I expect we all will."

"I will find someone to take you to Macau, Miss Kolbe," Huang fu pledged.

"Thank you, Huang fu, from the bottom of my heart," said Leah softly, her voice mixing with the fall of rain.

Huang fu nodded solemnly.

Truly, Leah thought, the world has shifted on its axis.

～

TUNG left, grateful for Leah's gift of a hundred Swiss francs and Huang fu was out, sniffing around the docks for a fisherman willing to take her to Macau. It was so strange to be the only one in the house. Always there were servants, quiet and unassuming, attending to this or that. Now, the house had stopped like a run-down watch. The fans didn't whirl, the lights didn't turn on, the telephone was out and water no longer ran from the taps. The house was dying.

There was a sharp rap on the door. Leah froze. It was the end. The Japanese had come and she was alone.

"L-e-a-h. It's me. Charlotte Cecil."

Overcome with relief, Leah hurried to the front door. Charlotte and she weren't friends. In fact, they hardly spoke at all, aside from hello and comments about the weather. To Leah, Charlotte was "the sock woman." A small, nondescript woman with mousy hair and glasses, Charlotte was out of her depth in the Colony. She had drifted into the Auxiliary out of a desperate need to be seen to be doing something worthy. Delia allowed her to stay because the little grey woman was a ferocious knitter. Every day she sat on a battered chair with skeins of wool and knitted socks. On a good day, she finished two pairs. Delia would sweep in and beam, "Charlotte, my treasure. Good warm socks win battles," and then sweep out, leaving Charlotte unnerved, but grateful that she had found her niche at last in the rigid social hierarchy of Hong Kong.

Now, an unblinking Charlotte with a determined mouth

said, "Some of us are going to look for our husbands. We know where the Volunteer Brigade was posted, near Kowloon. They may be wounded or dead. I must find Harvey. The Japs have taken over the hospitals and thrown out our wounded. Join us. If we're in a group, the beasts won't dare touch us." She was still breathing hard from the climb, her mousy hair pulled back into a tight bun. She was desperation in sandals and knitted socks.

At a loss, Leah could only stare. The woman was raving, despite her calm. She still believed the Japanese would recognise the superiority of white-skinned ladies in ugly purple dresses and allow them to pass. Crazy, going on foot, passing endless Japanese check points. After battle, Japanese soldiers went on drunken rampages of victory; look at Nanking.

"It's not that simple. We'd have to smuggle the men back through the lines. We'd have to hide them in Chinese squatters' huts. How would they eat? I don't have any food. Do you?" she argued, attempting to inject rationality into Charlotte's lunatic, dangerous plan.

Charlotte screwed up her face as if she might explode. "I might have known," said Charlotte, icy with rage. "It's people like you—"

"—Charlotte, it won't work. It won't save them."

"Do you have a better idea?"

"No," conceded Leah in a hoarse whisper.

"Coward," hissed Charlotte. She turned on her heel, her back ramrod straight, and strode down the driveway.

Leah watched Charlotte's knitted socks disappear. Maybe she was a coward. She was running away, leaving Jonathan behind. She sank to the floor and buried her head in her hands, crying, glad there was no one home to see her despair.

～

"MR. FONG is adamant," said Huang fu, sitting on the chintz sofa, looking helpless. "He insists. He doesn't understand banks. Besides, they are closed. He wants gold and jewels."

Leah nodded and trudged upstairs to return with her jewellery box. She opened the marquetry box and stared at its contents. "I haven't got much," she apologised.

She dumped out a thin gold chain, a bracelet of small cut rubies and a necklace of graduated pearls. "Is this enough?"

Huang fu shrugged. "Fong is worried about mines."

"Take everything. I've given up dressing up," and gave a sour laugh. It was true. She still wore the dirty black Chinese pyjamas.

"But for this man, you must wear good clothes. He must think you are an important person."

"Can Mr. Fong be trusted?"

"He was the only one willing to go to Macau. I have not met this man before. When you are on his junk, you must open your suitcase and let him see you have no other valuables. I think this would be best. You are paying him well."

"Is he a pirate?"

"No. Only a greedy fisherman." Huang fu collected the jewellery into a cloth bag. He sighed heavily. "It is the best I can do. There are such rumours." He shut his mouth. He was not about to repeat them, even if they were true.

Leah surveyed the living room. Out of sense of loyalty and duty, Huang fu had restored the porcelain, carvings and pictures to their rightful places, a brave, useless gesture. "Take whatever you want from this house. I leave them to you."

"The Japs steal everything. I'm sorry. It is too dangerous," said Huang fu, drooping with fatalism. He looked at his watch.

"You must hurry and change. My cousin comes at six to take us to the dock."

Leah fled upstairs. She stripped off the pyjamas and changed into a black suit, sensible shoes, no makeup and a hat with a veil. Adjusting her hat in the mirror, she realised she was dressed for a funeral. On the bedside table was a framed picture of Jonathan in his Volunteer uniform. He looked dashing and capable, but as her fingers traced over the glass, she thought his soft mouth held traces of weakness and she was afraid. She shivered and slipped the photograph into her handbag, snapping it shut.

Midway down the stairs, she paused, overwhelmed by regret. For a moment, she heard her own bright childish laughter as she hurtled down the stairs and Theo's long dead voice urging her to be careful. How could homesickness start before she even locked the front door?

She felt compelled to return one last time to Theo's study, now hers. A duck-bottomed Japanese officer would soon be sitting in her desk chair. Well, he'd get a surprise. She cut deep into the ancient cracked leather seat with the letter opener, dug into the stuffing and inserted it point up. It was a stupid, childish act. She didn't care. She hoped it would puncture the officer's balls. She slammed the door, leaving old ghosts behind.

HUANG fu's cousin cut the headlights in the narrow alley leading to Aberdeen harbour, *Heung Gong Tsai*, Little Fragrant Harbour. All three sat, hardly breathing, listening intently. The quiet was unnerving. Usually, the place was mobbed with street hawkers, and stall holders and reeked of dead fish and sewerage. It still smelled. Aberdeen Harbour was home to the junk people who lived in their own small world, selling their wares, marrying each other, bearing children who never slept on land. Police avoided it. It was the last place anyone would look for a missing European woman.

Huang fu's cousin remained in the car. Huang fu shut the door with a noiseless click and, despite Leah's emphatic whispered protestations, carried her suitcase. Their steps echoed in the silence of the deserted street market. Nothing was left, not even the empty boxes usually littering the cobblestones.

A shriek of laughter broke the silence. Leah and Huang fu exchanged looks of fright and froze. In the inky dark, they saw the outline of two laughing Chinese boys carrying a table between them. The boys halted, making a joke about what else they could steal. Huang fu told them to get lost. They should be ashamed of stealing, leave that to the Japanese. The boys hooted their contempt, but left them alone and hurried off, still lugging the table.

Mr. Fong, a flat-faced man in a threadbare singlet and loose trousers, shone a kerosene lantern on them. He nodded at Huang fu and said, "Pay." Huang fu handed the man the cloth sack. Squatting on his haunches, he bit the gold and scraped at the pearls with dirty fingernails.

"Good," he said. "You come."

With a sigh of resignation Huang fu said, "Mr. Fong knows these waters well," and set the suitcase down.

Leah nodded and embraced Huang fu. She whispered, "I wish you good luck and good fortune."

Impatient, Mr. Fong picked up the suitcase and trotted off.

"Go, Miss Kolbe. Be safe," said Huang fu.

Leah had to run to keep up with Fong. Ten feet along, she turned around and saw Huang fu's shadowy figure sagging under a weight of worry and sadness. She waved and he flapped his hand as if urging her to hurry. She ran on.

7

THE SEAT WAS still wet from the day's rain; moisture leached through Leah's skirt. She shifted uneasily, unable to find a dry spot. Fong's wife held a kerosene lamp to guide the skiff towards the junk. The thin track of light cut a wavy path through the water and illuminated a body, face down, riding a gentle swell. Fong grunted and pushed it out of his path with his pole. The body drifted away, into the dark.

Fong manoeuvred the skiff alongside the junk and motioned Leah to stand on the wet seat. Short, stocky Mrs. Fong reached over, grabbed Leah under the arms and hauled her in like a large fish. Stunned, Leah lay spreadeagled, inhaling the stench of fish, greasy timber and mould. A small boy poked her in the ribs with his bare toes and giggled.

"Hey," said Leah.

Mrs. Fong yelled at the boy to stay away. As Leah sat up, Fong tossed up her suitcase. It landed with a loud thump, narrowly missing her head.

"Watch it," cautioned Leah.

Fong grunted in reply as he clambered, monkey-like, up the hull and jumped neatly onto the deck. "We eat," he declared, as he hovered by Leah's side. She gagged on his sour smell.

Mrs. Fong lit the brazier. Children came out of the shadows to stare: first a small boy, then his older brother, and finally a scrawny girl. Under their watchful eyes, Leah ate and tried to forget the body in the water. No one talked as they slurped down fish and rice.

After eating, Fong wiped his fingers on his trousers, then cast off. He steered the junk skilfully around a clot of other junks and sampans. Soon, they were in open water. The clouds cleared in the gentle wind and the stars were visible.

Leah pointed at the stars. "Bad?" she asked.

Fong shrugged.

Leah wasn't certain if the shrug meant there were no Japanese patrol boats on the prowl for escaping Europeans, or it didn't matter—he'd been paid.

Mrs. Fong clouted her daughter on the ear for trying to touch Leah's hat. The child roared in pain.

"It's okay," said Leah and began to unpin her hat.

Mrs. Fong hit the girl again and shoved her in the direction of the hatch. "Sleep now," Mrs. Fong ordered Leah.

Leah wondered if Mrs. Fong might hit her too, but she only scowled and disappeared into the hold dragging the youngest boy with her. A few minutes later, Mrs. Fong reappeared with a fetid blanket. When Leah didn't immediately wrap the filthy thing around her, Mrs. Fong mimed sleep, pillowing her head on her clasped hands and closing her eyes.

"Soon," promised Leah.

Mrs. Fong grunted and went to consult her husband at the wheel, hissing and whispering in agitation.

Leah thought they were arguing about her. Maybe Mrs. Fong resented putting her children in danger even for a price. Fong growled something, raising his hand as if to strike. Mrs.

Fong sprang back with a torrent of abuse in a patois Leah couldn't understand. Like a squall that had run out of wind, Mrs. Fong abruptly stopped her tirade, shrugged, and walked nimbly over the deck to disappear below.

Leah wrapped the rancid blanket around her. Unable to stand the smell, she threw it off and grew cold, her feet icy. She opened her suitcase and Fong swivelled round to look. She found a small flashlight and shuffled her belongings around under Fong's snake eyes so he could see she had nothing valuable hidden away. She pulled on a coat and socks, then shut the case with a bang. When she looked again, Mr. Fong was staring purposefully at the stars as if plotting his course.

At last she slept. She dreamed of red fish with enormous teeth, emperor fish that pursued her with amazing speed even as she swam faster and faster. She woke in a panic to Fong's loud snores. He was curled in a heap by the rudder and the anchor line was out. Even colder now, she wrapped the reeking blanket around to stretch out again, wishing and worrying that dawn would come soon.

The day passed achingly slow. She was always in the way. Mrs. Fong shot her dagger looks. She retreated to sit atop her suitcase, barefoot in her good suit with her hat on her head to keep the broiling sun off, her handbag on her lap. The children made a game of stepping inside an invisible boundary line, causing Mrs. Fong to shriek, Get away, every few minutes. Leah developed a headache from the shouting, menacing looks and whispered conversations between the couple. Mr. Fong continually tacked and changed course. When she dared to ask why, he spat out, Mines. She shut up, willing the children to go away, refusing to meet their curious eyes.

By nightfall, they still hadn't reached Macau. Because of

mines and the threat of patrol boats, Mr. Fong refused to sail after nightfall. "They steal," he declared without irony.

Everyone chewed through another silent fish dinner. Afterwards, the Fong family retreated to their 'cabin' below deck and left Leah to the cold, starry night. After a bit of yelling and sounds of heavy slapping, she heard Fong's loud snores and the junk was quiet.

The silence unnerved her. If the Fongs meant to kill her, surely they would have done it by now. She rubbed her throbbing temples. Hadn't Theo drummed into her, Don't anticipate, only deal with things as they are? She should be grateful. She was safe, lying on the deck, listening to the water break against the boat. At last, she allowed herself to be rocked to sleep.

In the grey dawn, Leah awoke to a distant shadowy Macau and her misgivings evaporated in the fresh salt air. She smiled at Fong. He smiled back, gesturing toward Macau. She sighed with relief. She had been a suspicious fool.

As they neared the harbour, Fong towed the skiff to the side of the junk. "I come too," announced Mrs. Fong as she rounded up the smallest boy to bind him to the mast so he wouldn't fall overboard. Then she tied a gourd to the older boy's back so he would float if he fell into the water. Impassively, the daughter stood and watched.

"What about your daughter?" asked Leah.

Mrs. Fong shrugged. "Girl."

Leah frowned. Reluctantly, Mrs. Fong knotted a gourd around the girl. Mrs. Fong cackled her annoyance. The loss of a son was a tragedy; a daughter, a blessing—no dowry to pay.

The woman was a devil and her husband, a scoundrel. Leah pictured the flat-faced Mr. Fong and his bulky wife wandering around Macau, bargaining hard with a pawnbroker to get the most cash for her jewels.

Mrs. Fong grasped Leah by the wrists and dangled her over the side; Fong's strong hands caught her around the waist. Then, Mrs. Fong planted a wide foot on the rope and slid down into the skiff with a heavy plop. The boat wobbled, then steadied. Mr. Fong sat on Leah's suitcase in the bottom and allowed his wife to pole them toward the harbour. From the rough wooden seat, Leah kept her eyes on Macau.

A hundred yards from shore, Fong stood up and flung the suitcase into Leah's back. Leah pitched forward against the side of the boat, banging her knees hard. Stunned, she whipped around, but Fong was quicker and shoved her up to a standing position. Leah grasped the side of the boat, her feet planted wide apart, trying to steady herself. She shouted, Stop. Ignoring Leah's pleas, Mrs. Fong smacked Leah on the head with the bamboo pole as Fong's strong hands grabbed her by the ankles and heaved her into the sea.

The water was so cold. She flailed her arms and sunk under the murky brown water, twisting and turning. She couldn't breathe. To die like this. No. She kicked furiously, desperate to right herself. She exploded out of the sea: coughing, wheezing and kicking, her throat on fire. She took in more seawater and spat it out. Somehow, she got her arms working and turned to glimpse the Fongs briskly poling back to the junk.

Mrs. Fong threw something high into the air. Her shoes. They arced, then plummeted. She hadn't the strength to retrieve them. For a moment, she saw her shoes ride a wave and then they were gone. She turned, kicking out her legs and slicing the water with a determined, bloodthirsty stroke, and swam to Macau, cursing the Fongs all the way to shore.

She heaved herself onto the sea steps and stood dripping and shivering. She peeled off her sodden jacket and stared up at the broad avenue, gawking at the imposing houses with their wide verandas and fairy-tale colours—turquoise, lemon yellow and faded rose. From one of the houses, she saw a pair of hairy male hands open a pair of second storey shutters. A dark-haired man stuck his head out the window and inhaled deeply. He gazed at the harbour and the junks bobbing serenely on the water. He couldn't see her standing below the sea wall like a drowned rat with rivulets of brown water pooling at her feet. He smiled at the rosy morning, promising a sunny day, and was gone.

She let out a yelp of loss. A woman on one of the bobbing junks looked at her curiously, but offered no help. A terrible burning itching sensation swept over her. She pulled at the buttons on her blouse to stare at her chest covered in small red blotches. Sea lice. Scratching made them burn. Her legs hurt too; irregular bruises were beginning to puff and darken on the backs of her legs. She moaned softly, afraid she might collapse on the stairs, another bit of flotsam and jetsam washed up on the shores of Macau. She forced herself to move, dragging her aching body up the steps to the street and stood barefoot and bereft, unable to decide where to go.

In a faded soutane, a thin priest with a large nose raced towards her, calling out consoling phrases in Portuguese. The priest opened his arms. She nestled in. In a singsong voice, the priest said *"Eu vi-o. Terrível Eu vi-o. Terrível."* I saw it. Terrible. I saw it. Terrible. He patted her back, oblivious to how wet she was and how bad she smelled. Afterwards, smiling and gentle, he motioned her to follow.

Carefully, Leah picked her way, head down, afraid bits of loose stone or glass might cut her feet, avoiding the curious glances of strangers. At last, they came to the door of a large stone building with a sculptured Mary over the archway looking sad and doleful. The priest knocked hard. A young Chinese girl in a clean white blouse and dark blue skirt answered. Her face registered shocked surprise as she stared at Leah, bruised and battered, reeking of the sea, and her blackened bare feet. The priest coaxed Leah inside. An old nun draped in heavy white linen, an enormous rosary with a crucifix looped around her waist, glided sedately like an ocean liner towards them. Leah tried to explain in Cantonese what had happened. The nun and the priest shook their heads, not understanding a word. The Chinese girl hesitantly translated Leah's words into Portuguese. Finally, the Chinese girl said in Cantonese, "The Mother Superior says you can stay for now. But first, you must bathe. You smell."

Leah murmured her heartfelt thanks. The priest beamed, blessed them all and left. The Mother Superior issued an order in Portuguese. The Chinese girl tugged at Leah and led her down a long hallway with pictures of saints, their eyes wide with religious fervour.

The girl opened a large cupboard to extract a clean towel and clothes. She led Leah to the entranceway of a large tessellated tiled bathroom. Leah turned on the taps and watched with satisfaction as hot water gushed out. In the bath, Leah used the nun's harsh yellow soap and scrubbed hard at her skin as if through washing she could rid herself of the thieving Fongs and her murderous thoughts. Exhausted from scrubbing, she lay in the warm water and worried, What now. The water grew colder. She tried the taps. The water wouldn't heat up. Perhaps the nuns only had a ration of hot water and she had lavishly used it all. Chilled, she eased her bruised body out of the tub. The sea lice rash on her breasts had disappeared, but the bruises on her legs were blossoming into large purple patches. Her heart sank as saw the clothes the girl had brought in. It was either a mended mission dress decorated in swirls of green or a faded outfit like the Chinese girl's. There was also a set of sturdy underwear—thick cotton underpants and a sensible bra. They would chafe. She changed into the nun's uniform. It was less depressing than the hand-me-down dress. The black lace-up oxfords with thick heels were too big and flapped like clown shoes, echoing down the stone hallway as the Chinese girl escorted her to the refectory.

The nuns stood in two quiet lines in front of long wooden benches. They looked normal, except for a certain shiny clean-liness that Leah associated with never having worn makeup, a life without mirrors, and purity. The Mother Superior sat at the head of the table next to an old woman in everyday dress, Señhora Ricardo, who welcomed her and said the priest had asked her to come because she spoke English. During the long prayer, Leah salivated over the real bread rolls, butter, and sugary coffee. For a while, no one said very much. Perhaps it wasn't allowed.

With a look for permission at the Mother Superior, Señhora Ricardo began speaking. "Macau is only free because there is a large Japanese community in Brazil. Portugal threatened to freeze the bank accounts of these wealthy Japanese. Japanese officers are crawling over Macau. They swagger about like they own the place. We are still afraid they might blockade Macau or take us over. You can't trust the bastards," she said fiercely. Then she translated what she said. The nuns paled and blessed themselves.

Leah smiled at the word bastard. Señhora Ricardo looked like a nun without a habit: unlined face, no makeup and short square nails on her stubby hands.

"I must work," said Leah.

"European women don't work in Macau, except for teachers.

I am a lay teacher. They think we must live like nuns. You can't exist on your salary. I live with my brother and his family. You must learn Portuguese first."

"I need to work. I have nothing."

Señhora Ricardo thought about this and spoke to the Mother Superior. Finally, she said, "We think you must go to the British consulate. They may be able to help. After all, you're one of them."

Yes, she was one of them, but would they claim her? She held a British passport, or rather, had it stolen. Did new rules apply now? Could one just turn up, declare oneself British, and expect a handout? She had no choice and asked for directions. She would make her way there tomorrow. She was too defeated to do it today. It would be an excuse to leave the cloistered walls and see more of Macau. She had been in Macau before, spending her time in a gambling den and a pay-by-the-hour room. After Cezar died, she had blanked his memory out. She believed firmly in Theo's dictum: What's done is done. That was how she would run her life now she decided, looking at the soft-skinned women, who believed in goodness and mercy. The time of happiness was past.

The nuns gave her Sister Eulalia's old room. It was tiny and quiet. The Sister had been recently appointed to head a new mission in Angola. In the middle of the night, Leah awoke from a menacing dream. The actual events she couldn't remember, but what terrified her was Jonathan. He wasn't dead, but she couldn't fill in his face, the contours of his body, the smell and touch of him. In despair, she turned on the light and stared at the crucifix on the wall: the gashes on the chest, the blood, the pain in the eyes. She got up, unhooked it from the wall and hid it, face down. Back in bed, with the lights out in the coffin still-ness of the convent, she reconstructed Jonathan piece–by–piece.

A lightning stab of lust overcame her and she touched herself until she came, and was calm. She fell asleep wondering if she were defiling Sister Eulalia's bed with such human desires.

◠

AFTER two wrong turns and asking directions for the third time, Leah found the icing pink British Consulate on Travessa do Paiva behind the old hospital. A thin, bald man with the white skin and freckles she associated with redheads sat behind a handsome wooden desk. Behind his thick glasses, his eyes were the palest watery blue. He had almost no eyelashes and white blond eyebrows. He must live like a mole, never daring to go out, because he would be horribly burnt by the sun, she thought. The man eyed her novitiate outfit. She asked to see the consul. The man asked if next week suited.

"Next week does not suit. I am Miss Leah Kolbe. I've escaped from Hong Kong, been robbed and nearly killed. I live on Victoria Peak. I need assistance *now*."

The man stood up and stammered an apology. "Well, the truth is Mr. Albemarle is His Majesty's sole representative now in the entire Pacific. He's been working day and night, but I'm sure he will want to see you. I'll just go inquire," and he pointed to a reception room through an arched, open doorway. "Please wait there. It shouldn't be long."

Sitting on a chintz-covered chair, Leah flipped through three dog-eared copies of *Country Life*. The most recent issue was dated December 1940. On the wall was a portrait of King George VI. The picture hung in every colonial office in Hong Kong. Its presence was oddly reassuring; the king didn't seem to mind losing Hong Kong to the Japanese. An hour passed before the bald man reappeared and solemnly conducted her to the consul's cream-coloured office with gold-framed paintings of thatched cottages and English country scenes. It was another world here, she realised.

Stephen Albemarle rose to shake Leah's hand. He was a middle-aged man, with silver grey hair. His eyes were red with tiredness. He apologised for keeping her waiting. The pale, thin man hung around the door

"Mr. Talbot is my right hand," said Albemarle. "He's been here for fifteen years. Knows everything."

"Can you send these telegrams, please?" he requested.

An angry flush crept up Talbot's skinny neck as he realised he had been put in his place and dismissed. He left, fanning the papers in disgust.

"Now, Miss Kolbe, let's talk about your situation."

Leah's heart sunk. Her situation? Her situation was terrible. At first all she could speak about was the battle for Hong Kong, how she had been cut off from news and hardly knew how it was going. He took copious notes. He was going to use what she said in his report. To Leah, his note taking was an excuse to not look at her stricken face. She stopped and couldn't go on.

"I haven't got anything," she confessed. "The Hong Kong banks are closed. There were such terrible rumours about the Japanese." She saw him studying the novitiate costume. She fumbled: "The nuns have been kind. I thought a letter of credit might help to establish my bona fides."

The consul looked uncomfortable. "We haven't planned that far ahead."

"How am I to live?

He chose his words with care as he watched her face. "We are discussing a system of small allowances for people in your circumstances, without papers." He shrugged. "Governments like things to be clear cut, all the boxes ticked. You understand. I could advance you a personal loan."

"I don't want charity and I couldn't pay it back." He was going to hide behind his rules. Here she was, penniless and needy and he wanted to advance her a bit of money, while he lived in his government provided residence with servants, food and the officious Mr. Talbot to do his errands. Arguing wouldn't help. He was her only hope. He must be good for something.

She spoke with emotion, not caring what he thought. "I'm engaged to an Englishman, Jonathan Hawatyne. He's a solicitor . . . That is, he was in the Volunteers." She heard her voice crack; she was going to cry. Awful to show this stranger how vulnerable she was, how out of control, her emotions seesawing from anger to despair. "Do you have information about the Volunteers? It was terrible to leave, not knowing . . ." Her voice faltered. She pressed her hands together and blinked hard to keep from breaking down.

"Tea," the consul announced as he responded to a discreet knock on the door and a polite servant bearing a tray of tea things entered.

"Thank you, Moy," said the consul.

Moy left as silently as he had come.

Albemarle poured and handed her a fine bone china cup. "Milk, sugar?"

Unable to think how she could ever force herself out of this chair and wander back, empty-handed, to the convent, she stared.

The consul stirred his tea and said in a sad voice. "I have no information yet. Not even rumours. They have to abide by the Geneva Convention."

"Do they? We were to be married on the 23rd of December."

"It's an awful time to be young," said Albemarle, shedding his diplomatic shell.

Leah started to cry. He was kind. It was so unexpected after the rules, the statement of the risks, the note taking, the sipping of the tea.

Albemarle yearned to do something. He didn't want her to walk out the door and then, later, see her on the street or hanging out in the casino seeking the protection of a man who would use her and, when he got tired, throw her away. It was a real possibility. There were no jobs fit for British girls. And Macau was as corrupt as could be. He knew it and he knew what Whitehall thought about Macau. A clever British journalist had written a diatribe against Macau in one of the quality broadsheets a few years ago. Some wag had sent it to him, with an unsigned note: Thought you'd like to know. He remembered it word for word: 'Macau is an obscure fishing village, slowly rotting away under a crust of filth, stench and rice punctuated by the baroque splendour of half a dozen cathedrals, living off gambling and prostitution. There is a massive amount of money circulating around the gambling tables.' He'd torn it up before his wife, Mildred, could see it. His posting was so hard on her. He wished he could have consulted with Mildred. That wasn't possible. Mildred had returned to England with the children and now they were getting the hell bombed out of them. He was baffled by his sudden overwhelming need to discuss this young woman with his wife. Mildred did not have opinions. Or rather, she had opinions and they were all negative. 'You're the diplomat,' she always said with a bland expression on her face. They both understood it was a dig at him for his backwater postings. Still, he missed her and the children. He felt miserable, telling this beautiful young girl she was to go and mix with the sordid low lifes of Macau. War corrupted everything.

"Can you type?" he asked.

"A bit."

"Macau is going to be squeezed by the Japanese and by refugees. They're going to flood in and we are going to be inundated with work. At the moment the staff consists of Mr. Talbot and me. We won't be able to cope. I can offer a small salary."

"Yes," she cried. "Thank you."

"Don't be so sure," he responded, getting up and walking to a window. He snapped up the blind with a bang and Leah jumped. He pointed at the window of the building facing them. "That's the Japanese Consul Nagotchi's office. We used to be friends. Life here is going to become unpleasant. Still want to join us? They don't play by the rules."

"Yes. I hate them."

Albemarle continued to stare into the empty office. A man in a Japanese naval uniform entered the room. He saw Albemarle staring in. The officer jerked the curtains closed, his face laced with contempt.

"A carpenter is coming tomorrow, Miss Kolbe. We'll get a little less fresh air, but we adjust."

"Yes," agreed Leah. "We adjust.

"We start work at eight. I'll sort out an office with Mr. Talbot." A shadow of doubt crossed his face, then he brightened saying, "I look forward to working with you."

Leah pumped his hand and said, "Thank you, sir. I am so grateful. I will do my best."

Albemarle smiled. He had chosen a superb candidate. Mildred would have been pleased.

8

IT WAS EARLY evening when Leah returned from work, dead tired. She stopped in the tiny courtyard, its flagstones forced up by the roots of the banyan tree, and fished around in her handbag for the key. With Albemarle's help, she had found the flat; he knew someone who knew someone. She was extremely grateful because, as Albemarle had predicted, the population of Macau had swollen four-fold with the flood of refugees escaping from Hong Kong and China. Now, five months later, sleepy Macau was unrecognisable. Every square inch of housing was taken. Old women squatted underneath city shop verandas and begged. Hungry children roamed the streets with their hands out and their bellies distended. Snatchers scouted the streets ready to grab wallets, suitcases, anything of value that could be sold or traded for food.

Her fingers ached from typing and always were smudged with ink from changing ribbons. The consulate had been transformed into a social services centre. It was easy to be dispassionate about other people's problems. Albemarle praised her efficiency; Talbot tolerated her presence.

She unlocked her door. Flat was too grand a name for the elongated room with a battered inlaid mother-of-pearl screen, blocking off the kitchen from the bedroom. The kitchen contained a basin and a decrepit stove surrounded by ancient blue and white Portuguese tiles. The tiles held the wall together. There was also an old fashioned bathroom with a claw foot tub and rusty water. She kept the bathroom window propped open to combat the creeping mould. It was too small for even child thieves. The main room contained a single wrought iron bedstead painted white with a lumpy mattress, a battered table, and a rickety chair. She liked the screen, despite its missing sections of inlay. The women were gracious and wore long flowing robes. At night she held conversations with them. They never answered, only looked wise and thoughtful.

Stripping to her petticoat, she arranged her body around the lumps in the mattress. She tossed, unable to sleep. Hunger. She hadn't stopped working for lunch and hadn't bothered to buy anything off the stalls because deciding what to eat took too much energy. Now she was ravenous. She must go out and find food.

She slipped on her crushed dress and slung her handbag over her shoulder. The streets were crowded with people passing, by hawkers with miserable offerings shouting their merits. On the pavement, a man was hunkered down mending broken shoes by the light cast from a shop window and touting for business. Leah caught a glimpse of a slender Chinese man in a suit a few feet in front of her down Avenida de Almeida Ribeiro. He was moving fast, looking neither to the left or the right, manoeuvring through the crowd as if it should part for him. But what caught her attention and caused her to stop was the pungent scent of the clove cigarette he was puffing. Dizzy, she simply stopped moving; people detoured around her. It couldn't be. Her mind was playing tricks. She was in Macau, not

Manchukuo or Hong Kong. Chang must be in Free China, plotting someone else's downfall, murder, destruction. She had paid the price for double-crossing him; or rather, her darling amah, An-li, had. Only, here in Macau he could pull strings and not fear being shot by the Japanese. She scanned the surging throng, and caught sight of the man again, farther ahead. No. The man was too short. Breathing easier, she began to move.

A skinny cigarette-smoker in shorts and a threadbare singlet bumped into her.

"Watch where—"

She was cut off as a sinewy arm darted from behind and throttled her. The man in front flashed a knife and cut the strap to her handbag. He took off running. The other man flung her aside and raced off in the opposite direction.

Recovering fast, Leah called in Cantonese, "Thief, snatcher," and ran toward the cobble-stoned alley. A man in a white suit tackled the thief. The men tumbled to the ground. The thief kicked viciously at his attacker and managed to roll free. He ran off, leaving the other man sprawled on the ground, hugging her purse and gasping for breath.

Leah rushed to her saviour's aid. "Are you all right?"

Triumphant, the man held her broken handbag aloft. "Got it." He had a gash on his forehead and limped as he walked toward her.

"Mr. Ito!"

"Miss Kolbe!"

"I can't thank you enough."

Ignoring her thanks, Ito attempted to clean his filthy suit. There were two buttons missing from his jacket, the sleeves were streaked with dirt, and the outline of the robber's sandal footprint was clearly visible on his trouser leg.

"You're bleeding."

He touched his forehead and dabbed at it with his pocket-handkerchief, frowning, distressed by Macau's lawlessness. "There should be more police. This would never happen in Hong Kong."

It was this man's fault she was wandering the lawless streets of Macau. He was of *them*. "Refugees have no money. The price of rice has quadrupled."

He picked up his ruined hat. "It doesn't give them the right to steal. Are you all right, Miss Kolbe?"

Leah touched her neck. It hurt. Refusing to admit she was in pain, she watched Ito hunt for his missing buttons.

"Found them!

She stared.

"They're hand carved and can't be replaced," he explained sheepishly.

"I don't live far. I'll clean your cut and sew on the buttons," she offered. He had rescued her. He couldn't help being Japanese. She was still a human being.

"Thank you. I feel so conspicuous walking around like this."

Leah understood that he meant: It was beneath his dignity as a Japanese to be in an unfriendly crowd and look as if he had been attacked. It might give others ideas.

Indoors, Ito remained standing, amazed he had found Leah amid the squalor and chaos of Macau. He watched a cockroach crawl up Leah's wall. True, he'd left his hotel room early to trawl the streets to discover if the combination of Chinese and Portuguese ancestry yielded beautiful women. Several passed his test, but he hadn't had the time to pursue his study in depth.

Ignoring Ito's fascination with the cockroach's journey, Leah opened a drawer to retrieve a needle and thread. She slammed the drawer hard; the cockroach scuttled out of sight. She sat on the bed and sewed.

"You have beautiful hands," he said. "Hong Kong has not changed much," he ventured.

Leah stuck the needle hard into the cloth. "Ha!"

He gave a tight smile. "Well, maybe a little. But it is safe."

"Safe for whom?"

"I like Western women. They speak their mind. We Japanese are never direct. But it makes for harmony."

She bit off the thread and handed him his jacket. "Except for bombing, making war and killing people."

He shrugged. "May I?" he asked, reaching for a rag, and dabbed at the stains on his trousers. "That's politics. I'm a businessman and not at war with anyone," he said head down, appraising the damage.

Leah debated hitting him over the head with the chair. How dare he think that the war was nothing to do with him? Look at his fine suit, his shitty hand-carved buttons. He was making a fortune out it.

He turned around with the cloth in his hand, confessing, "I've never lived in Japan. I was educated in Europe. In my own country, I'm considered a foreigner."

Why was he telling this? For a romp on her mangy bed? "I think you'd better go, Mr. Ito. My fiancé is in a Japanese prisoner of war camp. I don't think he would appreciate your distinction. I certainly don't."

For a moment he looked ineffably sad. "But you and I are not enemies."

She glared.

"It is very peaceful in Macau, despite the crowds and the thieves," he said putting on his damaged suit jacket. "It has a European quality—only the smells are different, and the sky. The light is not the same. It is often too hot, don't you think so?"

"I've never been to Europe. I don't think now is the time to go. Do you?"

He ran a hand through his dark hair and touched his cut. "I've acquired a very fine slip white figurine, a dancer. It's seventh century, T'ang dynasty. Her expression is like yours, mysterious. When I next come to Macau, I'll bring you a photograph. It is very rare."

"You'd better go."

"I was on my way to a dinner meeting of Japanese businessmen. It is too late now. I will call in the morning to apologise and send gifts. Gold lighters, I think. They make very good gifts . . . Have you eaten?"

He wanted to stay. She didn't have to do anything, only listen. It might pay off; he was nostalgic and unsettled.

"I was going to buy something off a stall."

"I could get something and we could eat here. I don't want to eat at a restaurant dressed like this."

She nodded. He didn't want to be seen in public with her. The Japanese only went to the best restaurants. Someone would be bound to see him and report him for eating with an English woman. There were spies everywhere.

"All right," she decided. "But use my *patacas*. The stall holders don't like Japanese military notes."

Frowning, she saw she had scored several points. He knew that she meant the Chinese hated the Japanese and their money.

They ate their meal—Ito balancing on the wobbly chair and Leah on the bed—and danced around the topic of war. Ito proclaimed that the war seemed far away in Macau; Leah retorted that Hong Kong was only forty-odd miles away. She grew increasingly impatient with his sly, calculating glances. Desire danced in his eyes. She finished the last of rice. "It's late. I have to work tomorrow."

He asked what she did and she lied. "I work as a translator for several Portuguese businessmen, wine merchants. It's boring, but jobs are scarce." She poured more Portuguese wine into his glass.

Ito rated his chances of getting her into bed as poor. Though he might have more luck the next time if she would only stop blaming him for the ugly, insect ridden flat, her lousy job, the poor food. At least, she'd stopped talking about her imprisoned fiancé. He came to Macau regularly. He could imagine spending time with her in the swayback bed. It would be something to look forward to. "I'm returning to Hong Kong, then to Hankow in a few days. They need steel for new railroad ties. The rail line has been heavily bombed. Someone has given the Chinese new airplanes. Maybe the Americans. We didn't expect the Chinese would be able to fly such complicated machines. They need thirty per cent more steel fast, twenty tons more. I have investors in Macau and will be able to buy more ships. I'll be back here in a couple of weeks. May I see you?"

Apparently bored by his talk of war materiel, she yawned. Inwardly, she memorised every word and gloated she hadn't had to ask one leading question. She rose to clear the table.

Ito cursed himself. He had rushed it. He didn't want to pounce . . . yet. He prided himself on his intimate knowledge of Western women. The next move was to show he cared. He racked his wine-addled brain. "I could check on your fiancé, if it would help."

Her face lit up with gratitude: "If you could—"

"Would you hate me if he were—"

"—Dead?" she supplied.

"I won't lie," he said, stubbornly. "Even if it suited me."

"No," she said softly. "Don't lie. You can't build anything on lies."

He kissed her.

She knew he was going to, saw desire flash in his eyes as he pulled her to him. She kissed him back, feeling his smooth cheek and tasting his wine breath. A conspirator's kiss. Then she moved out of his embrace to scribble Jonathan's details on a piece of paper.

Ito left, promising to return soon.

Stunned, she collapsed onto the bed. She knew where and when he was going to deliver steel and that the Chinese had inflicted damage on Japanese troops near Hankow. Only, how was she going to make use of her knowledge? The question tortured her. She stared at the silent, elegant women on the inlaid screen, trying to reconcile duplicity with love and Jonathan. Sometime around two in the morning, she gave up. It was war. There weren't any rules.

IN her hot tiny office, Leah doodled Chinese characters, racking her brain over whom to approach about her windfall of intelligence. Not Spencer Talbot. He was a terrible gossip, taking great pleasure in divulging which Portuguese officials or rich businessmen had mistresses or whose wife was addicted to gambling or opium. She was sure her west-facing office with its ridiculous small window was Spencer's revenge for daring to become part of his domain. He was a strange man, precise to the point of being pedantic and coldly polite. His voice was without expression, flat and dry. It was impossible to know what he was thinking, but he nursed his grudges. Certainly, Spencer resented her. He didn't try to disguise it, shaking his head in wonder at her typographical errors and insinuating she was responsible for the chaos in the office brought about by the exodus of people from Hong Kong or occupied China. He was jealous of her rapport with Albemarle. He made nasty cracks about her female wiles. Sometimes, the only way she could get through the day without causing a scene was imagining Spencer as a skinny scrawny schoolboy, no good at games, who was teased and bullied. Once he revealed his nickname at school was Foxy. He had bright red hair then, he explained, and she tried to look sympathetic. Boys can be cruel, he said, and she knew her image of him was correct. She suspected if he had power, he would be a thug. He had no generosity or compassion. Or if he did, he saved it all for himself. Albemarle had alluded to an incident in Spencer's past, a misunderstanding over money. Immediately, Leah thought fraud. He had the look of a forger; she had seen enough in the antiquities trade to identify the breed. That was why he had been shifted to Macau a long time ago. It was payback and revenge. Macau was an of end-of-the-line sort of place for a person like Spencer. He wasn't going any place else.

Albemarle was her best bet. He knew everybody and was discreet and, most importantly, went out of his way to help penniless Chinese refugees. Only today, Albemarle was uncharacteristically late. She heard Spencer say hello. The consul cut him off and asked him to come to his office. Then Albemarle stopped by her office and said, "I want you too."

He stood, fuming, as Leah and Spencer took their seats. "I've come from the governor's officer. The Japs are complaining I'm hurting Macau's neutrality. I've spent all morning with the governor. Teixeira is worried this time. The Portuguese government in Lisbon has received a formal Japanese diplomatic note. They accuse me of spying. Me!"

"Disgraceful, sir," said Spencer. "You're a diplomat."

"They can't prove anything. It's a bluff," Leah declared.

"Sadly, I've given my word. The Japanese have threatened to block all shipments of rice to Macau and divert them to Hong Kong. It may be a trumped up charge, but I won't be responsible for the Macanese starving."

"If I might say so, sir. You are not responsible for the Macanese."

"I'm going to forget you said that, Mr. Talbot," said Albemarle. "The point is, we are all being watched. Not by Consul Nagotchi, he would never sink so low. It's the fault of Sawa, his new military attaché. I've been warned."

Leah was tempted to ask by whom, but thought better of it.

"Sawa is the head of the *Kempeitai*, the Japanese secret military police. He's a thickset man, with a moustache, dead eyes, and always in full dress uniform. Have you seen him on the streets?"

"I always cross to the other side of the street, if there is a Jap around," said Spencer primly.

"Wise. Sawa is throwing a great deal of money around to get people to inform. Be careful, even gossip can be used to trick you."

Leah was impressed with Albemarle's tact. The consul had implied nothing, but had warned Spencer he knew about Spencer's weakness for gossip. The servant Moy knocked on the door with morning tea and the conversation switched to the day's business.

Leah slipped her tea slowly, determined to outwait Spencer, who left in frustration saying, "*I* have work to do."

"You wanted something, Miss Kolbe?"

"I was asked to spy for Britain."

Albemarle's teaspoon clattered to the floor. He bent down and eyed the spoon with something approaching misery, before coming back up for air and asking in a weak voice, "Tell me."

Matter of factly, Leah told Albemarle about her recruitment, careful not to mention Eldersen by name. "He found my knowledge of Cantonese useful and thought I could find things out," she said, not wanting to go into specifics yet. Albemarle looked pained, drained of colour and braced against the back of his chair, as if he wanted to disappear into it.

"You know Cantonese?" he sputtered.

Leah nodded. "I learnt it from my amah. Anyway, he asked if I could help gather information in Hong Kong because of certain contacts I had."

"You did this?" asked an incredulous Albemarle.

"Well, no. The war intervened and I never had the opportunity."

"Did your fiancé know about this?"

"No . . . It didn't concern him."

"I don't think it's right to recruit young women to spy. To put them in harm's way."

Already, Leah could see Albemarle removing her from the virtuous women category and re-filing her into another, dangerous one. What would he think of her relationship with Ito? Probably tie a bell around her and accuse her of being a leper. "If I were to find out information—"

"Too dangerous. Don't think about it. The Japanese are animals."

"Is there anyone else I could contact?"

"Certainly not. I don't want to be responsible. It will compromise us. And you, Leah, could end up dead. Sawa plays for keeps."

Leah nodded. She too heard rumours of untimely deaths, men and *women* who had 'gambling problems' or 'money worries' and were found dead in back alleys or washed ashore on the beaches of the nearby island of Taipa. The local police were stretched to the breaking point with the influx of refugees. They didn't investigate 'suicides.' It was all part of Macau's razor-edge neutrality.

"I'll send a coded cable and ask if they want you to be involved, Leah. I disapprove, but if I'm ordered to and we can do it without anyone else knowing, well, there are a few contacts . . ." He reached across and patted her lightly on the knee. His hand remained resting on her knee.

Wary, she shifted in her seat. Albemarle snatched back his hand as if burnt. He cleared his throat. "Now enough of this cloak and dagger stuff, what I want to know is how is the planning going for the king's birthday party? It's important to fly the flag."

Stymied, Leah discussed the arrangements for the gala. The party should be crawling with spies. She dismissed Albemarle's strange little advance. The man was lonely; he missed his wife. Spencer had no gossip about Albemarle's love life. He lived like a monk. The touch was avuncular, nothing more.

IN a hand-tailored lounge suit with wide-legged pants; a tuxedo jacket, fashioned from the heavy black silk mandarins wore; and a crêpe de chine blouse, Leah waited in the receiving line with the rest of wealthy and important Macau, the men in evening clothes and the women, their hair fashionably crimped or rolled, in flowing satin gowns or the occasional *cheongsam*.

She was a sensation. It was always best to hide in the open. Spencer was livid. "There are rules," he huffed.

"Don't you like it?" asked Leah sweetly.

Spencer walked away without replying.

A young Portuguese man asked her to dance. She had to be cautious. Everyone knew everyone in these elite circles. The longstanding Macanese Japanese business community had spies throughout Macau. They paid well for useful intelligence or helped favourites with trade contacts in the defeated territories. People turned a blind eye. Business first.

In Asia, the Portuguese were true middlemen. Middlemen had connections everywhere. After several months of tense negotiations between Portugal and Japan, those who had settled in Hong Kong had come flocking back to Macau in a special armada. There had been a formal pilgrimage to Guia Hill and the Chapel of Our Lady of Guia to give thanks for their deliverance from Japanese rule and internment. Leah watched the Bishop of Macau lead the procession. The sense of relief and joy was palpable. It hung in the air long after the returning Portuguese squeezed into the homes of relatives or were given shelter and a bed in church schools and monasteries. But for Leah, it was tinged with sadness: No one she knew could leave Hong Kong so easily.

The young Portuguese man twirled her around the large ballroom with its rosettes, green curtains and shining parquet floor. Over his shoulder, she watched a group of important Portuguese businessmen smoking and drinking while their wives sat on gold-painted chairs gossiping and, occasionally, training a watchful eye on their men. Leah thanked her partner for the dance and wandered over to the clutch of businessmen. They were polite and flirtatious, and perfectly correct. Casually, Leah talked war news. The battle of Midway was discussed and the war in China. In China, no one was quite certain what city had fallen this week to the Japanese.

"I keep thinking," said Leah, "I ought to be doing more to help."

One of the man suggested a benefit concert for refugees. Leah agreed to sell tickets, appalled at her stupidity. Useless talk to people in groups, no one wanted to stick his neck out and she would be marked as a volunteer for other charities, decorating a card table handing out raffle tickets.

A Chinese ear must be better. She spotted Mr. Kwong, owner of the largest firecracker company, the Celestial Brand, and known by everyone as Firecracker Kwong. Mr. Kwong ignored her implications, observing instead that she had finished her drink. Hurriedly, he went to the bar to fetch another. It was clear he did not intend to discuss anything in a public place, even if he wrote letters of indignation to the Chinese papers about the moral turpitude of the Japanese.

She drifted to the seated married women in their lace dresses, chatting contentedly in Portuguese behind their antique fans. A middled-aged woman with thick eyebrows and dyed black hair studied Leah, trying to place her. Was she someone's daughter who left for Portugal as a little girl and returned all grown up? Or a new young wife a lonely Portugese boy had married abroad, who was unhappy in small close knit Macau and played at dressing up? Diplomatically, Leah nodded at the woman and sipped a gin. The woman smiled. Together, they regarded the sedately dancing couples: a Portuguese lady with a Chinese man in a mandarin gown, an old man dancing with his elegant Eurasian daughter in a rose satin dress, the shared smiles between the Portuguese and Chinese. It was what Leah liked most about Macau. Unlike Hong Kong, there were no boundaries amongst people.

Then chaos. She glimpsed the face of Chang talking to the

Portuguese Minister of Finance, Pedro Lobo, a dapper little man who had his little hand in everything. She uttered a small oh of distress and swayed, collapsing into a chair, rubbing the cold glass of gin against her throbbing temple.

"Sick?" inquired the Portuguese woman.

The woman and her friends thought she was pregnant, not frightened. She took a sip of gin and fought to regain composure. The women clucked consoling phrases of Portuguese. She forced herself to look again and be sure. It *was* Chang, still tall and thin, but more polished than she had ever seen him in a dinner jacket, immaculate white shirt and knife-sharp pleated trousers. He oozed respectability. What secrets did he know about Macau and the double-dealing that lay just beneath the surface of Macau's complicated geography and neutrality?

Their eyes met. There was a blink of recognition in his pebble eyes. Chang's glance returned to Lobo. Lobo must have said something amusing, because she saw Chang laugh, or rather his mouth laughed, but his face resisted. The men shook hands and Lobo left to join young handsome Governor Teixeira and his wife.

Chang weaved amongst the crowd toward the bar. He stopped to exchange pleasantries with Albemarle and Spencer, who hovered, alert to the consul's duty to make the rounds. Spencer whispered something into Albemarle's ear. Swiftly and with seasoned professional courtesy, Albemarle left Chang to concentrate on other guests. Unperturbed, Chang continued his journey to the bar.

Chang was her man. He had direct links to the Kuomintang; or, if it were more to his advantage, he would convey her intelligence to the Communist Mao and his General Chou En-Lai who commanded the Eighth Army and the New Fourth Front.

In any case, he would not waste her information. But if she were truthful, if she had a gun she would not hesitate to shoot him dead. She drained the gin and said goodbye to the kind women who sat on the sidelines.

Waiting for his drink at the bar, Leah watched Chang take out one of his sweet-scented clove cigarettes, tap it on his gold case and light it with a handsome gold lighter. As she moved closer, a tongue of clove smoke lapped toward her. She gave a small cough of disgust.

"All right?" asked Albemarle, exchanging her empty glass for a full one as a waiter passed.

"Fine," she said and sipped her drink.

"Having a good time?"

"I'm so pleased it's going well," she replied. "Such a relief."

"I knew you would pull it off," he said like a proud father.

Indifferently, she asked, "Who's that tall Chinese fellow?"

"Ah," said Albemarle, "that is our esteemed Free China representative, Mr. Chang. He's the keeper of the Sun Yat-sen flame."

"Really?" Her voice squeaked up an octave.

Albemarle dropped the discreet façade to speak in a confidential whisper. "That's his official title. He's got his finger in lots of pies. Gambling, smuggling . . ." His voice trailed off.

"He's coming over," said Leah.

"Be sure to count your fingers and toes afterwards." Then he turned and said aloud, "Mr. Chang, I'd like you to meet Miss Leah Kolbe, the newest and most welcomed addition to my staff. She got out of Hong Kong in the nick of time."

"How wise of you, Miss Kolbe. May I welcome you to Macau."

Leah gave a pretty smile. "Thank you."

"Miss Kolbe organised the party and the band."

"Beautiful and talented," replied Chang.

As if on cue, the small Filipino swing quartet began to play again.

"Duty calls," said Albemarle as Spencer motioned him toward the Minister of Finance.

Younger couples regrouped and took up the challenge of the band's quick foxtrot. Leah led Chang towards the non-English speaking Portuguese ladies. She stood near them, as if their presence would protect her.

"Don't you go spreading lies about me. I could tell your consul things," he cautioned.

If the devil existed, he would be this thin dry man in a hand-tailored dinner suit. She began to walk away.

He caught her by the arm, "Out with it," he demanded.

She told him. Not about Ito, but about the destroyed rail-head and the shipment of steel. She ended with, "It must be bombed."

"I must know your source," he insisted. "I can't have bombers sent off on a whim."

"I can't say. Believe me, if I knew any other person in this room or Macau who could do it, I wouldn't be dealing with you."

They watched the elite having a good time. Now, tension pervaded the ballroom: the men were a shade too hearty and their laughter anxious; the women's eyes glittered unnaturally and many seemed to want to hide beneath a thick layer of makeup and rouge; a small brown-haired girl chain smoked incessantly; and a red-face Scotsman sat morosely in the corner with five empty whisky glasses neatly aligned, humming a sad tune about a dead beautiful girl.

Chang lit another clove cigarette. "You don't like these, do you?

"I don't smoke."

He gave a ghost of smile as he blew a curl of smoke. "I will use this intelligence and see what happens," he concluded, halfway between a promise and threat.

She walked away, towards the welcoming circle of Portuguese businessmen and found her young dance partner. "I like this song," she said. "Would you?" The young man beamed and led her triumphantly back to the dance floor.

Albemarle watched Leah dance under the chandelier, its light picking up the sheen of her black silk lounge suit, the glow of her face. She moved so well. She lit up a room. She was luminescent. Was she in danger? He had sent a coded cable to Whitehall about Leah. They had yet to respond. He was overcome with fear for her. He could not protect her. Guilt gnawed at him that he would be putting her in danger and could not help.

His own foray into the underground was feeble. It was composed of Portuguese and Eurasians still able to do business in Japanese controlled China. They passed him third-hand accounts about troop size, armaments and battle plans. By the time he sent the news to his superiors, it was stale. If anything, he was helping the Japanese cause because his intelligence was so out of date. He had one operative. Operative, what a joke. He was an oily Russian with the unlikely English name of Boris Harris. Harris volunteered that his father had been an engineer advising on the Trans Siberia Railway, met his Russian mother in the polyglot port city of Vladivostok and never returned to England. Albemarle checked his story because Harris seemed to be such a phoney and his passport had been reissued in Vladivostok. To his dismay, the news came back that Harris was indeed British. Albemarle had given Harris introductions to Macau moneymen. Since then, Harris intermittently provided intelligence that the Foreign Office had found useful. Harris was often in China. Thank God, he hadn't come tonight. He embarrassed him, ogled the ladies and made obnoxious, unfunny remarks. Harris was rich. How Harris got to be rich was unfathomable. Albemarle had made it his business not to find out.

Chang was different. Smoother, and without a doubt one hundred and ten per cent corrupt. Half the time the Nationalists were more intent on preventing the Communists armies from proclaiming victories than on winning any of their own. Thank God, Chang hadn't stayed long talking to Leah. He was being a nervous Nellie and overprotective. The girl had too much sense to be taken in by such a ruthless man.

What an introspective old man he was becoming, mad and lonely. It was his own fault. He had encouraged Mildred to leave even before the war. The fiction of wanting to return to England to be with the children had been an easy excuse. In truth, he and Mildred should never have married. He sighed deeply as Leah and her partner finished dancing and came to rest near him.

"My turn," said Albemarle gaily and danced Leah around the floor in a bouncy two-step that left him breathless and excited.

9

LEAH STARED AT a letter addressed to George Bentley in care of the consulate. From war-torn China, Bentley had made it to Macau. He was vague on the details—he claimed his business associates helped him. He declared he was destitute, his Hong Kong funds embargoed by the Japanese, and therefore he was entitled to the full allowance European British citizens received. When she explained how much he would get a fortnight he shouted he was not a damn coolie who lived on rice and asking who the hell was she. Ignoring his outburst, she replied calmly that it was generous given that Eurasian subjects received a quarter less and former Chinese residents of Hong Kong, even with families, only received half. Bentley thumped the desk and demanded to see the consul. Luckily, Albemarle was out. Bentley left in a huff, warning, "Mark my words, girlie, I intend to take this further."

By rights, she should simply re-address Bentley's letter, but the flap of the envelope was raised. She edged the blunt side of the letter opener along the gummy bit. The letter was from Bentley's comprador, explaining how he had arranged at Bentley's request a large transfer of funds through the Bank of Lisboa. The pig of a man was positively wealthy! Indignant, Leah went to Albemarle with the file.

Glumly, Albemarle explained, "We can't do anything about it. We aren't a court of law. You could ask him to provide his bankbook. He will refuse. That kind always does. He's taken the best suite at the Hotel Rivera. I can make a note of it. It won't make a difference. He's entitled to the allowance based on the information he provided. You shouldn't have opened his mail . . ."

"The letter was half out of the envelope, sir."

"Really?"

"Practically."

"Please sit, Leah. It's about that other matter."

Leah focused on the painting above the consul's head. It was a reproduction of a Constable landscape, she thought. A meandering river flowed through a tranquil peaceful countryside devoid of people. She wished she were there, sitting on the riverbank with a picnic, Jonathan lounging on a blanket, enjoying the hushed day.

"They want you to go ahead with your contacts. You're to establish your network. I can't help. There are a great many English stranded in Portugal. Reprisals, you know, and the Japs might make good on the threat to embargo rice here. We're all pawns," he said, attempting to be philosophical about her assignment, as if it were as ordinary as Bentley's file.

"But I'm so new," she stammered. "I know hardly anyone."

"They think you know *someone*."

She blushed and felt suddenly at sea and very young.

"*They* wouldn't tell me anything. I didn't mean to pry, only I feel damned useless. It must be hard to be part of such a world."

She could see it in his eyes. Albemarle no longer trusted

her. She was a liar, dangerous, and probably a whore. "I didn't volunteer," she retorted. "I was recruited."

"Blame the war. We all do."

"Yes," she sharply. "And I am no Mr. Bentley." She got up to leave.

He rose to his feet as if he wanted to hold her back from stomping out the door. "It isn't like that, Miss Kolbe . . ., Leah. I don't want—" But he couldn't bring himself to say, You can refuse. "I never thought you were," he said lamely.

There wasn't anything more to say. She said, "Thank you, sir," and left.

Later in the afternoon, she arranged for a boy to hand deliver Bentley's opened letter inside an official consular one. It was a very small victory. He would know that she knew and she bet the conniving Mr. Bentley wouldn't give a damn.

Albemarle turned a blind eye to Leah selling tickets for fundraising events in aid of Free China to consular visitors. It was a good cover, mixing with a crowd that might lead to something. She had heard nothing from Chang.

Tonight's event was a seventeenth century operatic play, *The Peony Pavilion*, about a young girl who dies pining for a lover she met only in a dream. Years later, the dream lover stays in her town, finds her portrait and revives her. The audience discussed the current adaptation and commented loudly on how well each actor played his role. The actors were used to it.

Leah let her thoughts drift until she caught the whiff of cloves. At the head of the row was Chang. He mouthed, "I want to talk to you." Then he focused on the play.

Here was the monster of her nightmares wanting to meet and she was driven to make him the linchpin of her feeble network. On stage, the couple sang their duet of everlasting love.

Their devotion made Leah feel small and mean. There was this gaping hole in her life and she was filling it with Tokai and now Chang. How could life be so complicated? She considered bolting, but it was too late. People were clapping.

Outside on the Rua Camillo Pessanha, young girls in silky dresses and high-heeled sandals laughed and flirted with young men with slicked-down hair, their mothers in modest *cheongsams* and their fathers in suits or the black traditional dress of Mandarins, beaming. Mr. Kwong of the Celestial Firecracker Company congratulated Leah on her ticket-selling ability. They had raised thousands of *patacas*.

"Miss Kolbe is dedicated to the cause," said Chang.

Kwong didn't take Chang's bait, saying instead, "Miss Mo Hang Sheng's performance was magnificent. A beautiful voice. It is one of the few good things about the war. So many wonderful performers have sought refuge in Macau. We are already planning the next benefit." With that, he handed Leah a roll of new tickets to sell and excused himself.

Chang waited until Kwong was far away to tell her: They had bombed the rail line as it was being mended. Many Japanese had died. Japan would have to make more steel. Her intelligence was good.

A shiver of satisfaction ran up Leah's spine. She was responsible. She could hate herself less.

"Benefit concerts do not win wars," Chang said sourly and held Leah's wrist tight. "We must meet. The beach on the island of Coloane is good. There are . . ." His eyes flicked toward the animated crowd and back to her. "Tell the consul you need the weekend off. I'll be in touch." Chang tipped his hat and walked away, skirting the happy crowd.

Abandoned, she crossed the road to wait for the bus that

would take her home. She knew she would lie awake all night with a wet facecloth on her forehead, unable to stop thinking about the past and cursing the fact that Chang was her network. It was a sick joke that she had escaped occupation and certain imprisonment, only to be trapped into making deals with the devil. There were all kinds of war.

Arriving home, Leah saw a man's shadow underneath the banyan tree. She called out in Cantonese, "I haven't got any money and I have a knife in my hand." She heard a low chortle. Tokai Ito stepped out from under the tree's sheltering branches with a large box and a briefcase.

"I surrender, Miss Kolbe."

"That's not funny," she snapped.

"I've been waiting a long time. May I come in?"

"It's late."

"I've got news about your fiancé," he said quietly.

Jonathan was alive, unhurt, in Shamshuipo Prison Camp at North Point. Unable to control her tears, she collapsed onto the bed.

Ito remained standing, uncertain whether to stay and comfort her, or leave and return after she had time to digest the news. She was sobbing to the point of hysteria like a tortured kabuki ghost. Sitting down at the table, he opened his briefcase, took out a bottle, poured himself a whisky, and waited for the storm to pass.

For Leah, time had ceased to exist. She was back somewhere. The light played on his golden hair, the weight of his leg felt good on her back as he lay sleeping, she rubbed her fingers along his arm and inhaled his musky scent. Then she saw him hollowed-eyed, propped up on a narrow bed, his blue eyes clouded by sorrow. Tears were useless.

Ito came over with the bottle. She took several pulls. "Sleep," he insisted and wiped her snotty, doughy face. She lay back against the lumpy mattress and fell into a dazed sleep. Carefully, so as not to wake her, Ito removed her shoes.

Leah awoke to Ito slumped in the chair, his head pillowed on his arms resting on the table, snoring softly. She got out of bed and touched him lightly on the shoulder. Startled, he cried out and sat up.

"I think you should go."

He nodded and rose unsteadily to his feet. "I almost forgot," he said thickly and pulled the light cord. Blinking in its glare, Ito untied the string on a long white box. Inside, lying cradled in cotton wadding, was a white slip dancer dressed in a tight bodice and a high-waisted pleated skirt that fell to her feet. Her graceful arms were raised as if holding a shawl overhead. There were still traces of red and ochre paint on the skirt.

"Remember," he said. "I told you about it. You can't tell if the dancer is dancing for the pure pleasure of dancing, or to please someone else. It's such a self-absorbed pose."

"It's beautiful."

He kissed her, pushing the hard statue against her breasts. His lips were firm and his mouth tasted of sleep.

"I can't accept this," she said, pulling back.

"Smile," he ordered.

"I can't."

"Please."

Her lips moved a little.

He nodded. "You have the same secret smile."

Liar. He's trying to seduce me with his gift. Yet, he looked so sincere and there was such longing in his eyes. She placed the dancer on the table. Such a mysterious being, rescued from the grave like Persephone rescued from the Underworld by her mother. The dancer was looking at her, as if she could see straight through her. Tokai came over asking, "May I?" and arranged Leah's arms into the dancer's pose. "Not quite right," Ito judged and tilted Leah's head to the side. "Perfect. Please dance a little for me."

She danced a small mournful waltz and came to a halt in front of Ito. He kissed her arms, the nape of her neck. She allowed his hands free rein, aware of the outcome and her growing desire. In between his kisses, she murmured, "Perhaps the dancer is dancing for herself *and* someone else who isn't there."

Gently, he twirled her around to fold her against his chest. "Please," he pleaded as he pulled the light cord and the darkness embraced them. Together, with tenderness and lust, they went through the intimate ritual of taking off each other's clothes.

Just before Leah opened her legs, she said, "I wouldn't be doing this if Jonathan were dead."

He studied her face in the shadowy darkness. She was wide-eyed and serious and the smile was hidden. Why should he care about her English lover? He kissed her sad mouth. The Englishman wasn't here; he was, and rock hard he entered her.

෴

AFTERWARDS, Leah snuggled against Ito's smooth chest, amazed at what she had done. "I didn't . . ." she began and stopped.

"Don't. Don't pick things apart. It was good. I'm happy." He grinned.

"I need to sort this out."

He closed his eyes. He didn't want to know her motivation.

He had plotted his seduction like a military campaign and he wanted to enjoy his victory, the afterglow of sex with a woman he had desired from the moment he set eyes on her in a dusty blue smock. He ran his hands over her white body and pulled her on top. "Enough analysis."

She propped herself up her elbows and traced her fingers over his diamond-slanted eyes. "I have to say this. There is no war here. Here, there is just you and me."

He let out a long sigh of satisfaction. She kissed him and this time they made love slowly. He was quite unlike Jonathan as a lover, more probing, more open. How differently they fitted together.

In the dark, squeezed against Leah's long limbs, listening to her quiet intake of breath, Tokai was happier than he had been for a long time. Here, it was like before the war when he revelled in being a *modann boi*—a modern boy—free from the straightjacket of Japanese conventions, safe from his father's designs. Tokai hated Tokyo. His father had become a militarist, banning European books, speaking only Japanese, denigrating the time they had wasted in the West. He was consumed by his devotion to the Emperor. He was addicted to his war work: plotting the expansion of his steel mills, buying small factories, cutting deals with the *zaibatsu*, conducting intrigues and lining the pockets of civil servants to be appointed to serve on important industrial boards. Swept away with military fervour, the only thing they did agree on was that this was not the time to cement allegiances by a strategic marriage for Tokai. His father was building an empire and the girl chosen had to match his ambitions. Until those ambitions were realised, Tokai was free.

The lie he told Leah didn't bother him. He had tried to find out about the fiancé and it had cost him dearly. Calculatingly, he had become a drinking pal of Colonel Noma Kennosuke, head of the Hong Kong *Kempeitai*. The colonel was a tyrant with a vicious temper and a fetishist's love for the pearl-handled pistols he wore strapped to each thigh. Tokai spent hours buying drinks at Heer Grau's Tokyo Club to establish a friendship with a man most people avoided. Kennosuke was a thug, a thug with power. Once on patrol, the colonel discovered a poor Chinese family illegally foraging for food on the Peak. Kennosuke ordered his men to kill the family on the spot. Enraged at his men's hesitation to commit murder, Kennosuke shot the family with his pearl-handled revolvers, then ordered his men to cut off their heads. It had a salutary effect on the Chinese. More left. In a strange way, Tokai admired the man's ruthlessness. He had no illusion about war. Still, the man was an animal. He should have been more cautious.

When Kennosuke and Tokai drank together—Tokai paid— he was amazed at the amount of whisky the colonel consumed without passing out. During the early drinking phase, Kennosuke talked exclusively about his military exploits. After half a dozen whiskies, Kennosuke became maudlin, extolling his primary school friends, his mother's cooking, the beauty of Tokyo. It was in his nauseating sentimental stage that Tokai had dared to inquire innocently about imprisoned British soldiers. An instant change came over the colonel. There was a wary narrowing of the eyes and a hardening of expression. Tokai was thankful the lighting at Grau's was dim. He must have looked ashen when Kennosuke pulled out one of his revolvers and pointed it at him growling, "Prisoners should be killed. They have no reason to live." Then he shouted Bang. Tokai nearly wet himself as Kennosuke howled with laughter.

Charming Grau, the owner of the Tokyo Club, wandered

over and invited them to dine with him, on the house. "You'll have to put the gun away. It puts the customers off," the tall German advised, indifferently. Like a lamb, a grinning Kennosuke complied.

Tokai had absolutely no memory of the dinner or even how he had gotten home. In bed he vowed never to ask Kennosuke any more questions about POWs . . . Now, it didn't matter. The fiancé might be alive, but prisoners often sickened and died. It was natural. Who could face such a disgrace and want to continue living? He had done the right thing. Everyone lied to prisoners. It was expected. He cupped Leah's breasts and fell into a tranquil sleep.

In the afternoon, the flat became a hotbox. Tokai coaxed Leah into going to the Camões Gardens to stroll its leafy, shady paths. "In the heat of the day," he said, "it will be empty." Recklessly, she agreed.

It was cooler. It was pleasant to sit in this secluded spot, thigh to thigh and breathe in the fragrant air. In the distance, she watched an ancient Chinese man in a sunhat shuffle along with his caged canary. The canary fluttered its wings and twittered. The man spoke to the bird as if it were a person, telling the bird how lucky it was to require only a little seed. The old man walked past them, stared for a moment and then hurried on.

"Do you think," began Leah.

"He's half blind," said Ito. "I love the gardens here. Peaceful."

They talked about gardens: Leah about Theo's scholar's garden and Tokai about the aesthetics of Zen ones. It was lazy lover talk, time away from their lust.

Back at the flat in the cool of early night, Tokai complained about the plague of cartels and bureaucratic red tape he had to endure. He was leaving Hong Kong at the end of the month and might be away for several months because he had to visit munitions sites in China.

Leah complained about being alone again for so long, not knowing where in the world he would be. Letters were out. They both agreed it would damage his career if, God forbid, his father found out about them, or his competitors. Without thinking, he rattled off all the boring places he had to visit and how he disliked many of the managers his father had appointed, mentioning them by name. They didn't dare countermand his orders, but he could tell most were only going through the motions and couldn't wait for him to leave. Leah was very sympathetic. He promised to return as soon as possible. Leah pulled Tokai onto the uncomfortable bed. Afterwards, Tokai left happy and pleased with himself.

From the doorway, she watched Tokai walk away with a jaunty rolling gait, his briefcase in hand. Here was a man who still wanted Japan to win at all costs, despite everything. And she was going to tell Chang the location and the name of every Japanese munition plant in conquered China. With any luck, many would be destroyed. Only why did she feel so awful and whom had she betrayed most: Tokai? Jonathan? Herself?

10

HÁC SÁ BEACH was deserted. In the hot sun, Leah sprawled in a faded canvas deckchair. She wore a floppy straw hat, dark glasses, loose cotton trousers and a silk-printed midriff top. The beach was poor, the sand brown and gritty. She had expected more after Albemarle's enthusiastic endorsement. Wistfully, he'd said, "Mildred and I used to take the children there." He made it sound fun. Then, he'd added, "All the beaches in England are cordoned off. That's the way things are now."

She didn't know how to respond to his sadness and settled for a head bob, acknowledging that everything changed in a war, even the relationship between boss and employee. He didn't ask any questions or volunteer how to catch the ferry to Coloane Island. Clearly, he didn't want to know anything.

As she stared at the fishing boats far out in the calm water, she fantasized she was actually on the beach at Repulse Bay. She had come early to escape the happy families arriving later, dragging their rugs, thermoses and picnic baskets. But the image wouldn't stay. This beach was too bare and there was no place for a hotel or obliging waiters. Still, she appreciated the longed-for quiet and the cooling breeze that came off a stand of scraggy pine trees. Soon she would drag her chair under the pines to avoid sunburn, but now it was too much effort and she simply sat and gazed at the low flat horizon, the seagulls and . . . She looked harder at the lone man walking over the sand. Chang. She recognised him by his height, his determined quick step and how he held his arms close to his body, alert to danger and the need to protect himself. Despite the heat, she felt cold. Already, she pictured him looming over her, exerting his will. She scrambled to her feet and waded into the water.

He stood at the water's edge and called, "Enjoying yourself, Miss Kolbe?"

Leah waved and smiled. "The water's warm."

"Enjoy it while you can. The Japanese want to claim Coloane Island."

"What on earth for? There's nothing here except fish."

"They have plans. They want to dredge it and make it into a deepwater port to rival Hong Kong. The British are worried. The Portuguese government is easily bullied or tempted. Everyone has their price."

"But they have Hong Kong." She wadded further into the sea, her wet trousers clinging to her legs, feeling the gritty sand give between her toes.

"But for how long, Miss Kolbe?" he asked, his voice rising to reach her. "Come back. I'm tired of shouting."

She trudged back through the warm water, allowing her hands to make little ripples. A school of tiny black fish darted away in fright. She wrung the water out of her pants legs. "Do you swim, Mr. Chang?"

"That is what boats are for, Miss Kolbe."

"Swimming saved my life."

"Most fishermen can't swim. They only go to sea to earn a

living. They don't have an affinity with water." He paused, looking at her and then out to sea.

She felt the conversation was strange, that she was indeed in dangerous waters. He didn't go in much for Chinese politeness. He was very direct. She wondered if she were being hooked and, resenting his power, asked, "What do you want, Mr. Chang?"

"Do you think we can win this war?"

"Don't you?"

"Take off your sunglasses. I want to see your eyes."

"Is it right to have one law for Europeans, another for the Chinese?

"It will be different in peace. We will be better people," she declared, noting how peace left no taste on her tongue and how her words were empty rhetoric.

He made a gun with his fingers and pressed his thumb down like a trigger. "Pow!" he said like an American gangster. "And what will you sacrifice for this peace? Allow Chinese merchants to buy a house and live on the Peak? Offer to sell them your house? Give it to coolies as reparations?"

She didn't answer.

"May I?" he asked and took her sunglasses and stared up at the sun. "Japanese colonial rule in Manchuria is no different from British rule in Hong Kong or the Portuguese in Macau."

What was he getting at? He wanted something. Whatever it was she knew she would hate it.

"Albemarle wants to establish a government in-exile-for Hong Kong, to assert the British right to it."

"I know nothing of this. I type and deal with humanitarian relief."

"How good you are."

"Listen, I have all the locations of the munition factories and the names of the managers in most of China."

"Let's sit," he offered, friendly and cordial, motioning toward the deckchair as he sank onto the hot sand and sat with his arms around his legs, as if he too were on holiday and they had been engaged in banter.

She sat with her damp legs outstretched, feigning ease, acutely aware of her wet trousers clinging to her legs and the itch of drying sea salt. She repressed the urge to scratch.

"All right. Tell me," he said, lighting a clove cigarette and smoking it down to the stump, unresponsive as she rattled off the names. Afterwards, he leaned in and casually dropped a photograph in her lap. She examined the fuzzy photograph of Ito and her sitting on the stone bench in the Camões Gardens. Their faces were in shadow, but they were recognizable. At Ito's feet was his briefcase. She didn't remember him bringing it. It made the picture sinister. They were facing each other. She had her hand out, gesturing, as if accepting something Tokai was saying. Objectively, it didn't seem compromising. She was a spy. Spies consorted with the enemy. Eldersen had instructed her to use Tokai. In a court of law, she could defend herself; against the tide of gossip in Macau, she was helpless. Or, she shuddered, Chang would sell the photo to the Japanese. They'd be very interested. Sawa would not hesitate to order Ito's death through the shadowy network of his Kempeitai agents. Certainly, *she* would end up dead. Forcing a disinterested tone, she said, "The lighting isn't good. What are you going to do with it?"

He took the photograph back. "Keep it. Such things have value. Mr. Ito looks very relaxed."

She watched his smug face, the shape of his thin-lipped mouth as he spoke, the sun pinning him down, and his long shadow lengthening. "What do you want?" she demanded.

"*We* must have Hong Kong back. The Americans want to return Hong Kong to China. Put a stop to colonialism. The British want their empire. We must know what is going on. You will keep us informed."

"How are the communists going?" she shot back. "The East River Guerrilla Gang in the New Territories is doing well. Maybe they will claim Hong Kong for the Communists."

"Propaganda. But see, you do know what is going on."

She leaned back against the deckchair and searched for response in the blue sky and high fluffy clouds. "Albemarle isn't privy to high powered policy-making. Macau is a backwater."

Brushing sand from his black silk pyjamas, Chang got up and hovered over her like a prosecutor making his case. "Please, don't lie. It's stupid. He gets secret papers."

"They are locked in a safe. I don't have access and some are in code."

His face was hard and unyielding; in his hand was the snapshot. He flashed it, picture side up, as he spoke, using it like a semaphore to signal his control.

She stood up to meet his eyes. "Albemarle always says he's the last to know," she said stubbornly.

Chang gave a low amused grunt. "English understatement, Miss Kolbe." He pocketed the snapshot and produced a tiny camera. "We want *everything*," he said. "Buy a bird. When you have something, hang the cage on the banyan tree and leave the film there. You will find new film there too. We want *accurate* information, not useless administrative drivel. After all, if you believe in equality with your yellow brothers, as you obviously do with your Jap lover, then you should want China and Hong Kong to be free."

She said nothing. There was nothing to say.

"Don't think about confessing to Albemarle."

His threat hung in the air. Abruptly, he turned and walked quickly back in the direction he had come, above the high water line. Twenty yards away, he stopped and waved.

Leah watched his black pants legs flutter in the sea breeze and his upright hand moving. Then he hurried on. Her hand gripped the camera so tightly it hurt. Opening it, she saw her sweaty palm was riddled with red indentations. The camera's impassive, all-seeing glass eye stared up at her.

BACK in Macau, she slept badly, dreaming of swimming in debris-choked water, struggling against a riptide that dragged her out until there was no horizon. She woke in a clammy panic, sweaty and miserable.

Under the yellow bathroom light, she examined her face in the pockmarked mirror. There were deep circles under her eyes and a new tension in the set of her mouth. Splashing water on her face, she pulled at her skin as if to pummel it back into shape. She still looked haunted, defeated. She slid down onto the terrazzo floor. The cold tiles cooled her face. Curled into a small ball, she keened softly, rocking back and forth. Rusty tepid water trickled down the side of the washbasin to land on her back. Roused, she rose to turn off the tap. She couldn't stay in this mouldy bathroom forever. She had gotten this far and she would have to take whatever came next. It's what Theo would have done. He always said that in this life one doesn't get to pick and choose. Sometimes one just has to get on with it.

She fiddled with the taps until something approaching hot water came out and got into the bath. At least she would be clean.

Walking to work, the streets of Macau seemed grimmer. Hollow-eyed refugees in their telltale hessian charity clothes hung about under the awnings begging; while on the other side of the street, three teenage girls and a boy dressed in their dazzling white high school uniforms hawked flowers in support of the Chinese army to well-dressed men and women. The hands of the refugee children remained empty, but the high school students sold a great many flowers. Men stuck them in their lapels; women twisted them into their hair. She shouldn't be so critical. Even the high school children looked under nourished. There were porridge relief stations scattered throughout Macau that everyone supported to feed the poor. Not that much food was getting in. There was a thriving black market. It was rumoured that the cook in the Hotel Centro did a good trade in children no one wanted, butchering them, then selling the choicest cuts to the public as tender young meat. It made her feel sick to think about it. She gave a begging woman a handful of small *pataca* notes and hurried on before she became a mark for more beggars.

At work, the keys on her typewriter continually jammed and she read the same page of a report ten times without comprehension. When Albemarle walked in, she looked up guiltily as he shut the door to her tiny office. The small fan couldn't cope with the heat and hummed noisily. Sweaty and uncomfortable, she wiped at her face as Albemarle asked, "Enjoy the beach?"

Such an innocent question. She smiled. "Good to get away."

Albemarle hurried on, not asking for any more details about her seaside adventure. "I've got someone you must meet. Boris Harris. He's English-Russian. He's not everyone's cup of tea, but he's . . ." he hesitated. "Valuable, yes valuable. He could help you a lot with that other business."

"Yes," she said neutrally.

"Harris will be here at three this afternoon. Come to my office a little before, that way your meeting will be accidental on purpose." Albemarle lowered his voice. "I'm sure he will be of great help." He gave a small conspirator's smile. "I've sent Spencer on an errand. It will keep him out of the office all afternoon."

Leah couldn't help smiling back, such a pleasant little conspiracy, so different from Chang. It might even make Chang laugh. "All right."

LEAH sat on the couch with a several letters about nothing much, discussing them with Albemarle. There was a discreet tap on the door. In his best English, Moy announced, "Mr. Harris is here," as a large European man hovered just outside the door in the shadows of the hall.

"Thank you, Moy," said Albemarle. The European man strode in as Moy withdrew, leaving the door ajar.

Boris Harris went straight to Albemarle and pumped his hand, saying, "So good to see you again, Consul. Such a pleasure."

All the while, Leah sat stunned, too overcome to stop the papers from sliding off her lap. She knew this man, had done business with him in Manchuria. Only then his name wasn't Harris, it was Vasiliev. He must have nine lives. She had thought him dead. Or, perhaps, he had a twin brother who didn't use cheap black hair dye, preferring instead his thick snowy white hair that gave him a grandfatherly air, if grandfathers were oily and fish-eyed.

Albemarle made the introductions. Harris turned to see

Leah, his eyes alert. He bent down to retrieve Leah's papers. Their eyes met. Harris winked as Leah struggled to contain her confusion. "How do you do, Mr. Harris," said Leah as she accepted the fallen papers.

"The pleasure is all mine," answered Harris in what passed for English vowels in his Russian accent.

His suit was good, but his old self leaked though in the flashy red and gold bow tie and his glossy white slip-on shoes. He had lost weight, but his eyes were the same, deep blue and lying. He insisted on holding her hand for an instant, covering hers with his large Russian paw and patting it. Then he released her hand and sat too close, crowding her on the settee, all smiles. "A flower amongst two thorns," pronounced Vasiliev with smarmy charm.

Albemarle rose from behind his desk and sat in an armchair. In a loud voice, he described the constraints the consulate was now working under since the Japanese had complained about helping the refugee Hong Kong community. Leah turned and saw Moy, as if on cue, with a tray of afternoon tea and *pasties de nata* (warm egg custard tarts) in the hallway. Albemarle motioned to him to enter.

Harris reached greedily for the egg tart, his large face alight with desire. "I'm touched you remember, Consul. They are my favourite."

Moy handed Leah a napkin with a winning smile. Leah liked Moy the best of all the consul's servants. He was good-natured and managed to be helpful without being obsequious. He eased the door closed as he left.

"You vet your servants?" inquired Harris in between mouthfuls of tart and tea.

"No," said Albemarle, offended. "Most have worked at the

consulate for years. They are reliable and *loyal*. Take Moy. Always obliging, knows exactly what I want." He looked to Leah for confirmation.

"Yes," she responded, "without trust, where would we be?"

"We English," said Harris thickly, "play by the rules. Sometimes, this is a disadvantage." He clucked in sorrow at his trusting nature as Leah choked on her tea, coughing and spluttering.

"Do you need water, Miss Kolbe?" asked Albemarle.

Leah shook her head; Harris patted her back. She flinched and took a small sip of tea to quiet her coughs. "I'm fine," she managed.

After more tea and Harris's insights about the degradation of Macau life—too many spies, counterspies and refugees fleeing all kinds of dirty lives, robbing the place of its considerable charm—Albemarle steered the conversation towards Leah. "Miss Kolbe has a special brief. The consulate is not involved in this. I thought you might make arrangements to meet . . ." His words trailed off. He nodded at Leah and excused himself, shutting the door with a loud click.

For a moment neither Leah nor Vasiliev said anything. Then Vasiliev pounced. "Aren't you the clever minx. What a set-up."

"Shut up. Why aren't you dead?"

"Only the good die young."

"I make reports. I'd have to tell him who you really are. I have to protect myself."

"I am Harris. Don't say anything. My passport is valid," he said genially, but Leah understood from the way he sat with his thick arms on his knees and his unblinking lizard eyes that he would make it very unpleasant if she didn't go along with his Harris disguise.

Vasiliev pulled out a card with a name of a Portuguese bar

printed in fancy red letters: *De Santareme*. It was on Rua da Felicidade, the Street of Happiness, the red light district.

"I can't go there."

He brushed crumbs off his lap. "Meet me there at eleven tonight." He leered.

Albemarle knocked and peeked in. "All settled, then?"

Harris stood. "Must go. Another appointment."

He shook hands with the consul and left.

"Harris can be a useful person, despite his . . ."

"I expect you're right, Consul."

"In this business, we have to deal with all sorts of people," said Albemarle, as if trying to convince himself. "I have to attend a state dinner at the governor's tonight. It's Republic Day. The Japs will be there. I don't want to go."

"Perhaps," said Leah with a wisp of a smile, "you could leave early."

"No. I'll stay to the bitter end. That way, the Japs can't plot behind my back. They'd bribe Teixeira if they thought it would induce him to arrest me."

"They wouldn't dare."

"Let's not give them the opportunity," he said meaningfully.

"Don't worry. No one will trace things to here."

"What you are doing is so important—" He stopped and couldn't go on.

"—I intend to work late here tonight. I'm behind in my regular work."

"I'll ask Moy to bring you dinner."

"I'll get something later."

"Nonsense."

"Fine. Thank you."

"Look," said Albemarle, taking hold of her hand and peering

into her face. "It's always difficult to know who you can trust, but I did ask around and Harris's story was confirmed." He kept hold of her hand, his eyes on her delicate bird-like wrist. Incredible that people so far away had put such a burden on this young woman who should be spending her youth with admirers, breaking hearts. He wasn't sentimental, but he fancied that already she had a haunted look. It both saddened him and made him angry. "Don't work too late," he said, releasing her hand and disguising his feelings with a look of cool disinterest. "Or do spies do their best work then?"

Stung, Leah let the opportunity to tell Albemarle the truth about Vasiliev slip away. The consul would be appalled by her troubled, complicated life. There would be a flurry of communiqués between Macau and London and in the meantime . . . In the meantime, her access would be restricted. She would be watched and a furious vindictive Chang would send the Camões Gardens photograph to Sawa. Desperately, she wished Jonathan would appear, like a genie, and her secrets and treacheries would disappear in a puff of smoke. Moy entered to clear away the tea things.

"I won't, sir," said Leah and returned to her office.

⊙

LEAH pulled the door almost closed. Albemarle's office smelled faintly of wood polish and the red velvet curtains were drawn. She snapped on the flashlight. The room was very neat. Moy must have returned after Albemarle left, tidying and polishing. She must find Albemarle's logbook. It would provide a detailed list of all the communications that been received. She doubted she'd discover anything really incriminating.

Spencer boasted that Albemarle was receiving dispatches from the British Army Aid Group (BAGG)—escaped British prisoners of war from Hong Kong who fought alongside the Chinese communist East River Guerrillas. Together they harassed the Japanese army in the New Territories. Leah didn't believe Spencer. Albemarle had no advice to offer. He wasn't a military man and certainly didn't know the Hong Kong terrain. Maybe, though, he knew about supplies, or radios or other things. Hardly breathing, she opened the long middle drawer of Albemarle's desk. There it was: a green leather notebook stamped with a gold insignia, the English crest of three rampant lions. She ran her finger down the inked columns.

The notations were difficult to decipher since Spencer didn't have clearance to read the coded papers, only to mark them as Secret or Top Secret and the date. Daring to turn on the desk lamp, she slipped out a piece of writing paper to list those communications that might yield something of value. Her list was growing longer. Someone might notice the light on in Albemarle's office. If she took pictures of the logbook entries, it would document her spying and convince Chang that Albemarle was a mere functionary, not party to plots or policymaking. She laid the camera on the desk. What on earth was Section IV replacing the former Section B.115 directive on enemy aliens?

So intent was Leah on determining what to photograph that she failed to hear the door being eased opened on its well-oiled hinges. Moy stood framed in the doorway.

His eyes travelled from the logbook, to the tiny camera and finally Leah's ashen face.

"What do you want?" demanded Leah.

"You're not supposed to have that," said Moy, standing easy, mildly concerned. "It's private."

"The Consul asked me to check on something."

Doubtful, Moy edged closer. "Let me see what you have written."

"Don't be absurd."

"It is not allowed."

"Shall we call him and find out?"

Moy considered this. He was no longer affable. "I've been watching you. People want to know many things during a war."

"Yes, they do," Leah conceded. "Who have you been telling?"

Indignant, Moy said, "I work for the Consul for five years." Then he looked at her slyly. "Not telling also has its own reward, Miss Kolbe."

"What do you mean, Moy?"

Moy walked to where Leah was sitting. He picked up the camera, examining it and looking through the viewfinder at the logbook. He made a clicking noise.

"I'm not going to bribe you," Leah asserted with more calm than she felt. "The consul has given me permission. You will be dismissed from service." She could bluff him. Moy didn't want trouble. She was not about to give him money. He'd bleed her dry. Maybe she could threaten him with Chang, but if she revealed her connection to Chang, she might be in more danger.

Moy glared. "My cousin works for the Japanese consul. The Japanese are interested in everything. I think they will be interested in you. They pay well."

"I don't think that is a wise idea," said Leah. She capped the pen, returned the logbook to the drawer and slipped the list into her pocket. "I'd like the camera back, please." She held out her hand.

"I like this camera very much," he said, pocketing it. "I know just how the consul likes things arranged." He moved the leather container holding scissors, a letter opener and a stapler back into place.

Defeated, Leah said, "How much?"

In one astonishing swift manoeuvre, Moy slipped one arm around Leah's neck in a choke hold and squeezed. Then he grasped the letter opener like a knife and held it at her throat. "It's a very short walk to the Japanese consulate. Sawa is bound to be there. He doesn't like official parties."

"You're well informed."

"Get up, Miss Kolbe." He pricked her neck with the letter opener.

They shuffled through the deserted hallway and out the rear entrance. Leah stumbled along in front, throttled by Moy's bent arm and prodded by the point of the opener in her back. They were in the tiny alleyway, bounded by the high walls of the Japanese consulate. Leah tripped on the uneven cobblestones, then jerked fast into a squat. Moy toppled over her. He fell onto his knees with a loud echoing thud. She kicked him hard in the back; his face smacked the irregular stones. She kicked him again and again. An odd gagging sound filled the night. Out of breath and fury, she stopped.

Moy lay unmoving in a strange, contorted hunched position, turtle-like. Crouching down, she whispered Moy's name softly. No response. No movement. She held her palm an inch from his bloody squashed nose. There was no hint of air against her hand. In the dark, it was impossible to tell if he was dead or pretending.

Gingerly, Leah uncurled Moy. She saw the glint of the silver handle of the letter opener, its point stuck fast in Moy's chest. She lifted up his heavy arm, running her fingers up and down his wrist, unsure if her own fingers were too numb to feel a pulse.

Not that it mattered, he was clearly dead.

She vomited. Sick landed on Moy, other bits on her shoes. Woozy, she felt the adrenalin surge and thought: escape. She knew the Japanese consular guards were stationed at the front, not here at the back. With any luck, the guards were hunkered down on their haunches, catnapping. She strained to hear any passing footfall. No. Quite alone. Gritting her teeth and closing her eyes, she wrenched the letter opener out. She wiped the point against Moy's black jacket. Then she rifled his pockets and found the camera.

It was best to leave Moy here. Let the police ponder over what might have happed. Rapidly, she walked back to the consulate, the loud tapping of her high heels crashing in her ears like bullets.

In the lavatory, she took off her blouse and skirt, scrutinising them for blood, dirt and vomit. She sponged at the stains. One of her stockings was shredded at the knee. Hastily, she took both of them off and stuffed them into her pocket. She washed her shoes with toilet paper and the letter opener under hot soapy water, carrying it back to Albemarle's office in a towel. She placed it point side down in the leather holder, then picked up the flashlight. Lastly, she inspected the room, making a circuit, reassuring herself it looked pristine and untouched except for the sour smell of her own fear. She turned off the light and eased the door shut.

11

On the street it hit her. She was to meet Vasiliev, no Harris—she must remember—at *De Santarem*. Right now, all she wanted was the safety of her own uncomfortable bed. Let the bastard wait. She couldn't imagine sitting across the table in some dive exchanging confidences with him. But if she didn't go, it might be worse. Vasiliev was the kind of man who collected tidbits and sordid events and nothing remained secret in Macau for very long. He'd hear about Moy. And even if he didn't suspect her, he would still hunt her down. He wanted something from her. She had no choice. She dumped her torn stockings into a reeking bin outside a closed restaurant and then hailed a rickshaw. The man said nothing when she told him the address and, grateful, she slumped into the canvas seat of the rickshaw.

The sign for *De Santarem* was neon lit, fancy for the Rua da Felicidade. Perhaps a better class of pimps and whores hung out here, like the highly prized lute girls with their tiny bound feet, painted faces, and their centuries-old charm. She must look a wreck. She ran a hand through her hair as she watched the rickshaw puller fade away. Neat hair wouldn't alter her anguish. She hoped the club was very dark and that Vasiliev would interpret her long face as simple tiredness. She felt ancient, like the old Chinese women she saw on the street with their thread-bare black silk pyjamas and their bowlegs so twisted by age they could only hobble.

She pushed open the door and was trapped in a fug of smoke, booze and the dreamy glances of men: Chinese, Eurasian and Portuguese. The women didn't bother to turn their heads. Through the gloom, she spotted Vasiliev at the bar talking to a European man while their pubescent female companions stood silent, a frozen look of boredom on their young painted faces. She waved.

She saw Vasiliev whisper into the ear of a girl, then he walked towards her, with a satisfied smile. He led her to a secluded table at the back. A waiter hurried after them with two glasses of port. Vasiliev sniffed each glass, contentment filled his large face. "It's the best," he declared, licking his lips. "From Douro in Portugal. The other stuff is rubbish." He eyed her. "You look like you need a drink."

"Long day."

He considered this. "That so?"

"What shall we drink to?" she asked.

"To us," he announced clinking his glass against hers and took a drink, savouring the flavours on his tongue. "Superb."

Leah drank. It was very good, warming her from the inside. She took another sip and the nutty rich wine calmed her enough that she could focus on Vasiliev. She gazed at him, and his transformation from Vasiliev to Harris, as around them the buzz of conversations hummed. He certainly seemed to have become more successful, if you called being well-presented in a low rent bar success.

Vasiliev was studying the colour of the port, turning the glass in his meaty hand. "Such a shame in this light you can't see the port's true colour. It adds to the experience. All one's senses are involved."

"I thought you were executed in Manchuria. I was pleased."

Vasiliev narrowed his eyes and stared. "What a terrible young woman you have become."

"You nearly got us all killed in Manchuria," she said, lowering her voice. "You're the fiend. Sonia died because of you."

She looked away and was overcome by sadness as her mind rushed back to that terrible day in the teeming train station. Poor scheming Sonia, shot, dying on its cold concrete floor. A whiff of cheap perfume hit her as a couple got up and made their way to the door. The man squeezed the woman's buttocks with force and the woman let out a screech of drunken laughter.

Vasiliev nodded approvingly. "Someone's happy."

Icy with contempt, Leah demanded, "I want you to tell me how you got out."

"You think I work for the Japanese," Vasiliev flashed back with a hurt look on his face. "I hate them. All they know is war." He paused. "I miss Sonia too. She was like a sister to me." He rubbed his eyes and looked despondent.

In another minute, Leah thought, he will allow one large tear to escape. The man was an actor. It was all an act. He cared only for his own skin.

"She was dying. What was I supposed to do, stay there until the Kempeitai came, holding her lifeless hand and wailing? You didn't. You escaped and you dare reproach me?"

"It wasn't like that."

"So you say, Leah. I remember it differently. I was caught and thrown into a Jap prison because of you. You got away and escaped back to Hong Kong. Me, the Japs wanted to execute. I was lucky. They could have shot me on the spot. The Kempeitai don't go in for trials." He sighed, took another mouthful of port and looked pensive. "Contacts." He signalled the waiter and asked that he leave the bottle. He poured himself another glass. "I arranged for certain shipments of weapons from"—he paused again and looked around the room as if searching for a particular face—"a variety of sources and they agreed to let me go."

"You supplied the Japanese with weapons?"

"We weren't at war, then, Leah. Besides, if I didn't, someone else would have. It's business."

"Business," she echoed.

"Are you really Theo's daughter?" he asked.

"Don't you mention his name. You never knew him."

Vasiliev sniffed the port wine. "Wonderful bouquet. And Leah, for your information Theo and I were very good friends before you were born." He smiled serenely, as if remembering a particular enchanting event from his youth when he and Theo were young.

"You're lying. And you are not Mr. Harris."

"I am a very good Mr. Harris. And you and I have much in common. Not the least a fondness for your father. I *did* know Theo and we were very good friends.

"Don't bring Theo into this."

Vasiliev ducked his head under table then popped back up. "He's not here."

"I'm leaving."

His massive hand came down hard on hers. "You mustn't mind my little jokes. I am pulling your leg. It's what we Englishmen do with our jolly sense of humour."

"Let go of my hand."

His face changed, congealed into a harsh set mouth and narrowed eyes. "We haven't discussed business yet, my clever girl. It is important we understand each other. The consul depends on you so."

He inched his chair closer and whispered compliments, his breath heavy with sweet port. He rolled his eyes in praise of her escaping Hong Kong and finding refuge at the British consulate. They were two of a kind, living by their wits.

He was repulsive: ugly, brutal, with his loose flesh and round face alight with salacious intent. If he touched her again, she would leave.

"Pay attention," he snapped. "What happened before is ancient history. We can help each other." He reached for her glass, touched it lightly with his and toasted, "To us." He drank.

Leah felt compelled to finish the last of the port in her glass.

"Better," he said. "I am a patriot now. I have good connections in China. Did Albemarle mention I've been in Chungking?"

She shook her head.

"It's not good there. The allies aren't doing enough to supply Chiang Kai-shek's army. The American General Stilwell is out of his depth." He smirked at his pun, then continued, deadly serious. "I'm in touch with," he paused, swivelled his head around to make sure he couldn't be overheard, "people who can divert Japanese weapons to the Chinese. It costs money, though."

"You can't be serious."

"You check with Albemarle; he'll vouch for me."

"But I know you and *I* don't trust you."

He shook his head, clucking his sadness. "The trouble with you, Leah, is that you don't trust yourself. I don't know where you get that. Theo trusted me. Theo and I understood one another." He saw her disbelief waver as he smiled knowingly. "I was the one who got him interested in Chinese antiquities," he boasted. He'd done it, found the key to this interfering bitch, her arms drawn protectively in front of her breasts. So what if she found him repugnant? He knew so many things about her and her wily old sly fox of a father. She'd do what he wanted. He had a personal vendetta against the Japanese. What he had told her about escaping from Manchuria was mostly true. He saw no need to tell her anything more unless he needed to. What he wanted was money. Money to help the Chinese, yes; but also money to line his own pockets. It was such a tightrope to walk between the Chinese factions. He had to grease a great many palms. Politics was an expensive business.

With even more cunning, he ventured, "I miss Theo. Such a shame, how he died." He saw the effect of his words. Leah had taken her arms away from her chest and was leaning towards him eager to listen. "Not now, it's late." He turned and his little bar companion came to the table, smiling sweetly and perched in his lap. He stroked the girl's bare arm.

"We can't discuss business here."

"No," agreed Vasiliev. "I'll be in touch. The consul will be pleased we had this little meeting."

Leah nodded, and without saying goodbye made her way out to the deserted street. A lone rickshaw man came down the road, scouting for men ready to go home to their wives. The rickshaw man grunted when she gave her address and eyed her up and down. She saw in his calculating gaze that she was an exotic European whore. Seated, she supposed he might be right. Vasiliev wanted to screw her for money and she was too ex-hausted to care.

⌒

THE thin, well-groomed Macau Police Chief Luis De Rey lounged against the wall in Albemarle's office. Albemarle sat behind his desk; Spencer and Leah in the visitors' chairs leaning forward, intent to catch De Rey's every word. To De Rey, the man Spencer, who had discovered the body, looked terrible, his skin grey and waxy as if embalmed. The girl was very pretty, a real beauty. Out of habit, he kept his eyes trained on her as he mulled over what to say. It was just another stupid, senseless murder, which might or might not be linked to politics. He prayed to the saints that it wasn't political. What an idiotic thing for a Chinaman to do, get himself killed in the alley between two powerful enemies. If the man were alive, he'd murder him again for his stupidity and for putting his job on the line. He'd been in Macau since 1935, when António de Oliveira Salazar declared Portugal to be an Estado Nova, a New State. He understood his job: steer clear of the gangs and keep the general peace. Now his job was messy. Macau was chaotic, overflowing with refugees who had nothing. And his men couldn't cope. How could they? There were only six of them, good men on the whole, but limited. A ridiculous number to combat this surge in lawlessness— and perhaps they were too ready to look the other way. He couldn't blame them. They had signed up for a quiet, easy job. Well, he could look the other way too. Already, he decided it was a case of robbery pure and simple. He was not going to make himself unpopular with the Japanese. He had met Military Security Police Attaché Sawa on a number of occasions. Now, he avoided him whenever he could. There were some criminals one just stayed away from. The man was an animal.

"We will, of course, investigate," said De Rey. "Terrible

for this to happen to one of your employees and then the poor man to be found by Senhor Talbot." He shook his head in sorrow.

Spencer nodded, glad now to have played a pivotal role in the horrid mess. "Most upsetting," he said and realised Leah was staring at him as if he were an exhibit. Stupid girl. Why shouldn't he look disturbed? He shot her an evil look.

De Rey was amused by the interplay between the bald ugly man and the beauty, but managed to keep his face straight and sympathetic.

Spencer said to De Rey, "Moy was such a fine fellow. We will miss him."

"What do you think happened?" asked Albemarle. "Moy didn't have an enemy in the world."

De Rey cleared his throat and said with authority, "My initial reaction, robbery. A thief sees your servant leave the consulate, assumes he has money. Moy resists and the thief knifes him. Desperate people without anything, what do they have to lose? They care only about their next meal."

"You are probably right," said Albemarle, genuinely saddened by all the unhappiness and wanton killing in the world. He sighed. "Sign of the times."

"But may I say, Consul, on behalf of the colony of Macau and Governor Teixeira, who asked me personally to convey his condolences, we will investigate the matter thoroughly and make a full report. You have my personal guarantee." He stood tall and saluted.

"On behalf of my country, I thank you and look forward to receiving your report," said Albemarle.

De Rey looked around the room, smiled charmingly at Leah and left.

As soon as the door closed, Albemarle said, "Mr. Talbot, Spencer, take the day off. Go home, take a few days rest."

"I can work," said Spencer, desperate to show he was able to put aside his feelings of distress and carry on.

"No," declared Albemarle, "I insist. Miss Kolbe and I can cope perfectly well for a few days." Then more kindly, "Please as a favour to me, go home."

"If the police need me—"

"—They have your address, Spencer."

Spencer sighed. "If you think it best, sir."

As he got up to leave, Spencer added, "I'll write my report of the . . . incident . . . at home."

"Splendid," said Albemarle with utmost diplomacy and seriousness. "Write it all down, how you found poor Moy. It will help the police no end. Thank you for thinking of it."

Spencer was pleased. He had a purpose. Already, he was explaining in his head how he took his usual shortcut to work and discovered the poor bugger. Nasty. He'd include how he was certain other people—Chinese people—too must have seen the body and ignored it, not wanting to get involved. He'd entitled his memorandum 'Foul Play on the Streets of Macau.' It had a certain hard-boiled ring to it, like something in detective novels. He liked detective novels. How everything came out all right in the end. Maybe, he'd use Moy's death as a way to concoct his own. He might even drop in to see the police chief, De Rey. See how he was coming along with the investigation. Lovely word, investigation. It had an official ring to it. Maybe he'd even take the whole week off. "I'll do that, sir," he replied and even smiled at Leah as he went out the door.

"Load of nonsense," said Albemarle to Leah when they were alone. "The Japs did it. No doubt about it. That's why they left poor Moy in the alley. Not a very subtle message. I think they wanted to turn nice young Moy into a spy. Loyal man wouldn't do it, so they murdered him. Teixeira has received more protest notes from that weasel Sawa about how I'm marshalling anti-Japanese forces here. All we've done is support the Chinese escaping Hong Kong and provide some real news about what is happening in China. The Japs claim it's propaganda. Teixeira is nervous. He's a rising young star in the Portuguese bureaucracy. He doesn't want a Japanese police action to tarnish his record. And it could happen. One regiment of crack Japanese troops and Macau would concede defeat instantly. Then it wouldn't be only poor defenceless Chinese servants who are killed." He looked shaken.

"It might just be robbery."

He stared her down.

"No, you're right," she conceded, breathing a little hard, worried that somehow he could read her face and see her guilt. She hurried on: "Do you think we could take a more active role in China?"

Albemarle looked suddenly old. "You met with Harris?"

She nodded. "He has some scheme. But mostly, I think he wants money."

He shook his head. "The Americans are supposed to be supplying China." He sighed, lowered his voice. "You didn't hear that from me."

"Harris says it's not working."

"I don't have those kind of funds. And the Japs . . ." His voice trailed off. "There could be leaks inside. They seem to know my every move."

Seeing his defeat, she ventured, "I'm not certain Harris can be trusted."

"He somehow managed to get trucks to bring wounded Chinese soldiers to Macau for medical treatment and helped get drugs to the battlefield.

"He did?" She was baffled. She didn't believe Vasiliev had a humanitarian bone in body or gave a damn who won the war as long as he came out on top.

"You mustn't rush to judgment about Harris. He's full of surprises. You tell him, I'll try."

"Okay."

"And one more thing, he mustn't come here again. It's too risky for *all* of us. None of us wants to end up like poor Moy."

"No," she said, wishing Vasiliev had stayed dead.

12

WEEKS PASSED. FOOD became scarcer and prices soared. As 1942 neared a close, electricity was rationed. The Japanese claimed Macau's coal for Hong Kong and had the naval power to enforce it. Meekly, the coal boats put in at Hong Kong. In Macau, electricity was available officially between ten in the morning and three in the afternoon and in the evening from seven to dawn. Often it was much less. Many people turned into nights owls, staying up late to enjoy the glitter of Macau's neon lights and the relief of working fans. Leah did her routine consular work until two in the afternoon, then went home to lie on her bed naked and sweating, waiting for night to come.

Once or twice a week she returned at night to work at the consulate. If there was no one around, she searched Albemarle's office for information for Chang. No one noticed the lights on in the consul's office; often they burned unintentionally when the electricity flowed again. She passed low-grade policy documents to Chang. It wasn't much. It was more like gossip, hard to tell if it were true or not. The Americans were holding their own in the Pacific; China was a disaster. The Kuomintang and the Communists were busy warring among themselves. Allied war materiel was to come through Burma—Burma was overrun. There were no supply lines. Whitehall was too busy fighting the war to be concerned about the Empire and what colonial Hong Kong would be like after peace had been declared.

Over the past few months, she had shot three rolls of film and killed one bird. Billie—named after the sad American jazz singer—died mysteriously. Perhaps she had forgotten to leave Billie enough water, or perhaps the bird died of fright when she left it hanging in the branches of the banyan tree. There were no cats around. They had all been eaten. Now she had a second bird, olive green to blend in with the leaves. She kept it covered up when she came home at night and didn't give it a name. The bird seemed happy enough with the arrangement. The information she was giving to Chang must have satisfied him. She hadn't seen him since their beach meeting.

Vasiliev remained in Macau. He lived off the black market and held extravagant parties. He invited important men and the prettiest women. Albemarle was invited, but never went. As consul, it might look as if he were condoning Harris's excesses. She was a regular. A contingent of well-to-do young Portuguese men gave Vasiliev's parties a veneer of respectability. The parties often devolved into sordid drunken revels that scandalised a small section of Catholic Macau. Albemarle was convinced it was Harris's way of being undercover. Leah knew it was because Vasiliev was a drunk, a liar and a lech, but she didn't tell Albemarle this. Sometimes, before the parties degenerated, she learned interesting things. Chang turned up at one and spent most of his time with the Minister of Finance Pedro Lobo and the Chinese head of the Committee of Refugees. He left before midnight and didn't bother to cross the room to speak to her. She was relieved. She made conquests amongst the young Portuguese men; most spoke some English and paid her outrageous compliments. She became a kind of mascot and they showed her off at dingy clubs and the casino at the Hotel Centro where she watched them gamble.

The casino was a good place for gossip: who was paying off the Japanese and getting goods through to China; or, who had a short-wave radio set to pick up Chinese war news. It was all useful stuff and her Portuguese admirers were fun and kept a respectful distance. Tonight, she watched three Japanese naval officers in full military dress with clanking swords steadily lose. Their faces were tight with disappointment as they exchanged angry glances. They hooted their disapproval at the fan-tan dealer, who did his best to ignore them as he scooped up the buttons and threw them down again in the cup while the crowd of Chinese and Portuguese gamblers shouted their bets louder.

The Japanese officer with the hint of a moustache screamed "Cheating" in mangled English while the other two officers banged furiously on the fan-tan table, yelling in Japanese. In Cantonese, the dealer, white-faced but calm, explained he wasn't favouring the locals. Not understanding a word, the moustached officer grabbed the dealer's arm. Several Chinese goons, who kept the peace, pushed in. The Japanese pulled out their swords and sliced the air. The goons backed off as the casino fell silent. The Portuguese floor manager raced in, using the few polite words of Japanese he knew as he bowed and bobbed his head like a marionette, repeating Sorry, Sorry. Then, he reached into his own wallet and made a small pile of large *pataca* notes. The Japanese stared at the growing pile with contempt. The manager added more. The moustached officer let go of the dealer's bruised arm. Wreathed in smiles, the manager signalled to three Chinese hostesses who inched forward beaming. The officers returned their swords to their scabbards. The moustached officer picked up the money and gave it with derision to one of the girls who, smiling prettily at the enormous gift, led the men away to the bar.

The onlookers and the gamblers grumbled loudly. The manager shrugged. It was better this way. The fan-tan dealer rattled his cup with his good arm and called for bets. Instantly, the casino was alive with a chorus of bets.

Leah's Portuguese friend Aubertin commented, "At heart the Japanese are bullies. They think they can get away with anything. If they threaten violence, we give them money. They are the thugs of the world." He looked to Leah for confirmation.

She tried to imagine Tokai wild-eyed and threatening. He wasn't like that. He was kind and patient and shared her love of antiquity. "They can't all be like that," she said softly.

Aubertin gave her a searching look. "Don't be fooled by their politeness. It's a mask they wear."

"Maybe only the bullies come here."

"Wishful thinking." Aubertin changed the subject. He wanted to go dancing in one of the small Filipino clubs he knew. It was a happy place. It made him forget he was stuck here in this tiny crowded colony until the Japs were defeated. He signalled to his friends and they nodded their approval. Leah begged off. Aubertin planted a brotherly kiss on her cheek. "Suit yourself." The Portuguese men left in a noisy high-spirited group. Leah took the bus home.

TOKAI managed to return to Macau in April. It was a rushed three-day visit. He took the precaution of renting an expensive hotel room, going there only to bathe and change. Leah remained indoors at her flat, not going to work even during his absences. She told Tokai that she had called in sick to her bosses at the wine merchants. They were very understanding. Tokai had long lunches and nights on the town, cajoling Japanese merchants and a few sullen Portuguese businessmen to invest in ships to transport more steel and war materiel. The rest of the time he was in bed with Leah.

Tokai had been ill in China—malaria—and spent several months in Tokyo recuperating. He looked very well now. "Your father must have taken very good care of you," she said and kissed his mouth.

Tokai had hated every moment of it, having to remain in bed, seeing doctors he didn't want to see, later accompanying his father to board meetings, unable to say a word as his father railed against his workers who weren't meeting his unrealistic quotas. "The only thing I liked was visiting the Zero plant." He became animated and made his hands into wings, flying them at her, ducking and weaving as she squealed in mock fright. "They are marvellous. I have begun taking flying lessons. Unfortunately, I am learning on out-of-date planes," he complained.

Horrified at his new hobby, Leah asked questions about the Zero factory and why his father's manufacturing plants weren't meeting their quotas. Later, when Tokai was out, she wrote about the labour problems and the place names of the plants on rice paper, wrapping it around an exposed roll of film. She hung the cage outside. The bird was moulting and regarded her with his unblinking black eyes. It seemed a reproach.

Before Tokai left that afternoon for Hong Kong, he demanded to know if she missed him already.

"Yes," she said and kissed him extravagantly.

"Good. Now, I have something to look forward to," he said

and she saw sadness in his eyes as he lingered by the door, unable to let her go. Sighing deeply, he hugged her tight and left. At the door she watched him walk away. He still had his jaunty boulevard stroll. She could imagine him high up in the clouds wanting to lord it over the world. Maybe he wouldn't come back. She didn't know if this would make her sad, happy, or simply relieved.

One hot airless spring afternoon after the electricity stopped and poor Spencer, panting from the heat had left for the day, Albemarle entered Leah's closet of an office. He closed the door, cutting off the last hint of cool air. "It's come through," he announced. "They've agreed Harris is to go to China and have allocated him five thousand pounds. It's marked as charitable contribution in my accounts."

"My God, five thousand pounds. It's too much. It will be noticed."

"There are so many charities now, who will notice?"

She didn't bother to answer because they both knew the Japanese would find a way. Sawa probably had two or three informers inside the bank, competing against each other for the juiciest morsel, busy checking for irregularities, anything out of the ordinary.

"They should have sent it to Firecracker Kwong. Then you wouldn't be compromised, sir."

"They couldn't do that. You're to give the money to Harris. They'll know you are the go-between," he said grim and scowling, his face flushed from the heat and the stupidity of bureaucrats who inhabited a place thousand miles away from Japanese suspicions and their strangled-hold grip on the policies of Macau. "It's British money and they don't like using foreign nationals as a conduit. Too messy." He pulled out a revolver from his coat pocket and laid it on the desk. "The Firecracker gave me this. It's a .38 Smith and Wesson. Luckily, I won't shoot myself in the foot as it requires a long pull on the trigger. It's called a 'New Departure' in the brochure that came with it. It makes me nervous. I can't bring myself to load it."

Leah picked it up and balanced it in her hand, its barrel pointed toward the door, the black grip smooth in her grasp. "It's no good without bullets."

Albemarle reached into his breast pocket and brought out a crushed envelope. He dumped twelve bullets onto the green blotter, staring at them as if wishing they would disappear. "It's enough," he said. "I don't think there will be a shootout. Macau isn't the Wild West and the Japanese are too smart to do anything in the open." He made a show of a wry smile.

She was certain he had thought of this line before he came to see her in a misguided attempt to disguise how troubled he was about Harris, the money, and the gun. "No," she agreed. "But they're unpredictable. They kidnapped that gambler from the hospital to make his family pay."

"—And then, there's Moy . . . Maybe you should have one, too. I can ask for another."

Shaking her head, she returned the gun and watched him slowly insert a bullet into each chamber. She felt such a connection to him in this quiet office. She had an urge to confess everything: the true villainy of Harris/Vasiliev, how he shouldn't be trusted under any circumstances and her own miserable Quisling existence: bedding Tokai, spying for Chang and killing Moy.

"I'm so glad you're here, Leah. I miss not having someone who understands." He dropped the gun into his pocket and leaned across the desk, earnest and solemn. "Your young man is one lucky fellow." Then he lurched from the room his face convulsed with emotion.

Her young man. Her young man would never understand, and he would never find out. It was the one vow she intended to keep.

⊙

VASILIEV had a suite of rooms at the Rialto Hotel. They were a mixture of gilt, gloss, and pillowed furniture that one could sink into. The only thing Leah liked in the room—though they were only copies—were sketches by the eighteenth-century English artist George Chinnery who fell in love with Macau street life. What would Chinnery make of today's crowded, hungry streets? He'd become a modern day Hogarth, she supposed.

Vasiliev was bemused. "You think this war would be won if I lived in a hovel?"

She shrugged. In the past few months, Vasiliev had grown a moustache, perhaps in a bid to be taken for a Portuguese, but he still looked Russian with his large head and peasant hands. He wasn't quite Vasiliev and he would never be Harris.

He played with the tips of his moustache, turning up the ends—he waxed the ends—and ogled the custard tarts set on a silver platter. "I'm thumbing my nose at war," he declared.

"It's what keeps the black market running."

"Don't be so high and mighty. Sit, eat my fine tarts, and drink my good tea. You don't fool me. You are used to the best. We eat; we do business."

She told him about the five thousand pounds.

Bits of tart clung to Vasiliev's moustache, his face alight with greed and congratulations. "Give it to me. I knew they would need me. They will give me even more when I return. Five thousand will not last long. With more money, all China will be in flames. The Japanese will be forced to clear out. Chang Kaishek will praise me. I'll go down in history books." He stared at her with immense satisfaction. "Take a hundred pounds. A present from me to you."

"No!" she said, furious that he considered her a low-rent thief.

"You want more? Okay, you helped. Take two hundred. But, you can get more anytime. I've seen how the consul looks at you."

Vasiliev was a fungus, infecting everyone with his own warped view of the world. "I don't want or need a bribe."

He winked. "I understand. You're his mistress."

She stood up. "If you don't bring back concrete evidence of how this money helped, you won't get another penny." She opened a briefcase and handed him a huge wad of cash in *patacas,* Chinese yuan and English sterling. "Otherwise, I'll tell the consul everything. He'll believe me."

Vasiliev leered. "Will he?" He cleared a space on the table, crumbs of pastry cascading onto the floor as he counted the money with a wet thick finger. In the higher denominations, he used Russian numbers.

She turned away and opened the door. He didn't stop counting or say goodbye.

⌣

LEAH had given Tokai a key to her flat after he'd had a number of incidents—that's what he called them—while hanging around waiting for Leah to arrive home. Once, a well-dressed Chinese man spat at him. Another time a group of teenagers, hissing loudly in Cantonese, plagued him. He didn't understand the words, but he got the message, especially after they pulled out knives and practiced throwing them near the banyan tree.

When Leah turned the key in the lock, Tokai sprang off the bed, calling excitedly, "At last." She fell into his arms and together they toppled onto the bed, pulling at their clothes. He delighted in the whiteness of her skin and the ruff of pale blond hairs on her arms. Their bodies found a common language and neither cared what boundaries they crossed.

Later, unbearably hot and sweaty, scrunched against Tokai on the narrow bed listening to him breathe, she was swept by remorse. How could he stir up such feelings of lust and desire? How could she be in love with one man and spend hours making love to another? She stared at Tokai asleep and was once again stuck by his beauty: his thick black hair, his straight eyebrows, his cheekbones, his smooth buttery body. She needed a bath, to sit quietly and let all her misgivings float away.

The water was clear and hot—a good sign. Sometimes, it only trickled out, stopping at her ankles, brown and disgusting. She sank down into the welcoming water, resting her back against the cool tub, a washcloth over her face. She drifted. Distantly, she heard Tokai padding around. A book fell to the floor with a heavy thud. She didn't like him rummaging around, but was careful never to bring anything from the consulate home. She relaxed, ducking under the water to wet her hair.

The door burst open. Tokai flapped a manila postcard madly in front of her, heaving with injustice.

"Why?" he demanded.

"That's mine."

He held the postcard above her head, his eyes on her wet naked body. "I've read it."

On the front of the postcard was a printed address in red: Japanese Prisoner of War Camp, Hong Kong. On the reverse side were her twenty-five heart wrenching words—the Japanese mandatory limit for POW correspondence to allow censors to monitor the mail efficiently.

In a tight voice, Tokai read aloud: Am safe in Macau. My heart in HK. Red Cross packages sent. Other wants? His voice cracked as he said, "This is followed by a question mark, I think." He shoved the card under her nose.

She nodded.

His face contorted, he spat out her words: "Am still engaged. Hopes and dreams. I love you Leah." He paused, struggling to keep his voice cool and indifferent. "You forgot: 'Am fucking the Jap Tokai Ito.' No, won't fit. Too many words. Leave out the word Jap. He'll know. No. Still too long, twenty-eight words." He ripped the card to pieces, then rushed out, slamming the bathroom door behind him.

Bits of postcard floated towards her breasts. Tenderly, she fished them out, only the printed red line still visible on the fragments. In the cooling water, her head was full of Tokai's voice as he mocked her words. She forced herself to get up, dry her body and face Tokai: the enemy, the Jap, her lover.

Tokai was dressed. On the table was a Hong Kong newspaper in English. "They're still printing in English," he observed.

She shrugged, careful to keep a good grip on the towel. She felt at such a disadvantage. He knew so much about her. What was he getting at? Was he going to humiliate her further? Even now, she thought he might be quite prepared to parade her naked through the streets of Macau with a sign around her neck, SLUT. Only she knew that he wouldn't dare. It would mean his ruination too.

He pointed to the headline.

Slowly she took it in: WORKERS TAKE PRIDE and the photograph. It showed Tokai at the Hong Kong ship building yards looking proud and shaking a Chinese worker's hand. The caption read: Steel magnate Mr. Ito congratulates a worker for building a ship in record time.

"It's a good likeness. You must be pleased."

"I shouldn't have shown it to you."

"Are you angry that I still love Jonathan?"

"We are going to win. No one knows what will happen to prisoners."

Appalled that he was bullying her with Japanese power, she raged, "You want to talk war, look at this." She dug out *The Macau Tribune*. It's headline screamed in 24-point type: ADMIRAL ISOROKU YAMAMOTO KILLED BY US P-38 LIGHTNINGS OVER BOUGAINVILLE.

"That's a lie," he said. "Propaganda."

"No, listen to this." She read, "It is widely believed that the Japanese Government has not released news of the Admiral's death in Japan because he was that country's master naval strategist and national hero. It is likely the Japanese will delay making his death public for as long as possible."

"It's all lies," Tokai shot back, not believing a word. The Admiral was his hero. He had masterminded the naval aerial bombardment of Pearl Harbour. He knew him personally. Well, not personally. They had met at a Tokyo reception and Tokai liked the man instantly. They had something in common. Yamamoto was western-educated, a Harvard man. They had discussed the pleasures of Boston. Tokai had confessed his admiration for Yamamoto's military successes.

Yamamoto, smiling benignly, had responded in English. "For

now, Japan will have many victories. But if the war continues with the US and Great Britain, I have no expectation of success."

At first Tokai had not believed his ears and grinned stupidly like an idiot. He'd even forgotten to bow deeply when the great man was whisked away by one of his aides. In his heart, Ito wanted to see his people victorious. It was a natural instinct, to want to win.

Even here in neutral Macau, Tokai saw the war was not going to leave him alone. How could he compete with a man imprisoned by his people? Not for a minute did Tokai believe Leah was still in love with this Jonathan, but women were sentimental. They cried easily and wanted to believe they suffered from deep emotions. It was an act. They played at being devoted. That's how they had been brought up. In Japan, it was art form handed down from mother to daughter. He'd had enough. "I'm going."

"Are you coming back?"

"Do you want me to?"

"Yes," she said in whisper. "And so do you."

He didn't answer. He slipped on his shoes, picked up his briefcase and left without saying goodbye.

Leah sank down onto the chair, her towel sliding to the floor. Naked, she sat and stared at Ito's newspaper photograph. Now, what? Then it came to her. He still had his key. It wasn't over yet.

That night she slept fitfully in sheets smelling of Tokai. She dreamed of Jonathan, sunburned and wearing tattered shorts. He was talking to other British soldiers who stood in a tight-knit group. She was some distance away, jumping up and down to attract his attention. Angered by his lack of interest—he waved once—she ran to him and tugged on his thin, tanned arm. The scene changed. She was swimming at Repulse Bay. The water was warm and bluer than she had ever seen it.

Jonathan was asleep on the beach. She must have stepped on something sharp in the water because there was blood all around, although she felt no pain. She called to Jonathan; he continued to sleep. She woke crying, trying to convince herself the dream meant nothing, but she couldn't get back to sleep.

She switched on the light and set the fan in motion. From her purse, she retrieved a clean POW postcard. Her first impulse was to scrawl love twenty-four times and then sign her name. But Jonathan would be confused when he read it, feeling that this excess of emotion signalled she was grasping at their love like a life raft. She reconstructed her earlier message, written in a frenzy of passion and longing, counting words frantically and discarding them. She had no idea when she might receive an answer. POWs were only allowed to write two postcards a year. Albemarle had shown her the English military liaison's cable outlining the Japanese policy that at long last allowed correspondence. She had been overjoyed when she read the communiqué. Now, her twenty-five words rang false, leached dry of meaning.

13

WORK WAS A relief from her conscience, but Spencer plagued her. He was there in the corridor with papers under his arms after Leah met with Albemarle alone to discuss refugee pensions or who to invite to help construct a new form of colonial rule in Hong Kong once the allies were victorious.

If there was a pause in her conversation with Albemarle, she was certain she could hear Spencer skulking just outside the consul's closed door, his pale face florid with resentment. Leaving, he always raked his watery blue eyes over her clothes, searching for a wrongly buttoned blouse or smudged lipstick—any evidence of an affair.

She tried being friendly, but this made things worse. He'd sneer and say "Aren't we bright today" and then revel in telling her depressing war news, implying that somehow it was her fault the Germans had liberated Mussolini and were now firmly in control of Rome after killing 7,000 Italian soldiers.

In front of Albemarle, he took digs at her, "Isn't that right, Miss Kolbe? "Or, Miss Kolbe may have an alternate view?" Last week, he waited by the door and dropped the miserable news that Japan had advanced into middle China and might even challenge its national capital, Chunking. She retorted, "The Chinese will never surrender."

"Ha!" Spencer pounced, "I've heard that before. Their army is in tatters. The Americans are propping them up."

Sometimes, she thought he hated her. As a security precaution, he introduced a sign-in notebook for staff. The consul, of course, was exempt because, as Spencer cunningly acknowledged, the system was designed to protect him. No one should know his comings and goings. There had been another increase in anti-Japanese sentiment and the Japanese consul formally protested to Governor Teixeira. The Japanese paid people to rough up those who openly supported the allies. Albemarle headed the list.

She resented Spencer keeping tabs on her. Often she scribbled any old thing in the book. Spencer complained. "Just make it legible," soothed Albemarle. "Let Spencer have this one small victory. He is trying. He wants to feel needed." He shook his head in despair. "I know he's difficult. But he has a good heart." Leah said nothing. Spencer's heart was probably full of charts, graphs, numbers and black marks against people he disliked.

She was late this morning and was annoyed to find Spencer rifling through her desk drawers. "Found what you're looking for?"

"I've lost my scissors."

She pointed. Her scissors were sticking up in her pencil holder.

"Must have overlooked it," he said unblinking. "I keep mine in the middle drawer."

"Next time, look before you search."

"Oh, I will," he declared smugly.

Albemarle walked in. He said good morning to both, but

his face softened when he turned to Leah. Albemarle asked Spencer to leave. Abruptly, Spencer grabbed the scissors and gave them a nasty snick as he marched out.

"Never mind about him," Albemarle said, "I was rummaging through the post looking for letters from home and found this." In triumph, he handed her a postcard, grinned widely, squeezed her hand and left.

Jonathan. She recognised his handwriting. Her heart stopped. Across the top of the card printed in red ink were the words: Japanese Prison of War, Argyle Camp and a number of unintelligible Japanese official stamps. He had written in pencil. The writing had faded in spots on the cheap paper or, perhaps, the censor's grubby fingers had rubbed at the writing in an effort to understand the abbreviated sentences. He wrote: *Am well now. Huang fu great help. Have a vegetable garden. Received your package. Relieved you're safe. Think always of you. All my love Jonathan.*

Tears ran down her cheeks. She rested her head on the blotter, watching her tears stain the paper in ever increasing circles. Struggling to decode his message further, she traced her fingers over his handwriting. What did it mean: Am well now? Had he been sick? How sick? Maybe he'd been injured in the battle for Hong Kong. But then, he would have written: have been injured, or have healed now. He might have typhus, malaria, dysentery, beriberi. Christ, it could have been cholera. How wonderful that loyal and kind Huang fu was helping. But mostly, she cried because he had survived without her help or love.

There was a discreet tap at her door. Albemarle poked his head around, his eyes on the floor. "Go home, Leah. We can run this place for one day without you. I'm happy for you."

She motioned him to come in and he kissed her teary cheek.

Spencer passed by and stared. Albemarle collected himself first. "Leah's had the most wonderful news. Her fiancé is alive and well."

"Great news," Spencer said without enthusiasm.

"Go home," said Albemarle. "Savour this moment. That's an order."

Under the eyes of both men, Leah collected her purse and hat. Spencer stood aside as she passed through the door. She had an uneasy sensation his eyes were drilling a hole in her back. To hell with him.

With an overwhelming sense of relief and joy, Leah opened the door to her flat and stopped, open-mouthed. Lying on top of the white coverlet was Ito, dressed in a cotton kimono. On the floor was flat box elaborately wrapped in hand-made paper.

"I wasn't expecting you for another six weeks. How wonderful to see you."

"Here I am. You're back early," he said mildly.

"Too hot. The fans stopped." She put down her handbag and bustled around as if to tidy, getting out a cloth, removing the breakfast things cluttering the table. "I'll go back later, when it's cooler. Not much wine is getting through anyway. Business is slow. Why does Macau always feel hotter than Hong Kong?" On and on she rambled, unable to stop. "You look cool. Had a bath? The water was all right?"

"I've brought you a present." He patted the bed. She sat next to him as he plonked the box into her lap. "Open it," he commanded.

Flustered, she tore at the string.

"Hey, take care."

Slowly, she undid the last few knots and smoothed out the

paper. Inside was the softest, palest rose silk kimono. On the front and back were painted life-like white lavender and orange flowers. They hung off branches so artfully painted they appeared to be blown by a summer breeze. Near the hem, larger flowers bloomed. It was an exquisite apology for his leaving in a jealous huff two months ago.

"It's *yuzen* dyeing," he explained. "It's rare and beautiful. It reminded me of you."

She leaned over to kiss him, but he jerked away.

"You'll crease the silk."

His face was closed. Straight away, she was on guard. She watched his eyes as they moved over her, searching . . . For what? She played for time. "What's *yuzen* dyeing?"

"A technique invented in seventeenth-century Kyoto. We must go there after the war."

"After the war," she echoed. Was he going to take her there as part of the spoils of war? Was he such a fanatic that he could see only victory? She stroked the silk, marvelling at its work-manship. "How is it done?" she persevered.

He began to lecture, sitting on the bed, his eyes focused on the kimono. "The artist prepares a mixture of rice paste and soy-bean. He uses this to draw free hand on the white silk. After the paste dries, he paints the areas on both sides of the line with brushes using the colours he wants. The rice paste prevents the dye from seeping into surrounding areas. See how subtle the colour gradations are?" He touched the silk, pointing out the different rose hues. His voice hardened. "I knew you would appreciate it. You like subtle things. Put it on."

She stood and stripped off. She felt his eyes boring in as she slipped on the kimono. "Well?" she teased, sashaying about.

"Stand by the window," he barked. "There is more light."

She did as she was told.

He circled around her, surveying the kimono's drape. "You're too tall."

"I love it. Length doesn't matter. It feels delicious."

He slapped her face hard.

She tore off the kimono. "Get out. Take it with you."

"You work for the British consul. All that shit about your Portuguese businessmen. What were their names? Oh, I know, Ricardo, Balboa, Braga. Did you get them off office signs? You've ruined me. Kennosuke knows. If the head of the Kempeitai in Hong Kong knows, then Sawa knows. You're dead," he said with satisfaction, glaring at her tits, as if they should be answering for her.

"Go to hell."

"We'll go there together."

"I'm a bloody glorified clerk. What can it matter?"

"It matters. You have to do what he wants, or we'll both be dead."

Was the kimono a shroud? Part of a bizarre Japanese funeral rite?

"You passed on information," he said, his eyes narrowing, his face rigid with suppressed anger.

"We spent our time in bed. We don't discuss the war here. Remember?" She threw the kimono at him.

And that was what gnawed at Tokai as he picked up the abandoned gift, stroking it absently. He could never recall anything that passed between them, except their bodies together, the smell of her, the rush of his own desire and the sweet sense of holiday time, that what passed between them was no one's business. Looking at her naked, his hunger for her was overwhelming. He grabbed her waist, enjoying the touch of her and how his fingers marked her flesh as he pulled her into an embrace. "Did you tell anyone?" he hissed into her ear.

She wrestled against his grip, saying, "Do you think I would tell anyone I had a Jap lover?"

For a moment, he hated her. He should kill her, get rid of this demon lover. Then, he remembered Kennosuke cold blood-edly, reading from notes, describing in graphic detail his rela-tions with Leah. His hunger turned to ash. "You've got to help me," he begged.

"No."

"The Allies have mined the waters just outside Hong Kong harbour. Very little food is getting in. What does, goes to us, then the Chinese, and finally prisoners. They'll starve," he said full of spite.

She got into bed, drawing the sheet up to her chin, wish-ing he would evaporate into thin air. "It's not my fault. You started the bloody war."

"Well, now you are going to help us. We are running out of ships. There is one good gunboat in Macau. We want it."

"The Macanese are not going to declare war on you."

"Don't be stupid. We are going to steal it."

"You're crazy. I can't steal a boat, can you?"

"Shut up and listen. We want you to hold a party at the consulate. Invite everyone from the governor to Police Chief Luis De Rey and all the high ranking military men including those in charge of the African unit."

"The Mozambiques? Is this a joke?"

"They fight well. Kennosuke is convinced the gunboat is helping the Chinese. It smuggles guns and other arms to China.

"I don't believe it. Beside the consul is not in a party mood. There is a war on."

"Guy Fawkes Day, November 5, suits us." A ghost of a self-satisfied smile played around his hard-set face.

"I can't."

He ripped the sheet off her. "Kennosuke doesn't know about your fiancé," he threatened. She struggled to get away as his hands grabbed her breasts. She gasped with pain. He let go. "You'll be denounced as a Japanese spy. It will be a living death for you. If your fiancé survives, I don't think he will understand why you were a whore. I certainly don't."

She sprang out of bed, intending to crush his head in with the chair. But he was fast and caught her upraised hand, unwound her fingers from the chair leg and set it down.

She raged, "You don't really believe you will win this war?"

"I'm only human," he glared.

"Get out," she said and snatched up the kimono.

"Don't hurt the silk," he said. "Give it to me."

He caught it before it hit the floor, smoothed the silk out, then folded it into a neat package. Calmly, he said, "You'll do it." He stared at her, naked and panting. "Though I will miss fucking you." He let go of the kimono, which billowed into a cloud of silk, then dug in his pocket for the key, dropping it on the ground at her feet with a hollow ring.

He dressed in a rush, then slammed the door making the whole flat tremble.

She stared at the key for a long time. Then she picked it up and vowed to get even.

14

LEAH BURBLED ON eagerly about her idea for a Guy Fawkes party. Albemarle thought it a brilliant idea, a morale booster, and inviting all the military brass and the police chief, a subtle slap in the face to the Japanese who had started another graffiti campaign blaming the West for the war. She smiled and nodded until she thought her face might crack and reveal the party's traitorous core. She arranged a meeting with Chang, using the bird, hoping he would agree to a counterattack. They were to meet near the fountain in Francisco Park, near the Military Club, a busy part of the city. Who would notice if she followed him up the footpath?

On the way, she ran into De Rey outside the Military Club. "On such a beautiful day, it would be an honour to dine with a beautiful woman," he said, gallant and a bit sheepish. Unable to produce any leads about Moy's death, he had stopped coming to the consulate late last year. He repeated his invitation, but she begged off.

"Just as well. The food is very limited since the blockade. I do miss the banquets we used to have. Twenty-five different dishes. When this war is over, you must promise to be my first guest."

She dropped a small curtsey. "It would be an honour."

A baby wailed. They turned to look across Rua de Santa Clara at a crying infant tied to the back of a young woman dressed in charity hessian. The woman stood in front of the Chinese Reading Room with its double stone staircase and little round tower capped with a pagoda roof—a melange of Portuguese and Chinese architecture—and held a sign written in Portuguese and Chinese. It read: 'Need money to bury my father. Baby girl to a good home. Very quiet and good.' To escape the sad sight, people crossed to the other side of the road.

De Rey sighed heavily. "Before the war, Miss Kolbe, you never saw this. Macau was a happy place. We will all be beggars before too long. The government is running out of money."

A group of four Japanese naval men came into view. "I must go. I don't want to talk to them today." He touched her shoulder lightly, gave a wan smile and left.

Deep in conversation, laughing and smiling, the Japanese officers walked right past the woman hawking the baby. The woman picked up her sign and hurried off, the hungry baby still crying.

Leah looked guiltily away, towards Francisco Park. There was Chang, sitting on the edge of the candy pink fountain, near one of its pink and white-striped colonnades. He ashed his cigarette and walked up the hill above the fountain, moving at a good pace. She found him sitting on a secluded stone bench and sat.

"Tell me," he demanded, lighting his clove cigarette.

Her mouth was dry as she confessed. "He knows. Kennosuke told him. Sawa knows too."

He thought about this for a while, blowing smoke rings, watching them float away. "You're still alive," he said mildly.

Three little girls ran past in bright dresses playing a game of paper, scissors, rock. Every few feet, the children would stop, calling out their choices and showing their hands. The one who won the round then raced ahead and the game began again.

"The Japanese are going to capture the Portuguese gunboat," she said. She kept her eyes on the frolicking girls as she told him about the party and the gunboat. "The Japs are convinced the gunboat has been used to smuggle guns and weapons." She turned to face him. "Has it?"

The little girls squealed with delight. The smallest girl won for a second time.

"If we save this boat, your life won't be worth much," he said, stepping on his cigarette butt.

She knew this. Already Teixeira, pushed to the limit by the Japanese, had caved in and allowed Sawa's men to search anyone's house in Macau. People disappeared. There were rumours circulating about torture, dead patriotic high school students, money stolen. Monstrous. She didn't stand a chance. She hung her head. "I didn't have a choice."

Chang pulled out a handkerchief. He lifted the tip to reveal a derringer. "Keep it with you always. I'll make arrangements about the boat." He left without acknowledging the gift or saying goodbye.

The derringer was heavy in her lap. An old woman creeping along on bent legs toiled up the path. She stopped in the shade to remove her cloth slippers. Raising her arms, she began her measured exercises, her leg raised, holding her balance, her face calm and at ease. Leah continued to watch the old woman as the sun moved across the sky and her shadow lengthened. Enough. She couldn't sit here forever. She opened her clutch purse, made a space between her lipstick and compact, and dropped the gun in. The clasp closed with a hard snap. The woman glanced up with a toothy grin. Leah gave a small, brave wave.

∽

THE party grew louder, noisy and fun. The servants had rigged a stone fireplace. The bonfire was tiny—it was much too hot to indulge in a raging fire. It was like a child's, but people didn't mind, they pushed closer to watch the flames crackle even as they fanned themselves. Together, Albemarle and Leah tugged at the small grass-filled Guy with its bamboo hat and threw the effigy on the fire. Sparks shot into the air; people clapped, ohed and ahhed. A group of young men threw firecrackers, women screamed in fake alarm. Even Spencer joined in, throwing crackers, his face red from the heat of the flames. Above the racket, high in the night sky came a loud boom and the crack of distant artillery from the port. The Portuguese military officers and De Rey exchanged confused looks, then raced into the street calling for their cars. Other partygoers rushed out from the garden and stood helpless, panicked and worried, wondering if the Japanese had made good on their threats to take Macau.

"I should be there," said Albemarle. "I must see this first hand." Spencer rounded up the chauffeur and the car. Leah hopped in beside Albemarle. Albemarle shook his head, and ordered Leah out of the car, when Spencer pushed in to sit on the jump seat and urged the chauffeur to go fast.

When they arrived at the waterfront, the shooting had stopped, but it was chaos. A battered truck containing a troop of Mozambique soldiers screeched to a stop. The men jumped out in full battledress. A group of onlookers shouted out "Japs" and pointed to the water. The troops ran around trying to find Japanese hiding in the empty buildings. They found nothing.

Navy men commandeered small junks and sailed out, training flashlights on the water trying to find the culprits. They too could find no trace. De Rey's men shouted angry questions at a cluster of thin Chinese men, many with scars and tattoos, outside a rundown warehouse. The men scowled and declared they knew nothing, a cache of guns at their feet.

Two Portuguese navy men aboard the ship struggled to provide a coherent story as a medic examined their cuts and bruises. They had been fast asleep. Men in hoods forced their way in, shooting, and tied them up. It was pitch black and they were captive down below. Mostly it was all noises: running footsteps, shouting and shots. Other men clambered aboard. They seem to be battling with the first group. There were more shots fired. They thought this second, larger group—maybe twenty men, perhaps forty—had chased the first group away or thrown some of them into the water. There was a great deal of yelling in Chinese, maybe Japanese. The sailors didn't know; they hadn't understood a word.

Later, Governor Teixeira conferred with Albemarle, as Leah and Spencer stood a little away. Leah heard Teixeira say, "The Japanese have been pushing me hard to stop using the gunboat. I should have known they wouldn't stop there."

"They'll stop now. They've been so inept," said Albemarle, hoping this might be true.

Glumly, Teixeira shook his head. "They're so tendentious. They won't give up. My army and navy amount to less than four hundred men. And we have only *one* gunboat. What can we do against the Japanese?"

"What are you going to do?"

Teixeira lowered his voice. "They've offered to buy the boat. Gold. Think of the rice it can buy."

Shocked, Spencer turned to Leah and whispered, "Judas."

Leah hissed, "Half the population of Macau is starving," yanking Spencer away by the arm. "You're eating all right. What about the queues of hungry people who wait patiently for their charity rice porridge? Gold will keep people alive."

"It wouldn't happen in Britain," sniffed Spencer.

Albemarle came over. "We should go. It's in the hands of the Portuguese now."

Leah and Albemarle sat on the wide backseat, swaying with tiredness; a morose Spencer on the jump seat. The chauffeur drove the Vauxhall slowly through the narrow backstreets as night was ending. The car swung onto Rua da Ribeira do Patane then turned onto Rua de Julio de Ataujo to idle as groups of workers in singlets and shorts trudged past.

Two men on bicycles came pedalling fast. At first Leah thought one might tumble onto the hood of the car, but he stopped with a screech. There was a glint of silver. The cyclist took a bead on the chauffeur, who squealed, throwing his hands into the air and taking his foot off the brake. The car leapt forward as the other cyclist came up to Leah's window. Spencer dived to the floor. In a sweeping gesture, Albemarle knocked Leah to the floor on top of Spencer who kicked out at her. The man fired.

Leah jerked her head up to snatch her purse and saw the driver slumped over the wheel. The cyclists kept shooting; bullets slammed into the passenger side of the car. Dropping back down, she struggled to open her handbag as the car careened wildly. The Vauxhall struck the curb, bouncing Leah out from under the cover of the consul's protective body. She let out a high piercing scream of pain and distantly realised it was her voice. The gunmen pedalled furiously, ducking into a narrow *travessa* to disappear in the grey dawn as the car crashed into a low stone wall with a bang.

Dazed, Albemarle called, "Oh my God, no," as he raised himself and tried to lift Leah off Spencer, who lay rigid with fear. "Come on, man," said Albemarle, "we have to get help."

His words roused Spencer and the two struggled to position Leah on the backseat as she moaned and appeared grey as the dawn. Albemarle ripped off his jacket and tucked it gently around her, then touched her sweat-soaked forehead and felt her cold skin. Already, his jacket was darkening with her blood. He leaned forward searching for a pulse on the chauffeur's neck. Nothing. Dead. Spencer stood in the road, shaking. The consul grabbed Spencer by his shoulders. "Get help," he implored.

Spencer groaned and was sick on the road.

"You've got to get an ambulance, Spencer. I can't leave Leah."

"They might come back."

"Get going man," urged the furious consul. "I don't want her to die."

The words seemed to penetrate and Spencer took off in a loping run. As he felt his own blood surge, he increased his stride until his long legs were going like pistons and his leather shoes hardly touched the bitumen.

Albemarle bent down by the open door to the backseat and murmured unceasingly, "It's going to be alright," as he clutched Leah's hand and she whimpered. Time moved very slowly. He began to doubt the wisdom of sending Spencer. The man might have collapsed from shock along the way. He looked at Leah's ashen face. He would never forgive himself. Faintly, unsure if he was fantasizing, he heard an ambulance siren. It got louder. He breathed into Leah's ear, "It's okay now, they're coming."

She muttered something. He thought she was saying sorry. He wanted to cry.

The ambulance driver slowed and steered past the increasing crowd of early morning gawkers. The Portuguese medic with his emergency bag rushed out the back of the ambulance. Albemarle retreated to hover near by.

Jumping down from the ambulance cab, Spencer barked to the gawkers to get back and shooed them off. The medic knelt and exposed Leah's bloodied chest. He started probing. Leah emitted a strange high whine of pain, her eyelids fluttering. The medic signalled the ambulance driver to get the stretcher.

"Will she live?" demanded Albemarle.

"She's lost a great deal of blood."

Awash with guilt, Albemarle climbed into the back of the ambulance with the medic who placed a blood pressure cuff on Leah's arm and looked gave. Albemarle crouched down by Leah's head and tried to keep out of the way. The siren's blare shocked him to the core. It seemed to be saying, Your fault.

Spencer stayed with the car and the dead chauffeur. The crowd milled around, then wandered off. He hoped De Rey would arrive soon. Desperately, he wanted to change his ruined evening clothes. He must look such a fool. Already he could see the sardonic eyes of the police chief, bemused at his distress. What would he tell him? It had happened so quickly. He had been deathly afraid. He was certain he was going to die in this hot little street in dirty Macau. And for what? He wouldn't even be a footnote to history. Even now, he could remember the sensation of his own blood draining away and how he crumpled to the floor, then his mad dash to get an ambulance. He kept imagining killers with slanted eyes chasing him on bikes and shooting, eager to claim the assassination of the British consul's right-hand man. And when he returned with the ambulance, the consul hadn't even thanked him, too concerned over one wounded girl, whom Spencer was certain was exaggerating. Women were like that. Weak. He knew her type—adventuress. The consul was gullible when it came to women, look at his wife. Mildred ran rings around the consul and he, poor man, tried so hard to please her: importing tins of potted meat, shrimp and marmite, and standing bravely by as Mildred insisted on inspecting the hands of the servants to ensure they were clean. Often, she spent the hot afternoons snoozing under her fan in the bedroom, a cool G&T not far away. She was unsettled by too much talk about business. It wasn't *nice*. She had used the children as an excuse to escape Macau. Of course, he'd been extremely cautious around her and treated her with the utmost respect. Sometimes, subtly, he'd even aligned himself with her against the consul in small matters like the traditions of a Protestant Christmas party even when everyone else was Catholic and had the *Consoda,* the feast where extra places are set for the souls of the dead. A morbid custom, like the Chinese and their bizarre ancestor worship. He did enjoy playing palace politics with Mildred as an ally. It had provided him with amusement when things were slow. Still, he was relieved when she had gone. Now, unhappily, life was all go and bullets and he felt sick.

He peered into the bloody car and spotted Leah's open handbag, its contents spilling out. Even as the bullets whizzed, she had struggled with it. Why? He retrieved it—the bag would only be stolen—and lying underneath it was a gun, a very small gun. What he supposed was a derringer. He had seen them at the pictures, carried by desperate women. Why did Leah have a gun? To protect herself against rampant crime?

He stared at the bullet holes. It was a miracle Albemarle hadn't been hit. The killers were aiming for the consul. Spencer was certain of that because he had opened his eyes for a second and seen their murderous intent. He touched one of the bullet holes that pierced the car door. They had aimed low, maybe that was because they were on bicycles, but they had come up on Leah's side. Why? There was something odd about the glamorous Miss Kolbe. He had sensed it from the moment she appeared in that ridiculous nun's outfit. How had she managed to escape Hong Kong so easily, when all the other British civilians were rounded up? He pocketed the gun. He would make his own inquiries. The police were bloody useless. Over two years, and they still had no leads on poor Moy's murder.

Two hours later, when a very drained Luis De Rey arrived, Spencer was livid. "An attempt is made on the British consul's life and you take two hours to arrive. Macau is a lawless madhouse."

Sighing and placating, De Rey asserted he would do his best. Spencer glared.

LEAH woke, woozy from the anaesthetic, to see Albemarle, still in his evening clothes, slouched in a wooden chair, his hands resting on the white blanket, holding a newspaper.

He blinked awake, "Oh, Leah."

She smiled and shifted her weight in bed, wincing.

"You're going to be all right. The doctor said the bullet glanced off your collarbone. There's some muscle damage."

Her eyes widened in alarm.

"No. It will heal. The doctor says it will take time, but with proper rest, then exercise . . . it will be good." He reached across the bed to hug her.

A nursing sister poked her head into the room.

Albemarle jumped, jostling Leah, and she cried out. The nurse frowned, then clucked with hostility. She tapped her watch pinned to her habit. Guilty, he pleaded to stay.

The nun said in stumbling English, "You leave now. Lady needs sleep."

Albemarle squeezed Leah's good hand. "It's all my fault," but already Leah's eyes were closing and she didn't respond.

"I'll be back tomorrow," he promised as he reluctantly left under the nun's cold stare.

⌒

LEAH read the article:

GUNMEN ATTACK BRITISH
CONSUL'S VEHICLE

The British consul, Mr. Stephen Albemarle, reported gun-wielding robbers on bicycles attacked his car, killing his driver Mr. Chau Feng and wounding his female assistant.

"They stopped us at an intersection and demanded money," said the consul, aged 51. "When we refused, they started shooting. It was terrible."

"It all happened so quickly," said the consul's brave assistant, who requested her privacy be respected and her name suppressed. "I supposed hunger drove them to it. What other explanation could there be?"

The Bureau of Economic Development concedes that there has been a 300-fold increase in the cost of a catty of rice. Police are asking anyone with information to come forward.

Then she searched again for news of the battle for the Portugese gunship. Nothing. Not a word. The governor must have clamped down hard on the press and, probably, the Japanese exerted more pressure. As for asking for information about would be assassins, no one would come forward. It would mean death.

The dragon-nursing sister bustled in. Grim-faced, she tugged at the *Macau Tribune*. "No read. Sleep," she commanded, shaking out tablets. Meekly, Leah put the paper aside and swallowed the pills.

In her dream, Theo was alive, though his skin was the colour of sludge. She was a little girl, peeking in from the doorway as he tossed and turned in a mound of bedclothes. The more she stared, the more it seemed as if he were having a fight with the sheets and couldn't escape their clutches. She knew she ought to do something, scream or run in and remove the coverings, but she was rooted to the spot, unable to move.

She awoke in a panic and the word that ricocheted in her head was Run. She half-draped, half-pulled the hospital dressing gown around her. A slice of pain ran up her shoulder. The dragon wheeled in the dinner trolley and let out a rush of Portuguese, her big nose becoming red with anger. Defeated, Leah sank back against the pillows and obediently ate her fish soup.

She had no idea where she could hide. Her flat was too vulnerable; anyone who wanted could break in. She could hire a bodyguard but he might be susceptible to bribery. In any case, he would eventually discover Tokai. Then what? Why, he would tell others how she had a Japanese lover unless she paid him a lot of money. Then, he would ask for more money. Had she talked about Tokai under the anaesthetic? Now, she was being paranoid. The doctors and nurses didn't speak much English.

Could Chang help her? Somehow, she doubted he would lift a finger to save her. It might put his organisation in jeopardy. Her shoulder throbbed. The odds were against her. Many people preferred her dead.

Albemarle entered with an enormous bouquet of peonies and the flat-footed dragon followed behind. The nun sniffed at the flowers as if they were unclean. Albemarle requested a vase as the flowers dripped water onto the polished floor. The nun harrumphed and hurried off.

"I'm getting you out of here," declared Albemarle. "You must stay at the consulate. It's safer. I'm sure the Japs are behind this. I've hired bodyguards."

Tears welled in Leah's eyes. "Thank you."

The nurse returned and plonked the vase down on the side table, expecting grateful thanks. Instead, Albemarle announced Leah was leaving.

"No *partida*," declared the dragon nurse, miming that Leah needed rest.

Albemarle gave the nurse a note. In Portuguese it said the doctor was releasing Leah into the consul's care and the governor had arranged for an ambulance to convey her there. The dragon stopped snorting and let out a rush of soothing Portuguese. Leah supposed she was saying that Miss Kolbe would be well very soon. Leah thanked the nurse. She was certain Miss Kolbe would feel a great deal better and protected at the consulate.

15

How PLEASED SHE was to wake in the children's bedroom. She admired the starkness of the room: its bare plastered walls, the wooden desk, the large globe and the windows covered by fluttering voile curtains. Nothing bad could happen here. Getting up, mindful of her painful shoulder, she opened the desk drawer with her good arm. Inside was a box of broken, half-melted crayons, their waxy smell instantly recalling hot days spent in dull classrooms. It was so different from her childhood room. There was no mystery here, no patterned wallpaper of misty Asian landscapes, no intricate Chinese boxes hiding secrets, no ancient bronze mirror to reflect one's changing face. No An-li, her amah, watching her every move as she navigated her stormy way through adolescence, growing up under Theo's tutelage in beauty and Chinese antiques.

Without warning, she ached to see Theo and feel his comforting presence. If he had lived, her life would be very different. It would be a domestic life, she supposed, although she had never craved a husband or spared a thought about children. In this alternate life, she would dabble in antiquities as she looked after a husband, and if she must, children, with of course, plenty of servants to lighten the burden. Or maybe, there wouldn't be any children she thought with a purr of satisfaction, just Jonathan and her, living together in a haze of rosy happiness. Yes, except now she and Theo would be imprisoned together at Stanley. And what kind of birthday would that be? She was twenty-five today. Theo always made such a fuss about birthdays, discovering the most ingenious presents—from a centuries old Chinese writing desk when she started school, to a whole collection of tin performing Chinese acrobats, to more grown up gifts like the ancient bronze mirror and fine jade. Jonathan was more conventional—French perfume and jewellery—but last year he had produced the most wonderful Nile green silk and she had it made into an evening gown. The gown was probably ripped to shreds now, or on the back of a Korean prostitute brought in to service the Japanese. No, she wouldn't think about birthdays and crept back into bed feeling low and incredibly old.

Albemarle knocked on the door and in a cheery voice asked if he could enter. He inquired how she'd slept, then roamed around the room, inspecting for dust, opening the curtains and staring out into the garden. The mess from Guy Fawkes Day had been tidied up, only a faint trace of blackened bricks showed signs of the fire. Uneasy, he turned back, unable to keep his gaze from her bare shoulders.

Leah pulled the sheet up to her neck.

"I thought it best for you to have this room," he apologised as he busied himself again, arranging a chair by bed.

"It's peaceful." She watched his eyes. They were far away. He was looking through her, perhaps seeing his daughter lying happy and content in her place. She waited, not wanting to hurry him.

"I worry when this war is over if Anne and Conrad will

regard me as an interloping stranger," he confessed. "I'll just be this man whom they must be kind to for form's sake."

He tried to make light of his feelings with a disparaging smile, but Leah saw the care and lost love in his eyes. She reached for his hand and squeezed it in sympathy.

He got up too quickly to pace around the small room. He came to rest and folded his arms, struggling to place the conversation on an impersonal footing. "The police haven't a clue. Too difficult. Too many political ramifications." He patted a bulge under his jacket. "See," he said, undoing his buttons to reveal a holster and the gun. "What a world we live in now." He ran a hand through his greying hair, a look of bafflement in his brown eyes. He blurted out, "Spencer is convinced it was you, not me, they wanted to kill. He's obsessed with it. Won't shut up about it. He thinks you were involved in that, that . . . port business."

"He knows about me?" she asked in a panic.

He sighed deeply. "No. He's got it completely the wrong way round. I just ignore him when he gets wound up. It's the way he is. Difficult. Always into plots and subterfuge. All in his own mind. He got into financial trouble—I won't tell you the details," he said, waving them away as if they were only annoying and not deeply disturbing. "It was easier to ship him to Macau and let him rot. He's bitter about that. If truth be known, he's bitter about most things. I'm afraid, my dear, he resents you. He knows nothing about your real duties, simply feels he's been passed over." Albemarle stopped, upset. Afraid that now was not the time to tell her. But he knew there wasn't a good time. He loitered by the window. "I have to tell you this," he admitted. "There is no polite way to say this. He thinks you're my mistress. Put here by the Japs or the Chinese—he's not sure which—to spy on me. He thinks you were involved in Moy's death too. He's mad, but I can't get rid of him."

"Oh," she said quietly, trying to take it all in.

"I've told him to stop. Macau is a small place. Rumours abound. I don't want your reputation tarnished. It's so unfair," he concluded, throwing up his hands in despair. "Anyway, I'm going to tell Whitehall and explain you're off the agent list. It's too damn dangerous. You could have been killed."

He perched on the chair by her bed. "I couldn't live with myself if . . . I feel so God damn responsible." He kissed her cheek. There were tears in his eyes. "I am so sorry, Leah."

The devotion in his face threatened to overwhelm her. "I'm fine, sir."

"Please call me Stephen. You're my guest here . . ." His words trailed off.

"I need to rest, Stephen."

"I'll see you at dinner, if you're up to it."

"If I'm up it," she echoed.

He closed the door quietly. "Rest."

Leah heard his footsteps fade. Evading Stephen's concern and guilt would be tricky. He was a man at loose ends. She didn't want to be the one to pick up the pieces, only rest and lie low. If she took a long time to get well, she could avoid many complications. She slept.

STEPHEN was a gracious host, bringing her leather-bound books he must have had since childhood: Robert Lewis Stevenson's *Treasure Island*, Charles Dickens' *Oliver Twist* and *The*

Arabian Nights. She sympathised with Scheherazade and enjoyed her stratagems. The consul shifted his large radio cabinet into her room so she could listen to music and radio talks in English by the Macau Radio Club. That's what he called it now, her room—no longer the children's.

He was preternaturally kind, anticipating her wants before she knew them herself. They ate as much seafood as the cook could scrounge from the market or local fishermen. Other days, they made do with a bowl of rice, occasionally topped with shrimp paste. It was dry and inedible, but they ate it with gusto, washing it down with good Portuguese wine. Stephen insisted the best china be used.

After a few weeks together, they had worked out their relationship: a jokey familiarity that allowed the consul opportunities to pay compliments and Leah to parry them and imply she was lovesick for Jonathan. At dinner, Stephen talked a great deal about his youth, as if he yearned to be a contemporary of hers; or perhaps she was reaching and he was missing his wife and was simply sad and nostalgic. He described the time he had Mildred down to Oxford and how once after a dance, they had walked all one summer's night through the town's quiet streets. He made jokes and Mildred laughed. He could no longer remember the jokes. Perhaps they were no longer funny? He looked to Leah for reassurance. And she laughed and said she thought they must have been very funny to evoke such happy times. In her room, he found music on the radio and danced by himself, his arms around an imaginary Mildred, demonstrating his ability to whirl her around the floor. She clapped and he bowed, out of breath.

The Macau Radio talks were broadcast after dinner. If he

didn't have other engagements, Stephen sat in a chair as Leah, fully clothed, lounged on the bed. Together they listened to the familiar cadences of the announcer as he proceeded to give erudite lectures on British history.

It was a lovely time together. They both relaxed, drinking more wine, letting the English words wash over them as if they were in a warm classroom on a summer's day listening to the buzz of the teacher. For Stephen, his working days were becoming more stressful. The Japanese were tightening their stranglehold on Macau. Teixeira had granted the Japanese the right to raid schools looking for anti-Japanese elements. The consul knew the small English school would be first on the list, followed by the refugee schools, especially Sang Tak Secondary School, a pet project for wealthy Chinese.

The radio announcer was stuck on the boring genealogy of the various royal houses. Stephen poured himself more wine and mused aloud about his marriage. "At the start we both wanted the same things. But as the postings changed, it became harder for Mildred. It's a slow rise through the ranks. Or perhaps she just missed home. She doesn't miss me." He stared into his nearly empty wine glass.

Leah didn't respond. She was not an expert on husband-and-wife matters. On the radio, the speaker finished. They eyed each other, now the important part came. They leaned forward to hear the announcer read out greetings meant for friends and relatives in Hong Kong in the hope they would be passed to those interned at Stanley or in POW camps. "You should send your fiancé a message. It would mean so much."

Leah paled. "No. I might hurt him. The Japanese are convinced the greetings are coded messages." If Sawa found out about

Jonathan . . . No. Sawa would demand she tell him everything about the consulate, down to the last thank you note and expenditure. And Jonathan . . . She erased the thought.

Albemarle sighed. "Are we that transparent? Harris thought it a good idea. He started it. Paid for the radio time."

She gasped. Who and what was Vasiliev telling? "You've heard from him?"

Stephan looked uncomfortable. "I was going to tell you when you were a bit better. We are getting reports of more organised Chinese civilian resistance in Sheung. I put it in my report."

"Are you sure its Harris's doing?"

"He says it is."

"He's back?"

"He's managed to get a few messages through. Seems he's working with our friend Chang."

"I'm feeling very tired tonight."

Stephen sprang to his feet apologising. "I've tired you out. That's no way to treat a guest."

"You're a wonderful host," she declared as he hovered. She reached up to give him a friendly kiss goodnight.

Stephen hugged her with enthusiasm. "I'm so glad you're here," he managed; then, he fled.

Leah heard him walk quickly down the hall, then the loud slam of his bedroom door. Taking the consul as her lover would make her bullet proof. She could live at the consulate for as long as she wanted. God, how calculating she had become, but war was about survival. If she crossed this divide, she felt there would be no going back. She heard the consul in the bathroom turning on the taps. She pictured him in striped pyjamas, his feet in carpet slippers. He would have bony ankles. Would his skin be wrinkly?

Stop this. Soon, she would be indistinguishable from Vasiliev. Jonathan wouldn't know her. She turned out the light and held the pillow over her head to block out the consul's gargling.

$\backsim$

THREE weeks later, a servant knocked shyly on her door. He handed her Boris Harris's calling card. On the back, was scrawled: Urgent!

"Tell him to wait," said Leah. The poker-faced servant bowed and left.

Leah ran a brush though her hair with her good arm and smoothed down the skirt of her dress. She looked in the mirror and noticed the fright in her eyes. She closed her eyes, opened them and breathed in and out slowly. The panic on her face disappeared.

Vasiliev sat ensconced on one of the high-backed, intricately carved armchairs, part of a suite. The wooden arms were carved like wheels, held together by spokes to give them stability; the cushions were covered in green patterned silk. They were beautiful to look at and very uncomfortable. Vasiliev's eyes went straight to her sling. He didn't bother to rise. He had shaved off his moustache. It was a mistake. Instead of genial blandness, it drew attention to his large greedy mouth and his hooded eyes. Now, he looked like a cunning peasant.

"You shouldn't be here. The consul does not want to be seen . . . How did you get by the guard?"

"He knows me," said Vasiliev, rubbing his thumb on his finger miming a bribe.

"Why am I not surprised?"

"Is that anyway to treat a comrade in arms?"

She ignored this and sat on the edge of the couch. The cushioned backrest made slouching impossible and the seat was too low, her knees were in danger of touching her chin.

"Have you heard about my successes?" he asked.

"I've been away," she said dryly.

He clucked, "I heard. Nasty. You'll be glad to know my boys have inflicted real damage, blowing up ammunition dumps and off-duty Japs." He licked his lips.

She couldn't imagine Vasiliev as a guerrilla. He didn't like Spartan living and his step was as heavy as a rolling cannon. In all likelihood, he had set up camp in a village guesthouse and paid others to steal Japanese munitions and then sold the weapons to Chinese resistance groups at immense profits and claimed all the credit. Or he had done even less, simply pocketed the five thousand pounds. No, he would have given a bit to the Communists and the majority to the Kuomintang and sat back and enjoyed the mayhem. Then again, maybe he only backed the Communists Mao Tse-tung and Chou-en Lai in a deal he brokered with the Soviets. Anything was possible. Whatever he had done, he had made a profit.

"How about a drink or tea and cakes? Ask your servants, I deserve it."

"They aren't my servants."

He winked.

If she fed him, he'd leave sooner. She rang for a servant.

"That's better," he said as the servant left. "Such a clever girl, Leah. You've landed on your feet," he said, his eyes roaming the consul's reception room, nodding approval at the rich furnishings and paintings.

"What was so urgent?"

The servant returned with a tray, placing it on the coffee table between them. "I'll play mother," he said, looking at her sling.

Delicately, he picked up the Wedgwood teapot in his fat paws and poured. He sipped his tea, used the napkin to blot his mouth, then bit off a piece of cake. "Not bad."

"What do you want?"

"You think I'm a terrible man. A man with a large appetite who can't be trusted."

What could she say? He was a man accustomed to using people. He cared for no one but himself, was grasping and dangerous. She had seen him in action. There was nothing to like.

He shrugged. "I can't convince you. But ask the Chinese guerrillas. They'll tell another story. I must have more money. The Japanese are losing. Look how they've lost their toeholds in the Pacific. Now is the time to demoralise them in China. Honan Province is where they will strike next. They need its coal fields."

"It's also the birthplace of Chinese culture. What treasures are you buying cheap and selling high?"

"I'm putting my own neck at risk," he protested. He pointed to Leah's sling. "Mr. Chang told me why it happened."

Her heart thumped and now there was an awful ache in her shoulder.

"And you begrudge me a little business on the side. There is a word for people like you."

"Get out."

"Hypocrite." He gave a nasty laugh and sniggered, "What did you think I was going to say?"

"Leave, or I'll call the servants."

"Your consul know about your Jap lover and how you helped him?"

"I've already told him," she glared.

He stared. "You know, Leah, you are a very convincing liar. But I know the British. You wouldn't be here if Albemarle thought he was harbouring a Jap whore and spy." He paused to see the impact his words had made. She was white and was massaging her shoulder. "A 100,000 pounds would be the amount to put our operation into practice. The results are guaranteed."

"I won't."

For a large man trapped in a difficult chair, he sprang agilely to his feet to stand over her, breathing heavily. He placed a restraining hand on her bad shoulder. She attempted to wrench away. His quick fingers found the bullet scar and applied pressure. She bit her lip and gasped. He released his hold and looked into her grey eyes. "You know, just for a moment, I could see Theo in you. I know how he was killed."

"You weren't even in Hong Kong," she shot back.

"You know nothing. Convince Albemarle to get the money. I'll keep your secret and tell you one in exchange. I'll make my own way out. You look tired."

He left, whistling a tune. After awhile it came to her: *Don't Sit under the Apple Tree*. He was a real bastard.

16

"I CAN'T," SAID Albemarle in the privacy of Leah's room. "I don't have access to those kinds of funds. I'd have to stop all refugee allowances for months. I can't let our own people starve. Even in war, there are channels." He sighed. "I don't think Whitehall sees me as the lynchpin in the Chinese resistance movement. Harris will have to be patient."

"Would it help if I wrote a report to Whitehall?"

"Too dangerous. Even in code. One never knows . . ."

"Could we get the Macau Chinese community—"

"—Don't even consider it. Sawa has the right to enter the consulate now. He can't search our papers, but he could have me arrested."

"De Rey would never—"

"De Rey is a good man, but he's political animal. If ordered, he will have to comply. You and Spencer could issue diplomatic protests on my behalf, but it wouldn't help. More likely, they'd arrest Spencer too. I might end up sharing a cell with him."

"God forbid," she said.

"My thoughts exactly. Harris may just have to use his own connections and keep away from here. He knows the rules. I'll speak to him. He shouldn't have bothered you." Deliberately, he changed the topic of conversation. "You are looking pale. You need fresh air, a change of scene. I propose you accompany me to Senado Square this Sunday, sit in the sun, enjoy ourselves."

"I don't think I'm ready for a crowd."

"I've been planning," he said, beaming, like a boy savouring a treat. "We'll take a guard. Don't worry, he'll be discreet. And, I've invited De Rey. He is most willing to help. The man likes you," he teased. "And feels responsible. We should let him help."

"You really think its safe?"

"Nothing will happen. I promise."

IN the hot bright sun of Sunday morning, Albemarle, De Rey and Leah sat at a café table on Senado Square. The Chinese guard stood a little way off, making an effort to look inconspicuous, even as he swivelled his head, scanning the strollers, his fingers twitching against the holster of his gun bulging beneath his ill-fitting jacket. The churches had just emptied. Families were taking their usual promenade, smiling and talking amongst the elegant pastel buildings bordering the graceful wide colonial square. A portly middle-aged father watched with indulgent concern his teenage daughter flirt with a colleague's grownup son. The young man had blue-black hair, good teeth and long lashes. The girl blushed under the handsome boy's attention. De Rey exchanged a meaningful glance with Leah over the couple's coy advances.

"They're young," said Leah wistfully, finishing her tiny cup of coffee.

"Are you so old?" asked De Rey, smiling.

"Perhaps."

"Nonsense," said Albemarle.

A murmur went up as people turned to stare as the Japanese car that drove by with its Rising Sun pennant and a Tommy gun bolted to the roof. Perched behind the gun was a uniformed Kempeitai, glaring at the happy crowd. The car halted on the far side of Avenida de Almeida Ribeiro. Nagotchi, the Japanese consul, got out. He was a small, neat man in a well-pressed dark suit. He looked straight ahead and kept his face a blank. Another man got out.

"That's Sawa," said De Rey. "And it was a beautiful day."

Leah had never seen Sawa close up. He was taller than Nagotchi and held himself ramrod straight. He wore a dark green tropical uniform, with an open-collared white shirt beneath his jacket, but her eyes gravitated to his high black leather boots. Like the Gestapo, she thought. Pinned to his lapel was an Imperial chrysanthemum. He registered no emotion as pedestrians threw him covert looks and young women moved rapidly out of his line of sight.

As the two men walked to the square, the crowd parted. Albemarle turned his chair away. Leah saw Nagotchi blink at the deliberate snub.

De Rey whispered to Leah, "This must be Sawa's informal day. He isn't wearing his cavalry sword."

Without the uniform and the military bearing, he might be mistaken for another round-faced Japanese businessman, only his eyes were harder and always on the move. She felt a twinge of fear and the hairs on the back of her neck stood up.

A small Chinese boy chased a runaway ball. It landed at Sawa's boots. Sawa picked it up as the boy approached. Courteously, he made a show of returning it, then ruffled the child's hair. The boy's mother waited off to the side, not quite daring to snatch her son away until Sawa passed. The child howled his displeasure. The mother swatted the boy lightly on the bottom; the child screeched louder. Sawa kept walking through the thinning crowd, the obsequious Nagotchi at his elbow.

De Rey shook his head at the pair. "I've had trouble with cockroaches. My landlord suggested using a mixture of borax, cornstarch, plaster of Paris and cocoa. You really should try it. Kills them dead."

Albemarle nodded, looking into the middle distance. "Nasty things cockroaches. Very difficult to get rid of. I'll keep it in mind should any turn up. Nagotchi and I used to be friends. I never thought . . . He gave generously when the first round of refugees flooded in . . ." He looked at Nagotchi's retreating back. "Sawa put a stop to that," he said.

"Now, they enjoy torturing the local population," said De Rey softly to Leah.

"Surely not," protested Albemarle. "This is Portuguese soil."

Embarrassed, De Rey said helplessly, "They won't report it. Even when they're in hospital, they say nothing, or that it was a gambling debt. You can't blame people for being afraid." He looked at Leah for support, as if she too would understand the need for caution.

"You think I'm a coward, too," she protested.

Albemarle soothed. "Of course, not. You were shot. It's a natural reaction."

De Rey looked uncomfortable. "Miss Kolbe, Leah, we have no leads in your shooting. People say they know nothing. Whoever was behind the attack on the consul's car, now I think, doesn't want to stir up more trouble. They don't want Allied bombers or troops coming to Macau. They have their hands full with Hong Kong."

"You think the Japs will leave us alone?" asked Albemarle.

"It depends on the war. No one can say for sure. It is all gossip and rumour and I'm only a poor policeman," he apologised.

"It's time I returned home, to my own little flat," declared Leah.

"Unthinkable," burst out Albemarle, red in the face, oblivious to De Rey's naked interest.

"I have to go home sometime." There she had said it. She was sick of cowering behind the frothy pink walls of the consulate. If she didn't do it now, she knew that one night she would give into Stephen's vulnerability and her own loneliness despite his bony ankles, after they both had too much good Portuguese wine. The repercussions of that would be messy and, yes, sordid. "My mind's made up."

"Tell her it's too dangerous," urged Albemarle.

"It's true. What I said, it is all speculation. No one knows what might happen," said De Rey.

"People have been killed in broad daylight. Look at what happened on Rua de Felicidade," argued Leah.

"No one can control Chinese gangs," De Rey retorted. "We are spread too thin and there are too many people."

"Precisely my point," said Leah, patting the police chief's hand in reassurance. "Anything can happen. And no one's to blame. But I have to live my life.

"Another fortnight," pleaded Albemarle. "When you get a clean bill of health."

Leah caught De Rey's private smile. He thinks it's a lover's tiff. Unfair. Here she was, doing the right thing, returning chastely home, and instead she saw in his eyes that he too believed she was the consul's mistress. And what would Macau society think of her if it knew about Tokai? Why, they'd bell her like leper. "All right," conceded Leah in a level voice. "Two weeks."

⟲

ALBEMARLE paid for the installation of expensive iron bars on her windows, a wrought iron security door and a grille. Spencer clucked when he saw the items listed under miscellaneous security improvements and Leah's address. On his own initiative, he went there one afternoon, before Leah moved back, to gaze at the grillwork. The flat was sealed tight, the black wrought iron gleaming with new paint. He pulled on the bars and left his smudged prints behind.

When Leah returned, the flat had a terrible closed-up feel and the bird was dead. Ants had eaten it down to the carcass, poor thing. She cleaned up the mess and opened the windows, resenting the bars. She refused to be spooked by the bird's death, convinced it was a good omen: she was finished with Chang. She had heard nothing from him since the shooting. She was a liability, too compromised by her association with Tokai, and Chang didn't want to risk his own network. She spent a day cleaning and scrubbing away the stains of her former life and talking to the women on the Chinese screen who commiserated with her. Surprisingly, she found it easier to sleep in her own flat—no more listening to Stephen's nightly moves and considering the inevitability of allowing nature to take its course and share his bed.

Preoccupied with retaining their Pacific outposts and the large parts of China they had conquered, the number of Japanese officers on the streets dwindled. Those that were left swaggered less and kept to themselves. They continued to pay shopkeepers with their worthless and hated military script, but more did make an effort to pay. Everyone still hated them.

Leah's day became work that stretched into evenings. Hunkered down, still recovering, she refused all engagements except when Stephen urged her to attend public functions with him. Always he sent his car and new driver to pick her up and deliver her home. The driver went armed.

She heard nothing from Tokai and was relieved. She rationalised the attempt to kill her as a warning. If she kept away from Tokai, she would be safe. She was determined never to see him again. After all, he might be dead or have returned to the safety of Tokyo to manage his munitions plants. But late at night, when she woke to listen to the rain or a tropical storm, she missed him and hated herself for missing him.

Back at work, she put up with Spencer's cynical gaze and general nastiness. He insinuated that the consul had grown weary of her and kicked her out, and continually chipped away with barbs. He'd say, "'The consul wants to see you, you lucky girl'" and smirk; or, "'Brighten up, do this and you can meet with the consul over it.'" Always exceptionally gracious, she thanked Spencer for passing on Albemarle's requests and watched him seethe under his pale white skin as a red angry flush crept up his neck onto his cheeks. It was a vicious game: the sweeter Leah's reply, the more acerbic Spencer's dig.

Albemarle caught them at it as he walked down the hall. "The consul hates purple. Mildred wore a lot of purple. You should change before your meeting with him at two. It will make him very unhappy and we wouldn't want that, would we?" said Spencer.

"Spencer, how kind of you to notice. But I'm going to lunch with Stephen at the Military Club. And the dress is lavender and brings out the grey in my eyes . . . Brought your lunch?"

Curtly, Albemarle asked Leah and Spencer into his office.

Spencer stood and gloated, expecting Leah to be dressed down. Instead, Albemarle said to them both, "I expect better."

Now, Spencer went out of his way not to speak to her. He scribbled notes to pass on the consul's comments and sat tight-lipped when the three of them met or said, "If I may speak," then looked pointedly at Leah as if asking permission. It was absurd in a three-person office. She was convinced she had seen Spencer lurking near her flat. She hoped he was visiting friends. Did he have friends? He lived far away, on the other side of city, close to the sea. Another time she recognised the back of his bald head as he hurried away in the early morning. He was spying on her, but for what? Evidence that Albemarle slept in her bed? He would be very disappointed. She hoped he would give up soon. She considered telling Albemarle, but if she told, her relations with Spencer would become truly impossible. Thwarted again, he might spread very nasty rumours. It would hurt Albemarle, who didn't deserve it. She said nothing.

She was certain it wasn't Spencer who had rifled her flat. He didn't have the rat cunning. She checked the locks and bars. There seemed to be new scratches on several of the locks. Perhaps someone had made a copy of the key. Or maybe they had a skeleton key. As far as she could tell, nothing was taken, but she was dogged by a sense of unease. Again, it was something she let slide. She had lost a bit of resilience after being shot; she wasn't capable of dealing with anything too disagreeable. It was so much easier to ignore it, like Macau and its uneasy peace with Japan.

One night, Vasiliev came to her door unannounced. "Barricaded yourself in, I see," he said as he stared through the iron grille of the door.

"I am tired," she said. "Go home."

"Now, now," he tutted. "You don't want me yelling through the door about personal matters."

She let him in. She could smell the alcohol on his breath.

In the light, his large nose was red, but his speech was unaffected. "I've missed you, Leah."

"I've told you, the consul simply doesn't have access to the funds you want. Besides things are changing rapidly in China."

"It could save lives. And for the British to be seen helping the Chinese would help their case to rule Hong Kong."

"What do you know?" she demanded. "Who have you been talking to?" But she already knew, Chang.

"It's an open secret," he said, cagey. "For a girl with your advantages, Leah, you haven't used them well." He stared at her body.

She was wearing a loose cotton shift. "Go to hell."

"You shouldn't have moved out. Intimacy is so important in delicate matters. In England, Albemarle isn't a rich man, but here in Macau, he lives well and spends little. What is there to spend it on? Nothing much gets through because of the damn Japs."

"He has a wife and family in England. That's where his money goes."

Vasiliev shook his head. "All the more reason you should convince him to use his own funds. He'd want to protect his family from accusations his mistress is a Japanese agent."

"You wouldn't."

"It would stop his career, full stop. Wives are never that forgiving."

"It's blackmail and lies. You don't give a damn about the Chinese."

"Tell him, I need another ten thousand pounds. I've got the rest from other sources. He'll find a way."

"I won't do it. I've never been his mistress."

"I thought a nice letter enclosing a photograph would do the trick. The mail is a bit slow, but one can still send letters to England if you pay enough. The people above him are bound to find it interesting reading. I might telegraph the wife. Maybe I'd telegraph Whitehall too. Forget about the post. The wonders of modern communication. Not having the pictures would be a shame."

"You are despicable."

"I will give you a fortnight to change Albemarle's mind. If he does, I'll tell you how Theo died. Consider it an inducement."

"Get out."

"You know me," he said, getting up, "I always keep my promises."

He thinks he's won. "Leave," Leah said.

"See you soon," he said. "Make sure you lock the door. There are thieves everywhere." He pulled it closed with a heavy thud.

As soon as he left, Leah thought of all the things she should have said. This vile man was manipulating her, twisting her life to use it against her, promising things he would never deliver. She was livid; a slow burn in her gut worked its way up to her throat and she wanted to scream. If she had the derringer, she would have used it. It would have given her great satisfaction to see him lying on the floor dead. Well, he wouldn't get away with it.

⤴

SHE knocked on Albemarle's door. The servant let her in. He seated her on the uncomfortable green silk sofa and went to speak to Albemarle. Albemarle rushed downstairs in his dressing gown, combing a hand through his hair to tidy it. "Are you alright? What's happened?" he said and opened his arms to embrace her, his eyes wide with alarm.

She took his hand and kept hold of it as if he were the one who needed comfort. His hand was soft, and fine grey hairs sprouted from his knuckles. "Harris is trying to blackmail us."

Albemarle's eyebrows shot up. "The bastard," he sputtered.

"He wants ten thousand pounds. He's threatening to send letters to Whitehall and your wife. He's also threatening to reveal something about me." She hesitated. "It's private. I will tell you if you ask, but I would prefer not to." She could feel her emotions welling up inside, ready to explode. "Harris is not Harris. He's Russian. His real name is Vasiliev. We must stop this man."

"Do you have proof?"

She let go of his hand. "No."

"Do you believe he helped the Chinese Resistance?"

"There is no way of knowing. Whatever he was doing in China, he was also making a tidy profit for himself. I'm sure he's doing black market deals."

"He could be arrested. It's a criminal offence."

"I have no proof."

Albemarle got up and started poking around in the liquor cabinet. "Whisky. We need whisky." He poured two large shots. She slugged it down as he toyed with his, sunk in thought.

"I still have my gun," he mused. "I could say I caught him stealing it and tried to take it away from him. And it went off."

Leah gave a sad smile at the preposterous plan. "There would be a scandal and questions about why the British consul required a gun. Your career would be ruined. Or, Vasiliev might have a gun. He'd have no qualms about using it."

"I could retire."

"Spencer would be the next in line." They laughed with gallows humour and drank more whisky.

"De Rey is a good chap. He could arrest Harris on a trumped up charge. Black marketeering or some such. As his consul, I could ask that he be released into my custody. Portuguese justice takes a long time. He wouldn't dare blackmail us if the threat of a Portuguese jail hung over him. It is a filthy place. There are no custard tarts there."

"Do you think De Rey would do it?"

"The man feels he has a debt to me. Two unsolved crimes and then he relishes his man of the world image. It only has to look official."

"It must look very real. Vasiliev—Harris—has a lot of friends. They flock to his parties."

"No one in the public eye wants to be connected with a scoundrel, even in Macau."

"Please don't tell De Rey I asked you to do this."

"I won't use your name at all, except that I have to protect both our reputations," he said, struggling to disguise his embarrassment. "I'll tell De Rey that Harris threatened to blackmail me. You know nothing about it. There is so much black marketeering here that I'm sure De Rey and I together can cook up a good story. Harris, or what's his name, Vasiliev, will never know who exposed him. He'll blame one of the low lifes. You'll see."

"It could work," she said, mulling it over, trying to determine if there were any flaws. "Especially, if you were quick. He'd never attempt blackmail if you were able to wangle his release on black marketeering charges. He's tried jail. It didn't agree with him."

"It will work," said Albemarle. Already, he had the telephone in his hand dialling De Rey's home number. The two men talked for a while, then Albemarle put his hand over the receiver, whispering, "I'm going to meet with him tonight.

The chauffeur dropped Albemarle at De Rey's, then took Leah home.

The next morning, Spencer took an urgent phone call and the consul left with him and a flurry of papers to rescue the British passport holder Boris Harris from the clutches of Portugese colonial justice.

Spencer returned crowing. The consul was attending to the details of Harris's release. The Macau police had very flimsy evidence. Albemarle had been able to duck and weave through all the Portuguese red tape. The charges, Spencer sniffed with superiority, would in all probability be dismissed. Leah wished she had been there to see it. Spencer thought about this. It was no place for a woman. And for once, Leah was happy to concur.

Later in the afternoon, Albemarle stuck his head around Leah's office door beaming.

"Done?"

"Done," he said and closed the door. "I insisted that I go with De Rey and his men and Harris as they searched his suite. De Rey was magnificent. He kept playing with a pair of handcuffs and inspecting Harris's garish hotel suite, commenting how comfortable the bed was and how somehow Harris, or whatever is name is, had the best food in Macau. Harris said nothing, just looked at us with his lizard eyes. I don't know how I could have trusted that man. There is something distinctly unsavoury about him. The word blackmail never even made it into the conversation. Harris won't be bothering us anymore."

Leah let out a whoop of joy and hugged Albemarle. He

smelled of lavender and toothpaste. She pulled back, flustered. "Are you sure?"

"Afterward, I mentioned to Harris that it has come to my attention that his passport might be a forgery. Without a passport, he'd be stateless. Have to remain in Macau forever. That didn't go down well. You could see he was trying to decide if he should try to bribe me instead of blackmailing me." Albemarle laughed. "We won't be hearing from him again. If he stays quiet, he knows I'll let him retain his passport."

"You're going to allow that man to remain a British national?"

"For now," he said.

She smiled a conspirator's grin. "Lovely."

Spencer stood at the doorway, resentful and accusatory, "Am I missing something?"

All business, Albemarle said, "I was just telling Miss Kolbe that the official Allied policy on Hong Kong had changed. We will continue British rule in Hong Kong. I'm going to write an article about it for the *Macau Tribune* and invite all Hong Kong refugees—Chinese, British and Eurasian—to meet and plan a new type of government for the Colony. What do you think?"

"Well done for us," declared Spencer as if it were a football game. Then he cleared his throat and looking only at Albemarle, said, "Do you think that wise, to let anybody have a say?"

"It's a new world order," declared Albemarle who couldn't contain his high spirits.

Leah glimpsed the boy beneath the man: his eyes alight with hope, the lines on his face softened. What an idealistic young man he must have been, full of goodwill, believing the best of everyone. Macau must have changed him, left to languish in this diplomatic backwater dragged down by an unhappy, complaining wife. What if she had met him when he was young? She could imagine him young and as her lover, the two of them lying together in his mahogany bed upstairs underneath the slowly revolving ceiling fan, sharing gossip, making fun of diplomatic functions. Now he was talking to Spencer, outlining the article he was going to write. He had lost a bit of his enthusiasm and was speaking slowly, reverting to his stiff, formal self, a bit diffident and anxious about how to represent this resurgence of British power. The momentary desire passed and she simply said, "Peace. It will be wonderful." She was liberated. Chang no longer had a hold on her. Everything was going to be done in the open. She would be happy; peace was on the horizon.

17

THE WAR IN Europe was turning. The newspapers proclaimed it breathlessly all through June 1944. In Macau, the streets were crowded with pedestrians, a sea of humanity. Everyone walked. There was no longer any gasoline for buses. People cobbled together radio receiving equipment. And above the hubbub of the street could be heard the high-pitched whine of radio frequencies as apartment dwellers twisted knobs and fiddled with wires to reel in information about far away battles.

For Leah, life had become routine. There was work, there were charity events and there was scrounging for food. Like everyone else, she was eating little. Still, she was filled with optimism during the long sun-drenched days of simmering heat as she devoured the heartening news.

It was only at home that doubt set in. To avoid the let down of her empty flat and still no more postcards from Jonathan, she walked the streets of Macau. Often she strolled through Tap Sec Square, skirting Cemitério de São Miquell where the dead slept peacefully, to the São Lazrus district. This was China with its cobbled streets and shuttered Coast houses with turned up eaves and terra cotta tiles. Walking the familiar path, she pushed away thoughts of Tokai. She told herself she would be glad if he were dead. Even as she considered this, she hoped it wasn't true.

At night when she lay on her uncomfortable bed, a wet face-cloth over her eyes and the soft humming of the fan moving the heavy humid air over her, she regretted taking Jonathan for granted. He was a gift. He had worked so hard to make her happy. Discounting the days and nights they spent in bed making love, she had done far less: swanning around oblivious to his worries about his mother and sister in England, teasing him about his inability to reproduce the tones of Cantonese and lecturing him like a schoolboy on the finer points of Oriental art. He had improved her life with his love; in comparison, her love seemed smaller and inconsequential. Often, she got out of bed and wrote postcards to him about nothing very much to provide tangible proof of her love. Even as she posted them, she knew they had very little chance of getting through. It was what made them precious. She had made an effort.

There were errant bombings of Hong Kong, as if to reassure people to hang on. The Macanese turned on their lights to guide Allied bombers towards Hong Kong. The Japanese sent a stern warning to Governor Teixeira demanding street and shop lights be turned off. The lights were dimmed, but many disobeyed and whole streets became beacons when planes were heard overhead.

An Allied plane bombed the Macau airport by mistake, or on purpose. It was rumoured the Japanese stored petrol there. A few weeks later, bombers attacked the Inner Harbour ferry building searching for more Japanese gasoline to destroy. It caused an enormous fire and ten Portugese and two hundred residents were hurt. The Japanese language paper was full of outrage. Men in their employ massed and paraded shouting death slogans to the Allies. Stones were thrown at the British consulate, breaking two windows. Spencer was incensed. He wanted to station Portuguese troops outside the consulate. Albemarle calmed him saying, "Why give the Japanese the satisfaction of knowing we are upset," and quietly called in the glaziers.

Then all hell broke loose. An American plane crashed near Guia Hill. Sawa insisted De Rey send out a search party to find the missing airmen. They were war criminals, invading a neutral country. De Rey's men scoured the countryside. They found nothing.

A few days later Fire Cracker Kwong stood in front of Spencer's desk with a grave face and insisted with quiet dignity he had to see the consul now. Spencer stared into the clear appointment book and was evasive. Mr. Kwong then asked for Miss Kolbe, perhaps she could help. Affronted, Spencer sat Mr. Kwong in the reception room and made him wait. Mr. Kwong did not complain, merely flipped through the consul's five-year-old magazines. They always put him in a good mood. He loved the pictures of the royal family.

Closeted together with Leah and Albemarle, Kwong dangled two sets of American dog tags. "They're safe for now," he said. "But they are big men and one is blonde. Even with hair dye . . ." He frowned. "We need your help to get them out. We thought a boating party. A junk will meet them further out and get them to safety. And Miss Kolbe would make it look natural. She knows this group of young men well. No one will stop her."

"I'll go in Miss Kolbe's place," Albemarle volunteered. "I won't put her in danger. She was shot."

Mr. Kwong looked at Leah. "It will look suspicious. You are never with these young men, Consul. And I would not ask, if it were not . . ."

"I'll do it," declared Leah, brushing off Albemarle's misgivings.

"Use my car," urged Albemarle. "It will be safer than walking."

"Are you going to have your chauffeur push it?" asked Kwong.

"I can find enough petrol."

"You would draw attention to us," said Leah.

"We will have other people in the street. No harm will come to Miss Kolbe. It is well planned."

Late in the afternoon when the weather was warm and windy, a group of young Macanese men—Chinese and Portuguese—entered the consulate in high good spirits asking for Leah. "We're going to kidnap Miss Kolbe," they joked to Spencer.

For a moment there was a cloud of doubt on Spencer's face, then he realised they were teasing. "She's working."

"Doesn't matter," said Aubertin. "It's a perfect day for sailing," and marched down the hall to extract her from the growing mound of paperwork littering her desk.

Out on the street, Aubertin draped an arm around Leah's shoulders and hurried her along. As they walked amid the boisterous men, two solidly built European men in tight suits—one with dark hair and blond eyebrows—popped out from a narrow *traverssa* and merged into the group. One kissed Leah on the cheek and she smiled her welcome.

There were four lounging Mozambique army men guarding the charred dock. Aubertin invited them along for a sail. The soldiers joked, "Next time," and let them pass without glancing at their papers.

A fisherman rowed the party out in two groups. When everyone was on board, a strong offshore breeze filled the sails and they left the confines of the Inner Harbour without tacking. A Portuguese patrol puttered past. The yachting party waved and sailed on.

By nightfall, they reached the waiting junk. The American airmen thanked everyone in their creamy Southern drawl. On the way back, Aubertin and his friends did bad imitations of the Americans' accents, adding words they had heard only in movies like Stick 'em up, Bad guys and Soda pop. Leah laughed and laughed, clapping her hands and added other words like Baby and Sugar. At the dock, the Mozambiques, who were eating, called out their greetings. Aubertin said they should have come along. The stars were fantastic. The guards were too busy eating their fish to respond.

�

ONE late summer evening when the sun hung low and her windows were open to the breeze, there came a loud knock on her door. Leah looked through the grille and saw Chang's face staring back.

"Go away," she said.

He remained at the door and signalled to someone. Up popped Vasiliev's large head. He smirked.

"I'll tell De Rey," she threatened.

"It's important. We can help you," said Vasiliev.

Reluctantly, she opened the door. The two men sat on her bed. Chang wore an elegant summer suit, a Panama hat and carried a rolled up newspaper. He looked like a prosperous businessman. Vasiliev was hot and sweaty; his tie had a stain on it. De Rey must be making things very tough for him. Good. She refused to even offer tea. Her shoulder ached. It hadn't hurt for months.

She turned on Vasiliev. "I don't know how you dare show your face here."

"I needed money," he said. "It was for a good cause." He turned to Chang for help.

"It's true. We needed to buy weapons and medicines."

"Two patriots," she said.

"Theo would have been disappointed to see his beloved daughter had become such a cynic."

"Shut up. I don't care what you are offering, I'm not interested." She knew they'd been conspiring, cooking up something together. "You might as well go."

"Don't be nasty," said Vasiliev. "We've come to help you."

"And," interjected Chang smoothly, "to offer you something. Mr. Harris is a reformed man."

"We both know his name is Vasiliev."

"I prefer Harris. Everyone in Macau knows me as Harris."

"Go away, Vasiliev."

"That is no way to treat a friend of the family. I knew your mother, Vestna. We were children together in Odessa." He sighed. "A lovely childhood. You should listen to Mr. Chang's proposition."

Vasiliev was telling lies. She was sure of it. Well, almost sure. She could never tell with Vasiliev. He could be very believable, his big Russian face full of the woes of his past and his endless, depressing fatalism. But he was so ugly. Her long dead mother could never have known such a creature.

"The Japanese don't stand a chance once the Germans surrender," said Chang. "It's only a matter of time. But the Japanese are fanatics. Already they are boasting their people will fight to the death. If they do, it will be on the back of millions of starving Chinese. We get daily reports from Hong Kong of how the Japs are hoarding rice. The Chinese population eat hardly anything; European prisoners starve. Many will die before peace comes. Even with peace, nothing may get into Hong Kong for weeks. The harbour is mined."

She nodded. Albemarle had relayed similar reports. Every time she sat down for another inadequate meal, she thought how little Jonathan would be eating and how her Red Cross packages were so inadequate or would probably be confiscated. She forced herself to buy whatever was available at the Red Market or from stalls and asked no questions.

"What has this got to do with me?"

"May I?" asked Chang as he reached for cigarettes.

"I hate the smell."

"It's relaxing," said Chang with a tight smile and lit up.

The smell of cloves was strong. She noticed he didn't offer one to Vasiliev. Somehow, she didn't think they were on quite such good terms as they pretended. But certainly they were united against her and they wanted something.

"As soon as the Japanese surrender, I can have access to rice for Hong Kong. Don't look like that, Miss Kolbe, the Macanese aren't starving, those in Hong Kong are."

"You're a black marketeer, if that's what you mean."

"Of course not," Vasiliev smirked.

"A modest profit. It will be a gift from the Kuomintang. We must all play by new rules now. Later, Hong Kong will return to us. We are realists. Our time will come," said Chang.

"Why are you telling me this?"

"The British will be in charge again. They will require confirmations, bills of lading, certificates of all kinds. They are trying to stamp out war profiteering."

"Good luck," said Leah.

"Not luck, Miss Kolbe. Hungry people don't care about that. But we must have the requisite forms and approvals."

She watched the clove smoke spiral towards the ceiling. She would have to burn incense to get rid of the smell. "No." The room went very quiet. She heard Chang's sharp intake of breath; Vasiliev drilled into her with his eyes. And she knew any minute now, he'd begin making threats.

"You won't get back to Hong Kong for quite a while, nor will food. Commercial shippers won't run the risk and, perhaps it will take several months until the mines are cleared. People," Chang said ominously, "might be dead by then. Especially POWs. Often they die just as they are being liberated."

She wasn't surprised Chang knew about Jonathan. He had an army of spies and informants. Some must work in the post office, waging a silent war of information gathering against Japanese informants. And Chang knew exactly which strings to pull to make his victims cooperate.

"We want you to get us the forms, all correctly filled in, of course," said Vasiliev.

"I said no."

Vasiliev looked at Chang. Into the silence Vasiliev blurted, "I'll tell you how Theo died."

Chang glared at Vasiliev.

"What?" whined Vasiliev. "We agreed."

"Perhaps, Miss Kolbe no longer cares," said Chang smoothly, covering up Vasiliev's gaffe.

"No," declared Vasiliev, "Leah cares. They were very close." He looked at Leah for confirmation.

"It won't bring him back," said Leah. "I won't do your dirty work."

"Go on," Vasiliev encouraged Chang. "Ask her about Ito."

"I haven't seen Mr. Ito for quite some time," she said dully.

Chang spoke in a calm voice: "Mr. Harris, how would you feel if you found out your fiancée had been sleeping with a Jap munitions dealer while you rotted in a Jap POW camp?"

She felt her hands inching up to block out their terrible words, forcing herself not to react as they played out their vile game. She kept her hands pressed tight together. The tips of her fingers whitened from the pressure.

"The English word you are searching for is 'aggrieved'. One would feel aggrieved, Mr. Chang."

"Is that all?" asked Chang.

Vasiliev mouthed, "Whore."

Leah raised her hand to slap him, but Chang was quicker, like a snake, and hit her a stinging blow with his rolled up newspaper. She cried out. Chang ignored her cries and opened the newspaper. There on the front page was a young woman with terrified eyes. Her hair was shaved off and a swastika had been painted on her bald head. An angry man held her arms from behind, parading his handiwork. "I think this is in France."

Vasiliev squinted at the caption. "You're right. The French flag is behind them."

They were fiends. They enjoyed torture. "I know about all your dirty dealings, both of you. After the war, I could have you imprisoned for black marketeering, financially benefiting from the Japanese in Macau, money laundering."

The men shrugged in unison. Chang blew a wavy smoke ring. "People are tried after a war. Everyone knows we all do things that we wouldn't normally do in wartime. If it feeds people, what is a little harmless corruption? Or, using our charms to elicit information? It's the same thing."

"The same thing, exactly," echoed Vasiliev. "Join us, Leah. It is a wonderful opportunity."

Chang lit another cigarette and offered one this time to Vasiliev. The men smoked, studying her as if she were an exhibit under glass.

How she hated them and their grubby disgusting schemes. "I want my cut and I want to be on that boat," she declared.

"You don't want to do that," said Vasiliev. "If anything happens you could end up in jail."

"So could you," she retorted. "If I'm on the boat, it will be a guarantee that the rice is legitimate. There won't be any questions asked. I have a diplomatic passport."

Both men brightened. "Five per cent," offered Chang.

"Who do you think British naval officers will believe, you two or me? Twenty per cent."

"No," said Chang. "Five per cent, take it or leave it.

She stared them down. "Fifteen per cent. You need me."

With begging eyes, Vasiliev looked at Chang. "Very well, Miss Kolbe, we'll split the difference, ten per cent.

"Done," she said, her voice sounding thin and hollow in her ears.

The men got up to leave. Chang left the newspaper on the bed. Silently, Leah handed it back. Vasiliev gave a weak smirk. "We'll be in touch," said Chang. He opened the door and followed Vasiliev out, pulling the door closed with a thump.

Exhausted, she lay on the bed, breathing hard. The pillow reeked of Vasiliev's hair oil and the clove smoke lay heavy in the sheets. She got up and changed them, flapping the sheet to dispel the smells.

18

TODAY, AS LEAH neared her street, a welcoming
breeze sprang up, puckering the shop banners. The
cooling wind made the thin people, who peddled their
few remaining pots or their six peaches artfully displayed to con-
ceal their blemishes, smile. Leah stopped to talk. Yes, she agreed,
victory was in the air, better times were coming.

She stopped cold when she saw Tokai sitting on his
haunches, squatting like a coolie under her banyan tree. His hair
was unbrushed and his suit wrinkled. Tottering to his feet, he
lurched and fell into her arms, murmuring "Leah, Leah," a
drunken grin on his face.

"You're drunk," she said, holding onto him and dragging
him towards the door. He fell through the doorway, pulling her
on top with sloppy kisses.

"Miss me?" he managed.

Leah pushed him off and shoved him onto the bed where
he lay stunned, hiccupping loudly. He patted the pillow, a crafty
sly look on his face as he fought to remove his tie. In frustration, he yanked it off over his head.

"How long have you been waiting out there?" she demanded.

"I want you," he said, his eyes wide with desire.

"Why did you come?"

"You're beautiful. I thought I made it up. But no, you're beautiful. Lie down. I'm going to stay with you forever." He smiled with satisfaction, closed his eyes, and began to snore.

His mouth was ajar. A line of spittle collected in the corner, then slid down his unshaven chin. He reeked of cigarettes. His skin had a bruised, unhealthy tinge. He must have been drinking for weeks. He resembled those sodden bankrupt gamblers, unhinged and unable to recall how they had lost everything despite their conviction they were on a roll. She had seen them reeling through the streets of Macau, blinking in the bright sun.

She listened to his drunken snores with growing rage and impotence. How dare he think he could come to her drunk and expect her to provide sanctuary. He could still destroy her. She should pay a couple of labourers a few *patacas* and have him dumped in a squalid *traverssa*. Chinese resentment would do the rest.

Rolling him onto his side, she hauled off his jacket. When she finished undressing him, she was breathless and sweaty. He could be a coolie in his unkempt state, only his undershorts were silk and his hands were soft. What was she going to do with him? He couldn't have come straight here. It had taken weeks of steady drinking to reach this state. He must have stayed somewhere in Macau where he could drink safely, away from prying Japanese informant eyes, plucking up his courage to come to her.

She rifled his pockets and found his wallet. Inside were his Japanese military identity card with his photograph and a great deal of military currency. In the photograph he looked very pleased with himself, an amused stare on his unlined face. The real Ito looked like a lost older brother who inhabited doorways and lived off the street. Why had she agreed to help Eldersen on that cloudless sunny day in her garden? Eldersen should have warned her out of friendship or love—she had seen his longing— that spying was an occupation that ended in wrecked lives.

"Get out," she hissed.

He didn't move. She made her finger into a gun, pointed and yelled 'Bang.' He snored louder.

The light in the flat was fading; Tokai was becoming a dark lump on her bed. His animal smell was everywhere. It filled her with a hopeless lassitude. She was so tired. Slowly, she undressed and, clad in only in her slip, eased his comatose body onto the bare floor. She closed her eyes as the alcohol seeped out of Tokai's pores and his snores filled the night.

In the morning, Leah stepped over Tokai and got ready for work. Tokai opened one eye and groaned.

"You should go," she said.

Tokai lurched from the floor to the bed to pull the sheet over his head. He peeked out, massaging his head with his hands as if struggling to collect his thoughts and stop the throbbing. "It's over," he said dully. "Tokyo is ash. Our latest shipment has been blown up. My father's had a stroke. He's an old man now."

As hung over as he was, Leah detected a new watchfulness in his face. He wanted to blame her for his misfortunes and he wanted a sympathetic audience. She said nothing.

Tokai stumbled on. "People cheered when Tokyo was bombed. It was a spectacular performance. We Japanese enjoy a good spectacle."

She looked at her watch. "I'm late. Make sure you lock the door when you leave."

After the door closed, Tokai made up reasons to hate her.

⌒

SHE let him stay. There was no place for him to go. No one would accept Japanese military notes, not even the long-term Japanese residents. Besides, they too had barricaded themselves in. Tokai lived like a hermit, only moving from the bed to the floor. She'd brought blankets and made a nest for him there. He did go out to buy whisky. How he got it was a mystery. When she asked, he only grunted or mumbled incoherently. She bought him food from the street vendors. He held the chopsticks in his hands and manoeuvred the food around his bowl, washing non-existent mouthfuls down with swigs of whisky. She took his clothes to the laundry and threatened if he didn't pull himself together she'd kick him out.

With the sly knowledge of a drunk, he replied, "No, you won't. I'm your dirty secret."

It was a standoff.

In the third week of his stay, Albemarle came running into the consulate, ghost white. The Japanese consul Nagotchi and his secretary had been shot at point blank range as they walked along Avenida de Praia Grande, enjoying the cooling breeze from the Inner Harbour. Nagotchi was dead. His secretary was expected to live.

"Serves them right," said Spencer with satisfaction.

"It's murder," said Albemarle. "He was a friend, once. He tried to soften Sawa's madness. Who knows if he isn't the reason Macau was spared a Japanese occupation."

"You can't believe that," argued Spencer. "He wanted Japan to win. If they won, all of us would be in a prison camp or dead. You can't trust any of them. They are born liars and torturers."

"After the war, we will have to learn to live with them," Albemarle said mildly, upset at Spencer's rage.

"Shoot the lot of them," responded Spencer, red-faced and fuming with moral indignation.

"Who shot Nagotchi?" asked Leah.

"Rumours are running wild. Take your pick. The Chinese—both the Kuomintang and the Communists—claim credit. Even the triads want to get in on the act. But my money is on Sawa. It has all his nasty little hallmarks. The man is furious Macau is not blacked out and is giving aid to the enemy. He blames Nagotchi for not insisting Teixeira jail those who kept their lights on or those who smuggle out money and material for the Chinese cause."

Calmer now, Spencer raised more theories and provocations, but Leah could only see Tokai, unwashed and reeking, dead on the pavement. If Sawa was on rampage, then Tokai might be next. She had to keep him safe.

When she arrived home, she opened the door to find Tokai sitting on a chair with a new half-drunk bottle of whisky on the table. "You've been busy," she said.

"I heard about Nagotchi. I'm mourning his death," he said, his forehead puckered into a frown, his face a study in defiance.

She handed him a large package wrapped in a Chinese newspaper. "Open it. It's for you."

He ripped at the paper and found a cheap shirt, cotton trousers, a straw fedora and a pair of dark glasses. "This my disguise?" he asked.

"Yes."

"Maybe I should pull a rickshaw too."

"I'm only trying to help."

"Have a drink."

She put the hat on his head and pulled the brim down. "It suits."

"Ha!"

She unbuttoned her blouse to reveal the bullet scar on her shoulder. "Sawa's men did this."

He touched the raised red lumpy scar, harsh against her creamy skin. Up till now, he had been too sunk in his own misery to take much interest in her sexually, had not even attempted to sneak into bed late at night. It was too much effort and he preferred his drunken stupor. "What was it like, being shot?" he asked, suddenly hungry for details.

"I can't remember anything," she lied.

"It's beautiful in its own way."

She took his hand away and began to button her blouse.

"Don't." He drew her close and took off her blouse. He no longer seemed so drunk.

"It's sexy," he said and kissed the scar, his hand cupping her breast. As he touched her, he said, "In Japan little girls are taught to sleep with their legs together. In the night, their mothers come and move their legs just so." He moved his hand down.

"Don't."

"You hate me. I see how you look at me," he said, his hand moving under the elastic of her underpants.

She held his wrist. "I let you hide here."

"I'm not hiding."

"No? Then why are you here?"

"To be with you, where there is no war," he said, removing her restraining hand and her underpants. In bed together, there was a relentless despair in their pursuit of pleasure.

⌒

A few weeks later, Leah read the newspaper aloud to Tokai. 'The Japanese government is unperturbed by Germany's defeat. Japan will never surrender. We will fight on.'

Tokai acknowledged the truth of the statement. "In Tokyo during the fire bombing, people remained with useless buckets of water as their houses burned and walls of flame trapped them. They burned to a crisp. It was a terrible smell. We don't know how to surrender."

"When are you leaving to fight?" she challenged, hating him today.

"Soon," he shot back.

THE swiftness of victories in the Pacific left her breathless. Whitehall's interest in Macau was aroused with the issuing of the Potsdam Edict calling upon Japan to agree to unconditional surrender or face prompt and utter destruction. Albemarle was to devise a plan immediately to aid Hong Kong. The plan was to be put into practice the moment Japan capitulated. The foreign office wanted an orderly transfer of power in Hong Kong, not chaos and retribution.

Spencer found an enormous blackboard and propped it up between two chairs in Albemarle's office. Across the top of the blackboard in chalk, he wrote: The Plan. He turned casually to Leah and announced with supreme pleasure that Albemarle was going to be the Acting Colonial Secretary for Hong Kong.

"Is it true?" asked Leah.

Albemarle looked embarrassed. "There has been talk, but things change very fast."

Leah stared. She had heard nothing. Her deal with Chang and Vasiliev was off. She could hardly turn up with forged papers bearing Albemarle's signature and expect to get away with it if he was in Hong Kong. The consul would arrest her; Chang would be furious. She hated to think how he would take his revenge. He'd think she'd kept him in the dark on purpose.

"Aren't you pleased?" asked Spencer, twisting the knife.

"I'm shocked," said Leah. "You were so looking forward to being reunited with your family, sir."

Albemarle gave a small shrug. "What can you do?"

Spencer sniffed. "Duty first," he bragged.

"Spencer," Albemarle explained, "will be Acting Consul in Macau."

Leah said nothing.

"Congratulations wouldn't go amiss," said Spencer.

"Well done," said Leah without enthusiasm.

A deep flush of wounded pride crept up Spencer's face.

"Now, now," calmed Albemarle. "It's early days and plans keep changing."

The telephone on the consul's desk rang. Spencer made a grab for it. He put a hand over the receiver, "It's the governor's office, sir," and gave the phone to Albemarle. Albemarle motioned for Leah and Spencer to leave.

As they walked down the hall to their offices, Spencer said, "When there is a change in consuls, people hand in their resignations. The new consul chooses his own local staff. That's protocol."

"You're temporary," she pointed out and hurried down the hall into her office. She could almost hear Spencer gnashing his teeth.

19

THE FLAT WAS no longer a refuge with Tokai
there. She could never predict if today would be one
of his good days: the flat tidy, he'd be dressed and full
of plans to rebuild his factories working himself into a frenzy of
optimism. On the bad days, he was drunk. Drunk was easier.

Today, she was hit by Tokai's sour alcoholic reek. He lay
spread-eagled under the thin sheet feigning sleep, one naked
arm dragging on the floor. His discarded clothes lay next to an
empty bowl swimming in fermenting soy sauce and a bottle of
half-drunk cheap port. She banged the door closed.

As though in a movie, Tokai sprang awake, rubbing his eyes.
"I'm sick," he whined.

Leah snapped the blinds up and opened windows.

"People can see in. You are cruel. You should understand
how I feel," he said, holding up a hand to protect his eyes from
the late afternoon sun.

With disgust, she stepped over his clothes on the floor.
"They need washing."

He muttered, "*Hazukashii.*"

"I don't speak Japanese."

He bounded out of bed and grabbed the rose silk kimono

off the wall to drape it around him like a geisha, the silk flapping about his legs as he minced and batted his eyes.

"I can't take this anymore. You'll have to leave."

He stopped dancing and took off the kimono, smoothing the silk, then folding it into a neat square, and returned to bed using the kimono as a pillow while Leah edged towards the door, uncertain what he might do next. "Go back to Japan," she begged. "There's nothing for you here."

With the cunning of the deranged, he pleaded, "Come with me."

"You're mad."

"No, you can't," he replied coolly. "I'm getting married when I return to Tokyo. Her name is Joji." He pawed through his discarded trousers and pulled out a photograph. "Isn't she beautiful? She's nineteen. She will be a very good wife to this very good Jap." He threw the picture towards her.

She caught it. Joji looked barely fifteen. It was a full length studio portrait. The backdrop was a painting of waving palms and a bright round sun. Joji stood in a kimono and obi, her head angled down, a demure smile peeping from her cupid's bow lips.

"Congratulations. I hope you will be very happy."

Snarling, Tokai jumped off the bed and grabbed it away. "She's prettier than you. Her family is very wealthy."

"Lucky you."

He raised an arm to strike.

She ducked and sidestepped him. "Going to bleat about the war now? How it was all a mistake? How Japan was forced to defend itself to aid its Asian brothers?"

He flung her onto the bed, pinning her shoulders down, a murderous look in his eyes. "You think because your skin is white, you're better? I never saw you as a patriot. You were quite willing to open your legs to me, a Jap." He dug his fingers into her scar, forcing her to gasp with pain. He smiled.

"Get off of me," she said. "The British Secret Service had you in their sights long before you came to Hong Kong. Perhaps in France, Monsieur Martin realised your usefulness. You belong nowhere and were easy prey. He leaked your weaknesses for European women to his contacts in the Resistance. This . . . this liaison was always in the cards. It was all an act. You mean nothing to me."

Staring down at her, he felt strange, as if another person occupied his body. He could easily kill her. He was stronger than her. He placed a tentative hand on her throat and tightened his grip.

She looked into his eyes, challenging him, almost urging him on.

"Demon," he hissed and eased his hold. "I'm still rich," he taunted. "My money is safe in the Bank of Lisboa."

He looked pleased, as if he had provoked this scene to prove his superiority and her stupidity and gullibility. He rolled off her and stood, gloating.

"Get out."

"Japan will need me," he boasted. "We will rebuild."

There was fierce pounding on the door, followed by hard rattles of the doorknob. Spencer's infuriated insistent voice filled the room. "Open up. I know you're screwing the Jap. You traitor." He began kicking the door.

Tokai looked at Leah with malice. "I'm not going anywhere. Let him in. He'll only get the police."

"He wouldn't dare," but she opened the door. A flash bulb popped and she staggered back, half blind.

Triumphant, Spencer crowed, "Photographic evidence," and

pushed in. He took another picture of Tokai in his underpants, his eyes wide with surprise. "I knew it," declared Spencer, taking in the disordered, pungent room, smelling sex and dissipation.

Leah lunged at Spencer and his camera. Spencer fended her off as they danced around the room, overturning the table, breaking the rice bowl and trampling the kimono.

"Enough," said Tokai and stuck out his foot.

Spencer fell to the floor, landing on his back, hunched over to protect his camera. He cried out in pain.

"Tokai," said Leah, "meet my colleague Spencer Talbot. Spencer this is Mr. Ito."

Spencer stared goggled-eyed as Tokai bent and wrestled the camera out of his hands.

"Don't hurt the bellows. It can tear," said Spencer as he rose, sullen and bruised.

Leah placed the camera on the righted table. "We won't hurt it," said Leah.

"Tokyo Rose," Spencer spat.

Tokai shut the door firmly and stood guarding it.

"I've got my evidence. You have to let me go," said Spencer.

"Had fun playing Sherlock Holmes?" Leah asked, amazed by his disguise. He wore a cheap blue suit, no tie and sandals. His toes were very long and pink. On the floor was a large squashed grey Homburg, its grosgrain ribbon half off. She picked up the wrecked hat and put it on Spencer's bald head. It was too large and rested on the top of his ears.

"Stop that," said Spencer, glaring, and removed his hat, laying it beside his camera.

"Have you noticed Spencer on your walks, Tokai?"

Tokai shrugged and eyed the port bottle that had landed by his feet. He picked it up and fiddled with the cork.

"Well, why not," said Leah and fossicked around to find three glasses. The men watched, full of suspicion and breathing heavily. She handed them each a glass of port. "Do you want to propose a toast, Spence?"

Spencer sniffed the port.

"It's not poison," said Leah. She took a swig along with Tokai who said, "Cheers."

Spencer growled, but allowed himself a small taste. He took a larger swallow, relaxed slightly and pulled out a small black notebook from his breast coat pocket. He flicked through the pages and his neat blue ink handwriting fluttered past. "It's all here. I even saw you with Harris once entering a bar in Rua da Felicidade." He turned to Tokai and explained, "Prostitutes live there."

A look of mock surprise passed between Tokai and Leah.

Incensed, Spencer said, "I've seen you with all kinds of disreputable men. Chang's been here." He looked in his notebook for a date.

"Don't bother," said Leah. "I'll take your word for it."

Spencer finished his port and delivered his judgment, relishing her comeuppance. "You are a double-dealing spy, obtaining information through sexual favours." He grimaced, flushing red to the top of his bald head. "Further, you were involved in poor Moy's murder and your wounding after the attack on the gunboat was a ploy to divert attention from . . ." He paused for dramatic effect, "this Jap. Lastly, you seduced the consul to put him off the scent. The police will be coming," he concluded, rocking on his heels with righteousness.

For the first time, Leah was alarmed. "You haven't? It's all nonsense. You've added two and two and gotten six."

Spencer remained silent. He'd expected Leah to try and wriggle out. He was determined to stay until he had her signed confession. He risked a glance at his camera. It sat waiting on the table like a contented cat. "You've consorted with the enemy."

"Miss Kolbe and I are just friends," said Tokai ignoring the fact that he was naked except for his undershorts.

"Ha!" said Spencer. "You'll be charged too. There is going to be a trial."

"Mr. Ito is returning to Japan as soon as the war ends and transport can be arranged."

Tokai nodded.

"Have you told the consul?" asked Leah.

"He hasn't seen this," he said with disgust, indicating Tokai. "You seduced and duped the consul. But now I have proof. Good God man, put some clothes on."

"It's hot," replied Tokai, returning Spencer's look, and crossed his arms defiantly.

Alight with the fury of retribution, his pale eyes blinking, Spencer proclaimed, "I'm making a citizen's arrest."

"Don't be ridiculous, Spencer. You're not a citizen of Macau. You don't have the power," said Leah, realising that he hadn't spoken to De Rey for fear of being ridiculed. Instead, he wanted to round them up like bad guys in a film and present them to De Rey in a neat package. The man was mad.

"I haven't done anything wrong. I had nothing to do with Moy's death. I didn't hire assassins to shoot myself. I nearly died."

"Slut," raged Spencer.

She dropped her glass. It broke, showering the floor. Ignoring the shards, she said in a tight low voice, "Who I spend time with is my own private business. And in case you hadn't noticed, Macau is neutral. There is no crime."

"I know who you are," said Spencer. "You're a munitions dealer. And Leah, you've passed information to him."

"Make steel," corrected Tokai.

"What could I tell the Japs? I don't know battle plans. No one in London cares what goes on here. We don't count," Leah said.

"He's a fantasist," Tokai concurred. "He's made the whole thing up."

Leah nodded. "You've had your fun, Spencer. Go home."

"It's all here and as plain as the nose on your face. You're the ones who should be afraid. They hang traitors."

"Gossip, innuendo, and your own crazy imaginings."

"Don't you dare patronise me. I know what I know," he retorted. He had spent months making his case, poring over his notes, skipping meals to trail her and watching from alleyways. Late at night, he had played out this scene many times. He had expected her to collapse into tears and the Jap to commit suicide later, after the trial when she was condemned to death. But there she stood, calm and collected. It was unnerving the way she looked at him. He was the one in the right. And now the damn Jap held a glass shard. He might stab him with it. Why hadn't he brought Leah's gun and informed De Rey?

She asked, "Aren't you tired of war?"

"I'm not militarist," Spencer declared with a scowl at Tokai.

"I haven't done anything wrong. I'm not a criminal," said Tokai.

"Others will see things differently," Spencer said with authority. This was better. He would get his picture in the paper. Everyone would know who he was in England. First, he'd be the Acting Consul of Macau and then he would move swiftly up the diplomatic ladder. Why he would have a whole group of undersecretaries bowing and scraping.

"People are so tired of war. The consul says so." She crunched over the glass and plucked a slim report off the kitchen counter. "Read it?" she asked, flapping the pages. "It's intended for released prisoners in Hong Kong to explain the mood in Britain.

"Usually guff," he declared.

"You don't have someone in prison in Hong Kong. I've read it three times. It makes you weep." Leah read, "The people of England are noticeably tired. The strain of the V-1 and V-2 bombs after a period of respite and the successes following D-Day were great on those living in Southeast England, who show their exhaustion the most." She paused. "You're from Kent, aren't you?"

"Lower Halston," he blurted. It was like an admission of failure.

Leah read on, "Politeness and consideration are appreciated." She let the words sink in. "People want to lead normal lives, Spencer. They will want to forget the war."

He considered this. "So?"

"The consul knows about me," she said looking at Tokai.

"Liar."

"Ask him."

"I don't have to. It's all here."

"Go away," said Ito. "I don't want you here." He made a feint with the glass shard and Spencer went white.

"Stop that," admonished Leah.

Barefoot, Toki walked back to the bed, careful to avoid the glass. The man Spencer was barbaric, from his long face, to his ugly freckled hands, to his white blond hairy toes. He was an ape, no, more like a baboon with the same shifty cunning: noisy, hideous and no doubt red-assed. Truly, he no longer cared about anything. He must have always known in some inner recess of his mind that Leah was a spy, but he hadn't cared, mesmerised by her beauty and the world he had left behind. If he were more Japanese, he's say she was a demon. Looking at her now confronting this bizarre Englishman it could be true. She was icy, reasonable, not upset. She had used him. She *was* a demon. She had cast a spell over him. He had never loved her. It was only her body he craved. He didn't want it now. He shut himself off, no longer minding what the demon and the baboon were saying, dreaming about a rebuilt Tokyo and an adoring wife.

Leah could see that Spencer was beginning to have doubts. His hands hung down uselessly at his side and his pale blue eyes were blinking fast.

"Spying on a colleague is a strange way to get a promotion. Albemarle will be very unhappy when I tell him."

"Your fiancé should know the truth. Having a Jap lover is obscene. It's my duty to tell him."

"You and I have swanned around Macau well-fed and free. Do you want my fiancé to suffer more?"

Spencer shuffled his feet. "Heroes shouldn't marry sluts."

Incensed, Leah unbuttoned her blouse. Spencer blanched and stared pop-eyed.

"I'm stripping so you can photograph Tokai and me naked in bed." She stopped. "Or are you more the anonymous letter type? Here's a magazine and scissors. Start cutting."

Spencer rubbed at his face, mopped his brow. Somehow, he had lost his advantage. "I have to leave now," he muttered and picked up the camera, collapsing the bellows and closing its red Bakelite cover.

Leah blocked the door. "The film, please."

Spencer pursed his lips and let out a strangled "No."

"Why hurt an innocent person? You aren't a monster. Don't be that cruel."

Spencer stood poised to push past and leave, but Leah remained unmoving—really imploring. She seemed a lot smaller here and her face had a ravaged intensity. He wished she looked more like the enemy, yellow and ugly. A news photograph of British POWs released from a German camp flashed through his mind. In the photo, a few men grinned and mugged for the camera, but underneath their gaiety, he'd seen their worn uniforms hung off their gaunt frames and their eyes were tinged with sadness. It was the reverse image of a schoolboy class photograph. Not his, of course. He was the one shoved out of the frame or with fingers held up behind his head to make him look stupid. No doubt, Leah's fiancé would have been the sort of boy who would have plagued him. But, he liked to think he wasn't a petty man. He was a Christian, after all. He turned the camera over to press the release button. The bottom half of the camera came away, exposing the film to light. He took out the spool of film and dropped it onto the floor.

Leah took Spencer's hands in hers. "Thank you."

He pulled his hands away, amazed at his own actions. He handed her the black notebook. "You might as well have it. I might be—" He didn't finish the sentence because he could envisage himself alone at night sulking over a slight, slipping the notebook into an envelope and posting it off to someone important. The notebook fell with a soft thump as he walked out the door. He didn't look back.

"Fool," said Ito.

"I want you to leave now. Take your money, everything, and go away. We are through. There is no going back."

"I will forget you," promised Tokai, pulling on his pants.

She turned her back and watched the women on the inlaid screen as they chatted amongst themselves.

"I will have an ordinary life now," he said as he left.

She didn't know if it were a threat or a curse.

She spent the evening cutting the soiled kimono into small strips. It didn't matter: all the beauty had gone out of it.

20

PEOPLE STOPPED IN the streets to stare at the morning sky's eerie red glow. "Strange," said an old Portuguese man staring up, shading his eyes. A nun in a heavy white habit crossed herself saying it was evidence of God's power.

When Leah entered the consulate, Albemarle rushed down the hall, caught her in his arms and swung her high with joy, exclaiming, "We've done it. The Americans have dropped some kind of new bomb on Hiroshima. The Japanese will surrender any day now. It's over." He crushed her to him and they did a little dance.

In the doorway, Spencer stood agog, his stomach turning. The woman was at it again, working her powers. The last few weeks, Leah and he had maintained an icy formality that precluded all but the most mundane topics: the weather, the reporting of messages and briefest of interchanges regarding work.

"Don't look at me like that, Spencer," teased Albemarle as he let go of Leah. "It's wonderful news. Peace at last."

Spencer caught Leah's eye as if questioning her response.

And she laughed and popped a kiss onto his pale cheek. "Be happy for once, Spence. It's glorious."

"That's the way," said Albemarle. "Celebrate with a kiss from a pretty girl."

Under Albemarle's coaxing gaze, Spencer grudgingly, returned Leah's kiss, his lips only grazing her skin. "There," he said, looking for approval from Albemarle.

"Bravo, Spencer," said Albemarle. "And I've got other good news. I'm not going to Hong Kong."

Spencer's face fell—only this morning he'd been practicing calling himself Consul as he shaved. It suited him. He masked his disappointment by asking, "Who is going to run it, sir?"

"The interned members of the former colonial government."

Leah gasped. "What? But how can men held prisoner and starved for more than three years be well enough to assume control?"

"Truly, I don't know," said Albemarle. "But the decision has been made. It's a way to honour their suffering and demonstrate to the world we're back in charge. It's very symbolic. Japanese understand symbols. Personally, I think it's asking too much."

"No," said Spencer. "It's a grand gesture. A few days of proper food, a good bed and sleep, they'll be right as rain. They're British after all."

"They're also human," cut in Leah savagely.

"They're up to the challenge," declared Spencer stubbornly, his pale face aglow with British pride.

"Let's hope for the best," soothed Albemarle. "It could still be weeks or months away. We don't know what Hirohito might do. He might demand his people resist to the death and the Japs would follow like lemmings. How can a country wallow in death?"

"War is a test of character," said Spencer, his eyes trained on Leah.

"Tell it to the dead," replied Leah.

"Please," pleaded Albemarle, "on such a day, can't you two get along?"

"Sorry," said Leah. "You're right." She held out her hand.

Spencer shook it limply. "I hope they make Japan pay for through the nose for this war."

"Well," said Albemarle, "let's hope the negotiators can find lasting peace," and left them standing in the hallway. Spencer slunk back to his office; Leah returned to hers, wasting the rest of the morning daydreaming about Jonathan and pushing down her fear of sailing to Hong Kong with Vasiliev and Chang.

Albemarle stared at the boarded-up window. He could take it down soon. Things were going to change. He should lead the way. He took a ruler out of his desk drawer and tried to pry out a nail. The ruler snapped. "Damn," he said, his fingers stinging. He blew on them and it was like blowing his exuberance away. Just minutes ago the world seemed alive with possibilities and twirling Leah in arms had made it perfect. Anything was possible. But in the quiet of his office, he realised that for him, peace was not going to be a wonderful adventure. He would miss seeing Leah. He should never have allowed her to leave his house. Such a lost opportunity. They could have been lovers. From time to time he whiled away a slow afternoon with thoughts of her, and once or twice had wonderful sexy dreams about her, only to wake chagrined to find his bed empty. Then, when he saw her in the flesh he was overly formal and distant. Leah would be on the first ferry back to Hong Kong, might not even say goodbye. He sighed and wondered how Mildred had endured the war and what they would talk about when they were reunited. He hoped they would be kind to one another. Life in England was so very different to life in Macau. Was he up to the challenge? Today, he thought he might not be. Well, there was always divorce. No. He couldn't do that to Anne and Conrad. His children had survived a war without him. He couldn't inflict more suffering on them. Like poor daft Spencer, he knew he must do his duty. Leah would become an old man's dream that he would indulge in on cold winter nights as he lay in bed with Mildred between chilly sheets and hot water bottles.

⌒

Six days later, Hirohito agreed to unconditional surrender. On the radio, Governor Teixeira proclaimed a three-day holiday culminating in a celebration in Senado Square and a dragon dance. People poured out of offices, shops, and houses to celebrate. On the street, firecrackers exploded in joyous abandon. Children ran around waving any flag they could get their hands on. Gongs were hit and stringy men banged drums. An old woman with two teeth in traditional black Chinese pyjamas came up to Leah and gravely shook her hand as if she alone were responsible for the Allied victory.

Not even the threat of a typhoon could dampen their spirits. People cheered when the typhoon warning flag was raised so drunk were they on peace. Despite the wind, the nitric firecracker smoke of victory hung in the air late into the summer evening. Leah stood on the corner of the Rua do Campo with a group of bystanders watching workmen perched on a bamboo scaffold build the ornamental victory arch. The workmen laughed and good-humouredly disagreed on the colours as the crowd shouted their advice. People radiated happiness; it saturated the very air. Everything was wonderful. Happiness or hope magically plumped out the thin faces of the very poor. An urchin in hessian charity clothes threw down a string of firecrackers, making people jump. The men on the arch whooped their disapproval. Chang emerged from the crowd, grabbed the boy by the arm and shook him hard. The boy looked contrite. Chang eased his grip, allowing the boy to wriggle free. He ran off, laughing, as if it were the biggest joke in the world as he ducked past Leah. Chang waved and moved closer.

"I've been looking for you. We leave at dawn tomorrow," Chang said in a low voice as she stared at the men high above her.

"The typhoon," said Leah. "It's dangerous."

"We must get to Hong Kong before the British bureaucracy reassembles and before the Japanese rats escape. Don't come if you are afraid. Just give me the papers. We don't need you."

"You need me. Without me, the rice will be seized to prevent black marketeering. You won't see a penny. They might even impound the junk."

"Don't be so sure."

The men on the scaffold let out a cheer, signalling the arch was completed. Leah joined in the clapping as the men bowed. "I'll be there," she declared.

"Good," he shouted over the crowd noise and walked away, holding onto his hat, the legs of his suit billowing in the rising wind.

LEAH tugged a small brown rucksack from under the bed and blew away the dust, coughing. It was ridiculously small. Well, she wasn't going to take much. She hoisted up the end of the mattress and neatly cut the white stitching to feel among the lumps of cotton for the forged bills of lading, customs forms, and her new legitimate hardcover blue passport. She slipped the forged documents into the concealed pockets inside the rucksack, packed three sets of underwear, two silk dresses and pair of sandals, then placed her passport on top. She looked around the flat. Someone else could have the slip figurine. She didn't want to explain how she had come by it, besides it didn't look anything like her now. The L-shaped room seemed darker and dingier. The green-black mould had spread its hungry fingers up the blue tiled wall, making it bow and loosening the tiles. Twelve tiles now lay neatly stacked. She'd always intended to buy grout or mastic to reattach them. Now, she never would. The damp or the heat had caused two of the Chinese ladies' faces to crack and turn ghostly pale. They seemed to be urging her to get away. But first, she must explain her sudden departure to Albemarle. She owed him that.

Dear Stephen,

It may take weeks to get the ferries going—I can't wait. A fisherman and his family have agreed to take me back to Hong Kong. Don't worry. They are good people. I will not swim to shore this time.

I feel I must return to Hong Kong. I have had only one post-card from Jonathan. I am so worried. We both have heard such dreadful rumours.

I don't know how to thank you for all your kindness and understanding. You and I have had a good war. I am sorry that Mr. Talbot and I were not able to get along better. It must have been very wearisome for you in the midst of your own real worries and difficulties. I am so grateful.

I hope you will be very happy in England with your family.

*Should your boat home stop in Hong Kong, please do visit. I don't
know where I we will be staying, but Hong Kong is like a village
for Europeans and I'm sure you will be able to contact us.*

Ever in your debt,
Leah (Miss L. Kolbe)

Despite her resolve, she couldn't sleep. Images of Tokai
flooded her brain. Had she loved him? How much time had
they spent together? Was it even a month? Perhaps, she reasoned, it was like dog years—one for seven—a day in wartime
was precious and counted for more. A month of love and betrayal
equalled a lifetime of peace. She felt sorry for Joji. She would
have a terrible loveless life with Tokai. Tokai would be miserable. She was glad. Leaving everything behind was like sealing
up a tomb. Nothing could touch her now. She must think only
about the future. Desperately, she wished she were already in
Hong Kong, welcoming Jonathan home, in his arms, in his bed.
Only she had to do this one last thing. It might set them up
for life, a new beginning. If she did, Vasiliev had promised to
tell her how Theo had been killed and why. One last dangerous thing and she would be free.

Calmed, she slept until the bleat of the alarm sounded. She
sat bolt upright and heard the wind rattle the flat's wooden window frames. There was a loud crack of thunder and she jumped.
Let it come. She wasn't going to let the storm take away her
chance to have money and Jonathan. She pulled on dark trousers
and a blouse, then slid her feet into soft Chinese slippers. She
locked the door for the last time and sealed the key into Albemarle's envelope. No regrets, she decided, and hurried into the
grey dawn.

On Avenida De Rocha, under a verandah away from the wind, a sleepy teenage boy sat hunched, watching Leah push the letter through the mail slot. By the boy's side was a bicycle with hardly any spokes but two new tires. The wind was gusting hard.

"Strange time for a walk," the boy mocked in Cantonese.

"May I borrow you bike?" asked Leah.

The boy shook his head. "Hire only."

Leah emptied her pockets of *patacas*. They made an odd couple: Leah perched on the hard seat, a rucksack on her back, pedaling at a steady pace, the breathless boy running alongside, begging her to slow down.

Nearing the Inner Harbour, she handed the bike back. The boy rode slowly away, but driven by curiosity, he turned back to look. The European woman was waving to a tall Chinese man as five workers strained under ropes, hauling a wagon laden with sacks of rice to a waiting junk. It was a strange sight; he was certain he should forget what he had seen. The sky was an ominous smoky grey, the wind stiff. It was difficult to pedal against such a headwind. He got off and pushed, buffeted by the wind.

Chang only grunted at Leah when she clambered aboard the junk. He was busy arguing with the junk captain, Mr. Lee, a jowly man with liver spots on his face who was very worried. The rice was weighing the junk down and in this weather . . . It wouldn't be manoeuvrable, wouldn't be able to sail over mines. They'd be blown smithereens and then no one would profit. "Please," Mr. Lee pleaded, "no more."

"A few less sacks won't matter," interjected Leah.

Chang ignored her. "You've been well paid. No." Chang

signalled to Lee's two sons overseeing the loading to hurry up. "We can outrun the storm. It will veer off."

Lee looked at him as if he were crazy.

Chang dismissed the look and demanded to see Leah's documents.

"They're packed. In this wind . . ."

"Later, then," said Chang. To Leah, it sounded like a threat.

Vasiliev pulled himself up the ladder from the cabin and walked across the deck. "It will be a rough crossing," he said as a greeting. "It's not too late to stay in Macau and wait for us to get in touch."

Leah undid the top strap of the rucksack and took out her passport. "You need me."

Chang plucked it out of her hand, his eyes focusing on the words: *The bearer is part of His Britannic majesty's Diplomatic Service due all attendant rights, privileges and courtesies.*

"I have to be the one to show it," she said with cunning.

"Keep it safe," he said.

Both men stared as she fought the wind to keep her packed clothes from blowing away and tucked the passport in securely. Then she buckled the rucksack onto her back and went off to find a space protected from the wind by the rising stacks of rice. Sitting on the hard deck, she watched the thick clouds scudding across the oily grey sky. Loading was done. The Inner Harbour grew smaller and the pastel houses shrank. She felt the terrible dread of déjà vu. Again, she was leaving with people she didn't trust and in weather no sane person would sail in. She must be mad.

21

VASILIEV ROAMED AROUND the deck, a small canvas fold-up stool in his hand. "Found you," he said to Leah with a stupid grin and opened the stool, levering himself down with a grunt to sit with his thick legs apart. "I'm used to better."

The junk headed out to sea under motor power, belching smoke. Vasiliev squinted at Lee. "Tough as nails. He'll see us through," he said, but his voice had edge to it. His face matched the grey sky as he held his belly between his hands as if to stop it jumping as the boat ploughed through the unsettled sea, and muttered little yelps of surprise when it dipped. "It will take twice as long to get there now," he complained. "We'll have earned our money." His face was tinged with green. "You seem all right."

"I don't get seasick," said Leah, waiting for the right moment to quiz him.

"Ha!" he said. "You will." He pulled himself up, ran in a clumsy waddle to the stern of the boat and was sick. One of Lee's sons laughed.

"I'm going below," called Vasiliev. "Don't let my seat blow away."

She pillowed her head against her rucksack and used the stool upside down as a back support. In time, she dozed. She was awakened by a violent thunderclap. Vasiliev was hanging over the side, vomiting. He looked like a blow up doll losing air. He shuffled back and flopped down heavily. "It's worse down below," he managed. He closed his eyes as the junk slammed down. "Oh, God, we're going to die."

"Tell me about Theo. If we're going to die, I want to know."

Large raindrops hit them. Lee's sons ran nimbly around the deck in bare feet securing tarpaulins over the rice. Out of pity, one of the sons handed Leah a tarpaulin and Vasiliev squeezed closer. She smelt his sour breath.

"Where's Chang?" she asked.

"He brought a raincoat with him. He's helping with the rudder," said Vasiliev. "He could have brought two."

"You sail?"

"That's not the point. We're partners." He looked put out. "The Chinese only look after themselves."

"When did you meet Theo? I want to know everything."

Vasiliev stuck his head out of the tarp. "Chang is still working the rudder. In these seas, it takes two." It seemed to give him the impetus to begin. He talked rapidly, his Russian accent thickening until whole sentences were in Russian.

Lost in a maze of language, Leah interrupted. "Speak slower. Speak English."

Vasiliev backtracked and the story altered.

Leah had the distinct impression he was changing the facts or only telling some of the truth, embellishing his role to make himself central to the drama, but she didn't raise any questions, afraid to stop the words tumbling out in English and because he seemed very concerned to speak without Chang overhearing. The rain came down in sheets and the junk juddered through the heavy seas, weighed down with rice.

Leah's brain worked overtime, piecing together Vasiliev's story and judging it against what she suspected, what Theo had told her, and what An-li had hinted at. Vasiliev insisted he was a distant cousin of her Russian mother Vestna. As children, they had played together in Odessa. Vasiliev had worshipped Vestna. She was a beautiful child, full of energy and high spirits and very daring for a girl. Vestna called him her toad. Leah pictured him as a podgy boy, yearning to be petted by her beautiful mother. Certainly, he was an ugly man. He must have been a grotesque, ungainly child with his oversized head, lizard eyes. They had lost touch during the Great War. Separately, each escaped east to avoid the wrath of the Red Army, languishing in poverty in China and finally managing to reach Hong Kong. They rediscovered each other, eking out a living in the Colony, at the bottom rung of European society. Vestna traded on her beauty. Vasiliev was silent awhile, his face full of memories that narrowed his eyes. He wanted to go into salacious detail.

"Don't," Leah cut in fiercely.

He retreated, saying feebly, "We did what we had to do to get by." Vasiliev took credit for introducing Vestna to Theo. Theo was already deeply involved his antiquities business and Vasiliev had certain contacts. He rolled his eyes and looked coy. "One hand washes the other," said Vasiliev, letting go of the billowing tarp to let rain into their snug as he rubbed his large paws together, greed and calculation in his eyes.

There was something missing from his story-telling. Vestna's opium addiction. Theo had told her about it. He kept no pictures of Vestna, as if the memory were too painful to document, the descent of beauty into addiction. Tapping his heart, Theo had said, She lives in here. Leah had no memories. The only mother she knew was her amah, An-li. An-li lived in her heart. Leah could see Vasiliev as a procurer, as the person supplying Vestna with opium although Vestna could have found it on her own, or had it supplied by a Chinese lover, visited an opium den, or even bought the drug from a pharmacy.

"Anyway," Vasiliev concluded, "I don't think Vestna could have ever been happy. It isn't in the Russian nature. Fate."

He looked smaller, more human, his big body hunched over, the rain soaking his good leather shoes. He sighed and threw off his fatalism, pressing his fat thighs against hers, looking for sympathy. She inched away.

"You don't like poor Vasiliev who opens his soul to Theo's daughter," he whined.

"It's uncomfortable on this hard deck."

He thought about this, then said viciously: "Theo would have tired of Vestna anyway. He was only in love with lost things. He was so driven by his lust for antiquities. He had to have the best. It was a fever with him. That damn lawyer Everston used him. Everston knew his weaknesses. He became his private banker. It can take a long time to move old treasures. The lawyer was always upping his cut, raising the interest repayments. He was as greedy as the next man."

"Theo was too shrewd," Leah argued.

"You saw how Theo came alive whenever he got his hands on something rare and beautiful. Every man has his weakness. Before the Japs came, China was a riddled with archaeological digs supported by British, American or French financiers. There was a hole for everyone." He gave a dirty laugh. "Everyone wanted a share. I was the conduit. The middle man." He sat up straighter. "Even the Nationalists were in on it. Ask Chang, he knows. It set Chang's father up for life. It was total shit about returning China's legacy to China after that little devil Pu Yi was made puppet king in Manchuria and he colluded with the Japs to steal the jewels. Not one bead would have gone to the cause. They're all corrupt," he said without irony.

To Leah, Vasiliev's own corruption was so deep and black that by all rights his face should be a mass of boils and pus and his body riddled with pain like a sinner in a Hieronymus Bosch painting.

"Theo knew this. Knew they'd destroy the collection. If he'd gone to Manchukuo and not you, he'd have found a way to smuggle out the jewels to a third party without me. I couldn't have that."

"You killed him?" she gasped, her face bleached white with fury, one hand raised to push him out from under the flapping tarp and into the full force of the storm.

"Of course not," said Vasiliev and stuck his big face close to hers, as if demanding she look into it and see his innocence. "Chang knew what I knew."

Leah gagged.

"I have thought about this a great deal," said Vasiliev. "We both know Theo was greedy."

Leah opened her mouth to protest, but she had a vivid memory of Theo sitting in his study gloating over his latest acquisition, a jade pendant of a phoenix and quoting a poem about dragon seeds and phoenix birds guiding souls to heaven. It broke her heart.

"I can see from your face you agree. I think Theo's plan was to keep the jewels and use his own networks. Not share with anyone. Afterwards he'd keep Everston happy by paying off his debts. The lawyer didn't care about the jewels, just money. If Theo succeeded then Chang would be the one in terrible trouble. Theo would have spread rumours that Chang had made off with the jewels and screwed the Kuomintang. Chang would have been blamed. Another Nationalist, a pissed off triad member, or even a patriotic Communist furious at China's heritage being sold off to capitalistic pigs would have done for Chang." Holding his hand like a gun, he pressed it to the back of his neck and fell sideways onto Leah, his big head falling into her lap as the junk reared up.

"Get off," said Leah, pushing at his shoulders.

The boat rolled again, dipping down suddenly and banging hard against the force of the waves. Vasiliev gulped, then clamped his hands over his mouth. On his knees, he crawled outside to wash his hands and face in the pelting rain.

The tarp nearly blew away. She fought to control it in the drenching rain. Sickened and unsure of the state of her own stomach, Leah sat stunned, unable to make sense of what Vasiliev was telling her. It could be all lies, but parts of his story must be true. She had never liked the solicitous solicitor Everston. Even when she was young, she'd noticed how he looked at her. Theo had dismissed it as simple admiration. But she knew. Theo hadn't seen it because he revered Everston, an educated Englishman, from an old family, heavy with history and with the right contacts in the tight-knit colonial community. Displaced immigrant American Theo glowed in his presence and often told Leah the man was a gold mine for connections. It wasn't until after Theo's death that she learned Theo had been paying through the nose for Everston's help and reputation. In the end, Everston had taken everything but the house on the Peak.

Vasiliev crawled back underneath the makeshift shelter, reeking, his nose red and shiny, his hair streaming. Leah made a face.

"I may be dying," he said.

"Finish the story."

"Heartless bitch," replied Vasiliev, moaning. "I can't go on." His head sank onto his knees.

"Don't look at the waves. It will be worse. Look at me. If you talk, you'll forget about feeling sick."

He shook his head, but began to speak. "I don't know how Everston and Chang got together. But they did. I think each decided Theo wasn't to be trusted. Or maybe Chang had something on Everston. Everston had a succession of young Chinese mistresses. Chang is very good at blackmail," he said. Leah didn't want to probe and discover what sordid, repulsive incident Chang had used against Everston. Anyway, he'd only lie.

"You know the reason none of these Chinamen are seasick, Chinese medicine. But do they share, no. Or maybe it's not good for Europeans. Their drugs can kill us Europeans." He struggled to wink. He whispered, "*Ma huang*, it's a favourite of Chang's. It cures hay fever, asthma, the common cold. Its biological name is ephedra.

"How do you know this?"

"I know a lot about drugs," he admitted.

At first she thought he was confessing in his own devious way to supplying Vestna with opium. But, she realised, he was telling her something else too.

"You can make tea from *ma huang*," he volunteered.

A memory stirred in Leah. Sometimes she accompanied Theo to Everston's office. He was a great tea connoisseur, priding himself on his tea collection, brewing them up in wonderful teapots Theo had searched out specially for him. She could picture the Yixing clay teapot in Everston's hand as each man lifted his porcelain teacup companionably, sniffing the bouquet, consulting each other about the colour. Sometimes, three or four teas were brewed, each in its own pot.

"*Ma huang* is known to bring on tremors, perspiration. After taking it, people have died of heart attacks, especially if they go out in the heat of Hong Kong and are fat, unused to physical exercise. A man like Theo, with his business partner, who might be a solicitor, meets his partner's friend, a Mr. Chang. They have a tasting of teas. Despite the heat, they go on a vigorous walk away from prying ears or eyes to discuss their plans for Manchukuo and leave a poor perspiring Theo, dripping sweat, to recover on a park bench. It could have happened like that." He eyed her. "Later, this man Chang goes to Theo's daughter and persuades this now penniless girl to go to Manchukuo. Meanwhile, Everston continues to delight in his new tea. How soon after Theo died, did Everston take sick?"

"A few weeks," she said, recalling the absolute fury she had felt when she discovered Everston's perfidy and how pleased she had been to hear he was dying.

"Chang doesn't like loose ends."

"Why are you telling me this?"

He thought about it. "You know you look so much like your mother. Fairer, but still when I see you . . . Maybe I have a debt to Vestna's daughter. I have feelings too."

She was about to protest.

"I see in your eyes what you think of me. Doesn't matter. If I survive this storm, I'm Mr. Harris now, with an excellent passport. There will be so many refugees returning to Britain, I won't be noticed. The aftermath of war is always confusing. I will do well in England." He lowered his voice. "There will be no Chang there."

Together, they lifted the flap to gaze at Chang and Lee's

sons working the rudder, their faces straining to keep the junk on course, their hair plastered down and the rain falling off them in waterfalls while the wind whipped by them.

"Will it get worse?" Leah yelled to the captain.

The captain raised his head to look at the black sky. "Strong boat," he said in Cantonese and returned his attention to the waves.

"Have to lie down," said Vasiliev. "I can't feel any worse."

He crept out on his hands and knees and continued at a snail's pace over the slippery deck to the ladder. She saw the top of his white haired-head disappear below. His loud moans mixed with the storm and her revengeful thoughts.

When Chang stuck his head under her tarpaulin tent, she jumped.

"You can come out now," he said, "it's veering off."

She stared. He was soaked, from his soft cloth slippers to his hair, his suit clinging to him like tissue paper. He must have abandoned his raincoat during his fight with the rudder. Out of the corner of her eye, she saw the bare feet and wet trouser legs of one of Lee's sons. Then Chang collapsed backward with a thud. She fought her way out of the tarpaulin to see Chang with a rope around his neck. The oldest son pulled it tighter and flashed her an angry warning as he pushed Chang into a sitting position. The younger son squashed a rag into Chang's mouth and tied Chang's arms together. With a finger to his lips, the younger son stepped cautiously over the slick deck and descended into the cabin. She heard muffled cries and thumps. The older son went to help his brother, leaving Chang tied up, his back to her.

A few minutes later, Vasiliev's head popped up through the cabin opening and he flopped onto the deck, pushed from behind. The sons pulled him down next to Chang and bound him too.

Then, the older son relieved his father at the wheel. Mr. Lee rushed toward Chang and barked. "Traitor!" He aimed a deadly kick at Chang's ribs. Chang toppled sideways. Blood reddened the gag.

"He's choking," said Leah and pulled the rag out.

The captain raised his hand as if to slap her, then cursed her.

Vasiliev pleaded for his life. He had done nothing wrong, he wailed. He was a Chinese patriot. He had helped in the underground. All three Lees ignored him. "Do something," he begged Leah.

Helpless, Leah stood by the stacks of rice: wet, bewildered and afraid for herself. The wind gusted, the boat went into a heavy roll.

Lee's voice became triumphant. "We Communists will win in the end. Enough talk. How can you expect to find ivory in a dog's mouth? It has been decided."

Lee bent and grappled with the pistol buckled to his leg. It looked very ugly in his hard gnarled hands. The tips of his fingers were raw. "You should not look," he said to Leah. "This is nothing to do with you."

Her vengeful thoughts raced as she studied Chang, now pulled into a standing position, his dark eyes unfathomable, his face a mask. If she asked, would they hand her the gun and let her pull the trigger? She put out her hand as if to intercede and it grazed Chang's chest. His skin was warm. She pulled her hand away as if stung. Who knew how many deaths he had been responsible for? She remained silent as Lee and his younger son hauled Chang unto the gunwale. The son held Chang by his knees.

Vasiliev babbled incoherent phrases in Russian, whether cursing or pleading for Chang, Leah couldn't make out.

Chang stood and looked into the cold brown sea. Lee

pointed his gun at the back of Chang's head, Chinese executioner style, and fired. There was a loud splash, followed by a sickening thud as Chang's body crashed against the hull.

Leah's knees buckled. She landed hard on the deck, biting her knuckles to keep from screaming. Blood oozed up.

Father and son groaned under Vasiliev's weight as they hauled him up like a sack of rice. Vasiliev screamed his innocence in every language he could muster. The men held Vasiliev suspended above the deck and let go. Even after he hit the water, his piteous shouts could be heard for several long minutes. Leah covered her ears, rocking in fear.

Mr. Lee stood over her, strapping his gun back to his shin. "We need you to get the rice through customs. No one else but you came on this boat. You saw nothing. You will get your cut." He waited.

She nodded.

Lee ordered his sons to throw dozens of rice sacks overboard. "We must float over mines. People's stomach shrink when they starve. There will still be enough."

She made her shaky way down the ladder. In the tiny cabin, she couldn't stop trembling. She stripped off her sodden clothes and, naked, wrapped herself in a dry blanket to lie on the hard plank bed. Exhausted, she closed her eyes and blacked out to the sound of heavy rice sacks hitting the water. She didn't dream.

22

THE UNION JACK waving from a flagpole caught at Leah's heart, moving her to tears as the junk entered Hong Kong harbour in full morning sun. A group of sailors on board a destroyer waved merrily as they came within hailing range. Leah laughed and waved back; the men whistled and hooted.

It was the harbour she remembered, the same buildings, the same high mountains rising behind it, but it was eerily quiet, like a ghost town, without the boisterous hawkers crowding the docks, holding up tatty souvenirs and fresh fish and yards of silk and funny straw hats. The youngest Lee jumped nimbly onto the wharf and began securing the ropes. A stick-thin old Englishman in worn khaki shorts, tanned like a prune, made his slow way towards them. He stared at the sacks of rice. "You've brought rice," he said.

Mr. Lee dropped a plank over the side to serve as a gangway and urged Leah to show the old man her papers. On the wharf, Leah couldn't keep her eyes off the Englishman's doorknob knees. She thought she was inured to the ravages of starvation after the hunger of Macau, but she had never seen anyone alive so thin. How could the man stay upright? He had a clipboard and an official-looking pad. Immediately, she launched into her story about how the rice originated from Indo China and was a gift from the people of Macau as a gesture of goodwill to help the people of Hong Kong in their hour of need. She handed the old man her forms. He tucked them into his pad and wrote furiously, turning page over page in rapid succession. She rattled on to hide her surreptitious glances at the man's legs and at what he was writing so intently. He didn't look up once. She was completely unnerved when he ripped off the pages and gave them to her.

"It's a chit," he said in a quavering voice full of uncertainty.

She studied the forms. A series of large loopy circles filled each page. "Is this it?" she asked.

The old man nodded. "Rice is good. I hate rice." His eyes filled with tears, spilling down his concave cheeks. He wiped at them with the back of his hand. "I'm not myself," he apologised. "Stanley . . ." He turned towards the harbour to watch the wheeling gulls and the sun on the water.

Leah waited. There was something familiar about this wraith of a man, holding himself upright on his puny legs, his hands clasping her papers behind his back, a muddled dignity in his loss of control. She *knew* him. It was Hope Cuthbert's father. When last she'd seen him, his belly hung over his belt and he had a thick head of grey hair. The hair and the belly were gone. He looked like a chicken carcass boiled down to the bone. She laid a hand on his back and said softly, "It's me, Mr. Cuthbert. Leah Kolbe. Hope's friend."

The old man's sparse eyebrows came together in concentration, more tears clouded his eyes. He clasped her hands. "Yes, yes," he said. "Wonderful. You must come and visit us." He paused. "Mrs. Cuthbert died. Hope isn't here." He thought a minute, then said, "Yes, that's right. Hope is recovering in hospital. Her Charles—" and lost his train of thought as he searched Leah's face as if she could supply the missing information. He daubed at his teary eyes, then let his bony callused hands hang by his side, waiting for someone to tell him what to do next.

A young naval lieutenant in a bright white uniform came down the wharf at a half-run. He waved at Mr. Cuthbert as he drew nearer and saluted smartly. "Mr. Cuthbert, sir, I'll handle this shipment. You're wanted in the Customs Office."

Distressed, Mr. Cuthbert looked at the documents in his hand and threw them into the water.

"Hey," cried Leah, watching her papers floating away.

Lee hooked them with a grappling iron.

"That's my authorisation," she wailed to the embarrassed lieutenant as water dripped off the flimsy documents, now a soggy mass of runny ink.

Mr. Cuthbert waited to be hit, squatting on the dock with his hands over his head.

"It's not important," the lieutenant reassured Mr. Cuthbert. "We'll accept the shipment."

Frightened by Lee and his sons who swore at the stupid old white man in Cantonese, Mr. Cuthbert remained in a squat.

The lieutenant scowled at the Lees. "Can't you tell those fellows to be quiet?"

Bowing and apologising, Mr. Cuthbert slunk away.

Uncomfortable, the lieutenant and Leah watched the old man shuffle off. "Mr. Cuthbert gets muddled. Our orders were to give them jobs . . . It's too much for them. I'm sorry about your papers."

"It's all right. Mr. Lee," said Leah in English, "the officer is going to help us." She gave the lieutenant a brilliant smile. "We've had a terrible trip. We came through the typhoon. The men want to see their families and we are worried about the condition of the rice. The sooner it is in cooking pots, the better."

He stared in disbelief.

"We did really. We didn't get the full brunt of the storm. It veered off and well . . . here we are. The rice, I mean."

She saw the lieutenant trying to take it all in. He could still commandeer the rice and demand that she verify her story and then . . . And then, she was not at all sure what the murderous Lees would do. They would blame her and take their revenge. She blustered, "The papers are all in order. The consul, Mr. Albemarle, will verify this if you want to telegraph him."

The lieutenant held the dripping useless papers at arms length. What did it matter? Hong Kong was in chaos: people tripping over one another to restore order and the poor displaced Colonialists exhausted from starvation and ill treatment. He wasn't going to refuse food. It was his fault for letting poor old Cuthbert out of his sight. He was supposed to assist him in every transaction. If this got out, they'd throw the book at him.

Wreathed in smiles, Mr. Lee strode down the plank and talked rapidly in Cantonese to Leah who translated, "He has to see his agent about the unloading."

"Yes, fine. Do what is required. There is almost no food here. There could be food riots." He paused, embarrassed. "I know it's legal," he said, shaking the wet documents, "but do you trust these men?" He looked at Mr. Lee. "They won't price gouge? The black market . . ."

"The black market," huffed Leah. "I'm with the Red Cross. It's all in those papers."

The lieutenant reddened. "I wasn't implying anything. Tell him to get his agents."

Leah spoke rapidly and Lee nodded, showing how diligently he was following her orders. He saluted the lieutenant and bustled down the dock. His act didn't convince Leah, but the lieutenant seemed appeased.

"It's a blessing in disguise. I hate paperwork." The lieutenant grinned.

Leah gushed her thanks and flirted with him a little in the warm sun. The lieutenant suggested a drink later. Leah looked away and said in a halting voice. "I'm just so happy to be back in Hong Kong. I escaped before the civilian roundup."

"That was a piece of luck."

"My fiancé wasn't so lucky." She saw the light go out of the lieutenant's face as he turned somber and spoke more gently.

"I see," he said.

"He was with the Volunteer Brigade. Are they all right?"

"Some are; some aren't," he replied. He looked so young, vulnerable. He didn't want to expose his own feelings about the prisoners, too upsetting. She felt years older than him despite his war experience.

"Oh," she said, a catch in her throat, trying not to think in which category Jonathan would be.

"Are you all right, Miss?" asked the lieutenant, touching her lightly on the shoulder. "You look so pale."

"His name is Jonathan Hawatyne. Do you know him?"

He shook his head. "The word is once they get proper food and rest, especially the young ones, they'll be back to normal."

He was being kind.

"Seeing you, Miss, would perk any man up. Don't you worry

about this." He pointed to the junk. "There won't be any questions asked."

"Do you know where they put the—" She tried to say prisoners of war, but couldn't get her tongue around the words.

"They've put the officers up at the Peninsula Hotel. Try there. If I can do anything . . ." He let his words hang as Leah spoke rapidly in Cantonese to Lee's sons and told them where she was going.

"Don't expect to get what you agreed, we aren't capitalist gougers," said the older son, handing down her rucksack.

Startled, she nodded, unable to think about money or its terrible cost.

She kissed the dark-haired boyish lieutenant on the cheek. "Thank you, it's so good to be home."

He pulled himself to his full height and grinned, "It's been a pleasure, Miss." Even as he uttered the words, he was overwhelmed by a rush of homesickness and cursed the war, the Japanese and everyone else he had learned to hate.

On Nathan Street, Leah debated changing into a day dress, but she didn't want to meet Jonathan clean and washed. Neither of them were those two shiny people who had decided to marry on the eve of war. Hoisting her rucksack onto her back, she walked the familiar streets and saw the wounds the Japanese had inflicted on the Colony. A shop was gutted on Austin Road. Many houses had been stripped of their wrought iron, whole balconies torn away. Queen Victoria's imperious statue had been replaced with a monstrous Japanese memorial to its war dead.

It was a long walk. After so much time at sea, her legs were rubbery. Her emotions surged like waves: cresting with hope, followed by a trough of despair. He might be . . . No. He wasn't dead. She must not be shocked at his appearance. Inwardly, she rehearsed saying hello, looking only at his eyes and falling into his arms. There would be tears, but they would be happy tears.

The Peninsula Hotel came into view. A yard-high hand-painted sign in English read PENINSULA HOTEL followed by an exclamation point. It hung over Japanese characters on a brass plate. In places, the white stucco had worn away and the striped awnings were tattered. The windows were dirty and missing drapes. It was like visiting an old friend recovering from a terrible bout of illness who, while still pale and frail, was on the mend.

The doorman, in a plain black jacket, radiated goodwill and welcomed Leah in English as he held open the heavy door.

"Beautiful day," he beamed, ignoring her strange appearance.

"Yes, it is," she replied, disguising her surprise that the doorman and she had exchanged greetings. In pre-war days, doormen were as silent as totem poles.

Inside, she simply stared. The red carpet of the grand lobby was stained black in places, the furniture an odd assortment of chairs and sofas Leah recognised from the more palatial suites. The walls were pockmarked with holes where ornaments and paintings had been prised off. But the most disconcerting sight were the stick-like European men and women wearing shorts and faded dresses talking very softly in groups with a few suited Chinese men and women in pretty dresses. British military personnel bustled through the crowds looking in command and on schedule. She let her eyes roam over the thin faces and nervously walked around the clusters of people. She recognised no one.

Gathering courage, she moved to the unchanged mahogany reception desk. A middle-aged Chinese man in a faded morning coat and immaculate fawn gloves presided over the guest register. Leah asked for Jonathan.

"The men were brought in a group. We've converted a number of rooms to dormitories to accommodate them. They aren't registered. The Navy is handling that." He paused, his manner concerned. "They're on the fourth and fifth floors. Our telephones aren't working. I can send someone up there to check for you."

"May I go upstairs?"

"Of course. Just be a little quiet. The men like to rest during the day. The noise . . . If Mr. Hawatyne isn't there, I can arrange a rickshaw to the Prince of Wales Hospital."

His eyes slid off her face. He was trying so hard to be discreet. "Some require more than rest . . ."

"Yes, but I really think he is here, don't you?"

"It was just a suggestion. In case . . ."

"It will be fine," Leah said resolutely, struggling to remain composed, certain he was as fine as he had written in his one treasured postcard.

"If I can do anything . . . We want to help."

Leah thanked him, then climbed the wide stairs—the lift was out. She passed by a hotel worker on his hands and knees hammering in wooden treads to keep the carpet in place. He urged her to step carefully. The carpet was loose because the brass stair treads had been stolen. Her steps slowed. She told herself she was being cautious to avoid falling. Her heart was pounding too much to race up the stairs. On the fourth floor landing, she heard men speaking in English and her heart stopped. She saw a group of skinny men smoking in the middle of the long corridor. One of them commented, "Woodbines are better than banana peel." The others laughed.

Tony Pentley. She ran to him. He swept her into his arms,

tottered, and promptly set her down. The other men moved away, further down the hall.

"How?" he demanded.

"Doesn't matter. Where's Jonathan?"

"He's here."

"But that's wonderful."

He didn't meet her eyes. "He would bang on about the rules of war, the fuck—" He censored himself, "The damn Geneva Convention." He stopped. "I mean he was an inspiration, but . . ."

"But he must be all right or he wouldn't be here."

"He wouldn't go to the hospital. I mean who'd want more rules and regulations and no pretty nurses?" he joked, but his voice went down a register into worried concern. "He sleeps a lot." He hugged her again. "It's so wonderful you being here. Better than ten damn doctors."

He took her hand and pulled her along. "I'll get rid of the others so you can see him alone, lucky man."

He peered around the door and said quietly, "Get decent. There's a lady waiting. You lot have to leave. Let her wake him."

From the hallway came sounds of men dressing and running tap water. There was hardly any talking. Finally, four scarecrow men good-naturedly trooped past Leah, grinning and giving the thumbs up sign. She wanted to cry.

Tony touched her shoulder saying, "Just take it slowly, love," and kissed her lightly on the cheek, then joined the retreating men.

Even as she tiptoed into the room in her noiseless slippers, she was trembling. The blinds were down, the curtains drawn. The room was stale with the scent of men and had a naptime feel. She watched Jonathan sleeping. He was on his belly, the sheet across the small of his bare back, a spindly arm hanging off the narrow cot, his fingers grazing the floor. His blond hair was bleached from the sun—it was more white than yellow—and he was brown like tanned leather. His back was the saddest thing she had ever seen. It was a mass of raised ridges and ropey scars standing out in sharp relief. Despite the scarring and the dim light, she could count each vertebra.

She knelt on the floor by his head, listening to his even breathing, and matched him breath for breath. She held his outstretched hand and rubbed it along the side of her face. He stirred and murmured, but didn't open his eyes.

"Darling, I'm here."

He opened his eyes and stared, grumbling, "Christ, now I'm hallucinating," and sat up. "Am I dead?" He looked wide-eyed around the room trying to fathom why heaven had become this five-bedded room in the Peninsula containing a woman who looked like Leah, but was wearing filthy Chinese clothes and sobbing until her nose ran as she clutched his hand with an iron grip.

Leah's sobs subsided in Jonathan's arms. Minutes passed as they clung together. She pulled away to declare, "I'm home" and began to cry again. They kissed urgently and hungrily, tasting each other's tears. Leah was acutely aware of Jonathan's bones and his rapidly beating heart.

He cradled her awkwardly on the narrow cot and buried his head in the softness of her body. "It's wonderful," he said, his hands working over her clothed body as if she were a living sculpture, to prove that she existed, murmuring her name like a chant. She felt her heart melting into such happiness that she flushed red with pleasure and couldn't talk. They lay together on the cramped cot, their arms entwined, until finally Leah suggested they should eat.

Jonathan leaned on Leah's arm, her other arm around his waist, and watched where he placed his feet on the stairs. The touch and feel of him made her reckless and she kissed him on the first floor landing in full view of the teeming lobby.

He was a little shaken. "It's just not quite real yet," he said. The trip down the Peninsula's staircase winded him.

They wanted to sit quietly, away from the crowds in the lobby, and wallow in their happiness. Leah spoke to the concierge and asked if they could eat in the closed verandah restaurant. Delight filled the concierge's face and he agreed, saying he'd send a waiter and they could order food, not much, there wasn't much. Leah didn't care. They held hands, each reluctant to stop touching while sweet Jonathan watched her as if it hurt to keep his eyes trained on her for too long, like gazing at the sun. Finally, he looked away and focused on the people moving about in the lobby.

"Later, I'll get us a room," she declared.

"It's crammed to the gills. They can't make exceptions."

"Nonsense, everyone wants to help. There aren't those kind of rules anymore."

They ate omelettes and bread made with rice flour. The rice bread came with a curl of butter. "Butter," he said with satisfaction. He cut the bread into four neat squares and chewed each square thoroughly. "Maybe I'll save the next slice for later. Mustn't overdo it."

"Is that what the doctor said, darling?"

"It's best. Otherwise, I get bloated and can't eat. Nuisance, really."

She didn't probe any more, could tell he wasn't ready yet to tell her much. Instead, she told him about Macau, an expurgated version in which she emphasised her luck at finding a job and a flat. All the exiles had rallied around trying to do their best, she said.

He asked very few questions about how she got to Hong Kong so quickly. He seemed to assume that the ferries between Hong Kong and Macau were still running and that somehow she had wangled a ticket and ended up here to be with him. Anyway, his curiosity for now was blunted. He closed his eyes and she realised she was tiring him with her made-up tales.

"I am going to get us that room, now. You need rest."

"Huang fu said your house has been used by the Japs. It's probably disgusting."

"Yes," she said, determined to keep her tone light. "It probably is. The concierge is very helpful."

He stared out at the crowd in the lobby. "I don't think there are any rooms vacant."

"Anything can be arranged," she said, happy and confident. Then she stopped, noticing how silent and still he had become. "I don't want to rush anything . . . We both need time and quiet in a room of our own. I'm happy just to be near you," she said, capturing his roughened brown hands in hers. "We've both waited so long . . ."

Jonathan remained uneasy and uncertain, not like Jonathan at all.

"What is it?"

He tightened his hold on her hands and said in a shame whisper, "I don't think I can sleep in a bed yet. Would you mind if I asked them to move the cot in? I need . . ." He dropped her hands and took a long swallow of water.

"I'll go now," she said, and left him alone at the table as he meticulously cut another slice of bread into quarters.

They were lucky. There was an empty single room. A British officer was leaving for China to negotiate with officials there for rice. He would be gone for weeks. The concierge said it was his pleasure to lend it to Leah. He remained expressionless when she asked that Jonathan's cot be moved and agreed, saying, "Things will get better," and they both knew he wasn't talking about the shabbiness of the hotel. She thanked him profusely.

The cot gave the room a military air. There was only six inches between the bed and the cot, which was piled high with sheets, pillows and blankets. Already, it was an obstacle to manoeuvre around.

"Do you mind?" he asked. "It's only for sleeping," and he caught her up and held her tight, then fumbled with the clasps of her tunic. "It smells of the sea."

"It was a rough passage. Let me," she said and pulled the blouse over her head and stepped out of her trousers. Together they fell onto the bed. She burrowed in beside him, searching for the silky man inside the battered and bruised prisoner of war.

"I'm a wreck."

"No. You're the man I love."

He half pulled her on top of him, his cock stiffening.

"I'm not hurting you?" she asked.

"No," he said coldly.

"Don't," she said and put her fingers against his mouth.

He nibbled at them and began to explore her body with his hands. "What's this?" he asked as his fingers touched her gunshot scar.

She told him without emotion about how the Japanese

hated the British consul and tried to assassinate him. "I got in the way. It looks worse than it is. It's all healed now. There's just the scar." She showered him with kisses. "Not like your back. How?"

He closed his eyes. "I'm more tired than I thought." He slipped naked out of bed and began to make up the cot, falling asleep almost immediately.

She lay on the bed staring at the ceiling for a long time then she reached over and held his hand, seeking solace in the feel of his skin.

23

JONATHAN WAS PUTTING on weight steadily and regaining his health, but their lives together lacked a rhythm. It wasn't that they were awkward with one another; rather, Leah thought, they were too kind to each other, too polite. So much between them went unsaid. Often the sweetness of their lovemaking lacked passion or, perhaps, she was too sensitive to how his fingers always found her scar. Three weeks later, she still woke to find Jonathan asleep in the cot.

Huang fu appeared one bright morning and then visited them regularly. Leah liked having him around. He was their mediator and go between. He brought little delicacies from the black market and Chinese cures from the herbalist to restore Jonathan to health. He understood what Jonathan had been through and papered over their silences with his energy and good humour. Sometimes, she felt like an intruder, a visitor who returns from overseas and stares in disbelief that things have changed so much.

Today, the three of them sat in the hotel room having breakfast and finalising plans to see the Peak house. The Peak tram was working again. Jonathan looked at Leah and said, "You two go. I'll go another day."

"It doesn't have to be today. Tomorrow or the next day will do."

"No, really the walk up the hill, the people . . . I'm feeling a bit tired."

"Shall I send for the doctor?" Leah asked, searching his face for signs of illness.

"I insist. You two have been planning this for days."

She didn't want to argue in front of Huang fu. Jonathan had been consulted about the need to assess the house and make a claim for damages. He had reminisced about his first trip to her house and how An-li distrusted his motives, certain he was going to steal it out from under Leah. But now that she thought about it, he hadn't said that much as she and Huang fu made lists of tasks like check the roof, test the wiring, inventory the remaining treasures.

She couldn't claim for damages for her best pieces that she'd shipped to the Freer. No one knew what happened to them. She had spent hours telegraphing the States and making enquiries of the director. The ship had last been sighted off the coast of Japan. It hadn't been sunk. It could have been pirates. Japanese planes might have used it for target practice. No one knew. The shipping line had its offices in Singapore. There weren't any records left. It was all gone. Distraught, Leah had sought comfort in Jonathan's arms. He murmured blandishments and was pricked with real sorrow for her, but she could see he had forgotten what Theo's treasures had meant to her. It made her despair. Now, she said: "You're right. You shouldn't push yourself, Jonathan. Why look at ruins."

Jonathan's face filled with relief.

Guiltily, Leah kissed his cheek. It was petty to take her unhappiness out on him.

He squeezed her hand. "I'll visit later," he reassured her.

On the walk up the hill, Leah was grateful for Huang fu's company as her home came into view. The house had been blinded: its windows contained no glass and the frames were broken off or hacked at. The gravel driveway was barely visible beneath a thick carpet of weeds. Inside, the smell was revolting: urine, animal droppings—rats maybe—overlain with the heavy stink of gasoline. Several gutted engines rested against the mouldy living room walls. All the fittings had been stolen, from the chandelier to the copper pipes and the bathroom sink. There was, of course, no furniture and nothing of her collection. Upstairs, the plaster walls were sprayed with urine. She was loath to touch anything. Huang fu stopped making his damage report. The house was beyond repair.

They stood in the abandoned garden with the dead peonies, staring at the blackened circles on the lawn where trash or maybe Japanese military papers had been burnt. Her beautiful garden was a rubbish tip. She dusted off the patio bricks and sat down with her head in her hands. "It's unliveable. It's not even fit to camp in. Especially, not for Jonathan. I'm glad he isn't here."

"The banks will reopen soon," said Huang fu.

"I haven't got any money. No one will lend me money. Reparations are not going to pay to rebuild this. I'll be lucky to get enough to build a bungalow. I could always sell the land. It will break Jonathan's heart."

"Japanese occupation terrible," said Huang fu. "Impossible to make a living when those bandits stole whatever they wanted."

Leah hung her head. She hadn't been able to protect anyone or anything. She felt so guilty. Most of those who had been at Stanley saw themselves as martyrs and used it, even her old friend Delia. They implied Leah had let the side down by not remaining in Hong Kong to be interned. Delia, so changed, had lost her pre-war charm. She was hard and dictatorial. Or, perhaps, she was simply envious that Leah had not suffered deprivation, had emerged intact, still looking young and beautiful. She knew she was being unfair. She hadn't suffered. She had no idea what she would be like after years of internment and how she would view people who had escaped. Probably, she'd hate them.

Delia made it clear that Leah had been demoted from friend to acquaintance. Not that it mattered; everyone she had known was leaving. Delia and Carrington were to be on the first civilian boat to England. All the internees and most of the POWs were being processed and arrangements being made for their passage home, including the leaders of the old colonial regime. After the trauma of imprisonment and near starvation, they were unable to slip back into a work-a-day world. Leah felt sorry for all of them, Delia included. Hell, she felt sorry for herself in this burned out paradise, looking at the tatters of her life. She hardly bothered to listen to Huang fu.

"For years I care for your house, oversee your curios. Your curios are very old and beautiful. Then those damn Japs come." His voice shook and she saw the hurt in his face as he poked a stick into the blackened garden bed. "Terrible the things they did. When I visited Mr. Hawatyne in camp, some of the other soldiers pledged me money to buy food, medicine, other things for them."

It dawned on Leah that Huang fu had been a black marketeer. She gave him a penetrating look. He was better dressed than she remembered. Beneath his linen jacket, he wore a fine cotton open-collar shirt, his trousers were good and on his feet were real leather shoes. She ought to condemn him for profiting from war, but he had helped many people. Rules, she had learned, didn't apply during war. "It was war."

"No," Huang fu retorted, incensed. "Not black marketeer. I didn't make huge profits like those scum who preyed on those in Stanley. They added 200 per cent to their goods and had prisoners write IOUs."

In Huang fu's mouth IOU came out in one long diphthong. Leah puzzled over what he meant and what he was getting at.

Defensive, he said, "I did have costs."

She nodded.

"Many scum will be rich. The British Government has declared it will honour all the pledges of British prisoners."

"I'm happy for you, Huang fu. You are a good man. You deserve it. You helped suffering people and it was dangerous."

He seemed satisfied with her response. "We go now," he said. "Mr. Hawatyne will be waiting."

She felt in tune with Huang fu as they walked down the hill to the Peak tram. He had done his best in difficult times; she respected him.

Through the tram window, they watched the labourers with pickaxes, shovels and wheelbarrows clear a site of war debris.

"People will rebuild," declared Huang fu. "Building makes people rich. Many people will want pieces of China's history, not now, but soon."

"Yes," she said without interest. She wouldn't be building anything. "China believes in its history, its ancestors."

Huang fu beamed. "First customers will be Europeans, but later will be Chinese." He looked around the tram. It was empty except for three men in the back who dozed. "I hide many pieces

I buy during the war." He looked away and mumbled, "Some were yours."

"Oh," she said. She didn't want to embarrass him, better he had bought them cheap than someone else who might have used them for firewood, melted the brass down for cash, or donated them to the Japanese war effort. "I'm glad you have them." She didn't bother to ask which ones. They were like friends who had moved away. Now, she no longer remembered what they had shared in common or why they had been friends. It seemed so long ago.

He shook his head. "No. I bought them for business for the both of us. I supply the capital, the Peak house becomes our showroom and you and Mr. Hawatyne can live there."

Astonished, Leah sat opened-mouthed.

The tram stopped, its motor throbbing. Huang fu stood and put on his linen jacket. His eyes were bright and he seemed taller. Leah realised that Huang fu had planned this. Oh, not all at one time, but over the years as her antiques were pillaged and sold off in the market and as his friendship with Jonathan grew. It wasn't greed so much as making the most of an opportunity in a depressed market. "I have nothing to offer for this generous arrangement."

Huang fu gave a small cough. "The Peak house will become very valuable property. I will have a half interest in it. Of course, we will have to draw up a contract. Mr. Jonathan will want that." He beamed.

The uniformed conductor opened the door to the carriage. They walked down Garden Road. "I'll have to consult Jonathan, Mr. Huang fu Ping before I can agree."

"You do that, Leah," replied Huang fu. They shook hands, acknowledging they had crossed into new territory.

She was happy she realised, genuinely happy. She felt as though a weight had been lifted. In the noise and building dust of Hong Kong, it was a sign, a secret sign from An-li and Theo from beyond the grave: life goes on.

∽

HUANG fu was amazing. He found them a tiny temporary flat in Mid-Levels through another cousin of his. He arranged for a cook. Together the three of them visited the site with a builder and a geomancer. Leah and Huang fu talked endlessly about what should be built. Jonathan allowed their happy talk to swirl about him. If Leah asked Jonathan a direct question he'd shrug or say ask Huang fu. When she persisted, he'd say only that he wanted to be able to lie in bed and watch the clouds move. She asked the builder about a skylight in the bedroom. The geomancer said it was bad feng shui. She was still considering it. None of Jonathan's suggestions were practical or gave an insight into what he really thought. At night, she'd unroll the blueprints on the dining table, placing cups and saucers on the edges to keep them flat, and pore over the placement of windows and doors, power points and built-in shelving.

In the small flat, Jonathan and she rubbed along. A round of small celebrations was held to mark the departure of yet another group of soldier friends or long-term residents—old China hands that Leah thought would never leave—sailing back to England. After each departure, Jonathan withdrew a little more and spent the next few days mooching around the tiny flat hardly saying a word. She tried hard to be understanding and not pressure him.

In Huang fu's company, Jonathan brightened. He insisted that Huang fu obtain independent legal advice about his contract with

Leah. Leah exchanged a questioning look with Jonathan—she had always understood that the three of them were to be signatories. He was oblivious to her looks. Afterwards, in bed Jonathan turned away on his side and pretended to be engrossed in *The South China Post's* business page.

"Which do you want? A Christmas wedding this year or wait until next year, when our house will be ready?" she asked.

He turned and his face was animated, a look of hope and love. "We should be married in England. I want to see my mother and sister. They'll adore you. It will be perfect. A Christmas wedding at home."

"But darling, I can't leave now. There are so many arrangements to be made with Huang fu, the house, the business. We could have a registry wedding now and later we could visit your family."

"I want to go home," he said, looking at her intently.

"Oh," she said quietly, feeling it was a test and she was failing. "Hong Kong is our home."

In a rush he said, "No, it isn't. I don't feel comfortable on the street. I hate the crowds, the heat, people chirping away in a language I'll never understand. No one lives in Hong Kong forever."

"Jonathan," she gasped.

He hurried on, unburdening himself in a way he had never dared before. "Always, I think I might see someone who is Japanese. Then there is this flood of anger. I can't help it. I'm not proud of it. But that's how I feel. Even now those bastards believe Hirohito is a god. And our government is aiding them, shipping most of them back to Japan, not holding trials, sweeping everyone's suffering under the carpet and turning a blind eye to all the dirty dealing. I can't stand it. I hate it here."

She struggled to be reasonable. "But you've read the papers. It's all rationing, cold, and war damage in England. Where would we live?"

"It's home," he burst out. "Vanessa wrote inviting us to come and stay with her until we find a place. She's my sister. She wants to meet you. For God sakes, I haven't been home in nearly ten years. My mother isn't getting any younger."

"You never said."

"I can't stop thinking about leaving. I don't think I will be normal unless I—we go away."

"For a holiday, you mean. I guess I could leave for six months. Huang fu is reliable."

His mouth was set against her.

"A year," she offered.

"I need this," he implored, his eyes watching her every move.

He had never asked for anything. Now, he was asking so much. "Promise that not soon, but later we will return."

"No," he said and put his arms around her pulling her into his chest, close to his heart, "because you would always be waiting for that day, while I would be dreading it."

"But, Jonathan," she said reasonably, "what would I do in England?"

"We would have a family. We would lead a normal life. We would be happy and together." He started to kiss her hair, her face as if pleading.

She'd be a colonial wife, only not in Hong Kong, in England, filling up her days with ridiculous things. And then, there'd be *babies*. She didn't want to fill her days with children. They simply didn't interest her. She exited the room when people showed off their babies and small children. She hated the way adults were reduced to making ridiculous baby noises or engaging in stupid conversations with toddlers who always seemed about to cry. They were messy, needy, boring things. She recalled Albemarle's nursery room, so antiseptic and *mumsey*. Their children—Christ, hers too—would be sent to boarding schools. All those absurd games and schedules. She wouldn't have anything in common with them. They wouldn't want to learn Chinese. It would be cold, depressing, and she would hate it.

Sensing her distance, he stopped kissing and touching her. "You don't want what I want." It was a statement, not a question.

She reached for him, but he pulled away to stare at her face as if memorising its planes and angles. "I won't argue with you. I haven't the energy. In prison, my thoughts were always of you. Perhaps, I created a picture that never was." He paused, a far away look in his eyes, as if he were seeing his skinny self in a tattered uniform lying on a cot, daydreaming. Finally, he spoke— even as she hardly dared to breathe—"It was really the loveliest fantasy. And you were happy too. We were in love."

"I do love you," she insisted, pulling him close, holding his hand, pleading with her eyes.

"In your way, but not my way. I can't do this any more."

"You could come back."

He shook his head.

Leah felt her heart straining under his words and her mouth going dry under his penetrating gaze. Finally, she fumbled, "I don't mean now, but later. After some time . . . when you're better."

"I'm not sick. I can't live with someone I can't understand."

"That's not true. You know me. You know all about me. About Theo, about An-li. Everything that's important to me."

"Leah, you tell me so little. Take your bullet wound. I know you somehow managed to make a life in Macau, knew people whom you never mention. Then, you return to Hong Kong before anyone else, three weeks before the harbour was cleared of mines and a month before the ferry service restarted." He gave a grim laugh. "I made inquiries," he said in response to her flash of anger. "Also, I saw a strange Chinese man with liver spots and two thug-like bodyguards or sons come to the Peninsula. He gave you cash. When I asked you about the money, you said it was payment for your flat in Macau. I didn't ask questions because I naively believed that in time, in your own time, you'd tell me."

"You could have asked."

"Ha! . . . I rest my case."

"You never talk about your war experiences," she retorted, fighting for him, trying to win him back with words and reason.

"Mine don't count. I don't want to remember. Nothing good happened there. It was ugly and dirty and so God damned utterly pointless and fucking stupid. Why would I want to tell you that?" He stopped, breathing hard.

Leah could see he wanted her to capitulate, to tell him everything, to find the words to explain Tokai. But she knew if she told him, he would despise her. She didn't want his love to turn to ash. It would break her heart as well as his. She wasn't that cruel.

He held her face in his hands, as if willing her to reveal herself in one blinding flash of insight. She said nothing.

He took his hands away. "I always thought you would tell me voluntarily because there are no secrets between husbands and wives, only trust."

"I trust you," she said with passion. "Can't you do the same?"

"But you keep your secrets."

"They aren't that important."

"That's not true," he said, searching her face for clues as if it were a treasure map. "We were apart for such a long time. I think I could accept that you weren't faithful." He paused. "Where I was, there wasn't an opportunity." He smiled at his grim joke.

"If I told you, you would still leave. You hate it here."

"Yes," he acknowledged. "I have decided to go home with or without you. I booked places on the last detainee ship home."

"I'm sorry you'll have to cancel one." She hugged him fiercely. "I won't see you off. I can't walk down the gangplank alone. It would break my heart."

"Mine too," he rasped as he gathered her up.

They made love for the last time, saying their goodbyes with their bodies to keep from crying.

EPILOGUE

THE SITE FOR her new house was pegged out, the old house demolished. If she stood where the living room was going to be, she could see Hong Kong harbour. Down below she made out Jonathan's ship. She was glad she couldn't hear the nervous, excited chatter of the passengers and the shouts of the port hands as they loaded the ship.

It was a beautiful day. One of those really fine December days Hong Kong was known for: mild, a slight breeze blowing and the sky so blue and clear. It was her favourite time of year. She studied her plans and decided the new pond should be moved closer to the showroom. Water was good feng shui.

In the harbour, a horn hooted, long and loud, signalling departure. She turned to see Jonathan's dun-coloured ship travel slowly and gracefully like a grand old king cutting a foamy path through the calm water. She watched it until it was a black dot. She wiped away tears with her fingers.

Behind her, she heard footsteps and turned to see Huang fu Ping loaded down with plans. He was wreathed in smiles as he announced that the geomancer had declared that tomorrow was the day for building to commence.

She congratulated Huang fu and showed him where the new pond should be dug. He agreed. She gazed back at the empty horizon. She would miss Jonathan forever, but Hong Kong was home.

AFTERWARD: FACT AND FICTION

Few books in English describe Macau life during the 1930s and 1940s. For this reason, I am indebted to the Papers of Jose Maria Braga held by the National Library of Australia. Braga's collected papers provided a window into Macau.

A former Hong Kong businessman fluent in Portuguese and English, a teacher and a journalist, Jose (Jack) Braga was devoted to the task of telling the world the history of Macau and the role of the Portuguese in its development. He was active against the Japanese and helped to establish a spy network in Macau. His idiosyncratic accumulation of newspaper clippings, treasured books and his own secret documents were invaluable in my research.

Macau was the only place between Alaska and India where there was a European flag flying. The colony really did become a centre of espionage for nationals from Japan, China, Great Britain, the United States and Portugal. Leak Kolbe's story is fiction; Braga's was real.

Caroline Petit
Melbourne, Australia